J. L. Mihulka has been many things in their short life – a film grad, a theatre janitor, an NBC news anchor, a barista (to name a few) – and they aren't nearly done. Through every career, job, and hobby, they have always held onto writing, and hoped to make it their dedicated career. This is their first shot at it.

In their free time, J enjoys painting, sculpting, being a Plant Parent as well as a Parrot Parent, text roleplaying with friends, cooking, eating, watching The Office and the Watcher network on Youtube, and most of all, sleeping.

This book is dedicated to all those who believed in me, as well as all those who had their doubts and still supported me anyway (Looking at you, Dad ;) <3)

J. L. Mihulka

THE TIMEKEEPER CHRONICLES: BOOK 1

AUSTIN MACAULEY PUBLISHERS™

LONDON * CAMBRIDGE * NEW YORK * SHARJAH

Ordering Information
Quantity sales: Special discounts are available on quantity purchases by corporations, associations, and others. For details, contact the publisher at the address below.

Publisher's Cataloging-in-Publication data
Mihulka, J. L.
The Timekeeper Chronicles: Book 1

ISBN 9781647508357 (Paperback)
ISBN 9781647508364 (ePub e-book)

Library of Congress Control Number: 2021915594

www.austinmacauley.com/us

First Published (2021)
Austin Macauley Publishers LLC
40 Wall Street, 33rd Floor, Suite 3302
New York, NY 10005
USA

mail-usa@austinmacauley.com
+1 (646) 5125767

A big thank you to Tina Mihulka, for supporting me in my creative endeavors throughout the years, from Barbies to Books, and for being one of the first to read my story. Thank you to Erika Armstong, who helped me figure out the book process, and to Madeleine Koenigsberg, for being one of the first to read and edit my work, and for being the best friend in the world. Huge thank you to Sara Moake, who is the only reason my writing is where it is now (practice makes perfect, eh?) I promise the next one will be dedicated to you.

Those who don't believe in magic will never find it.

– Roald Dahl

Chapter One

Have you ever felt like something was meant for you? It can be something simple, like the last muffin at your favorite coffee shop, or finding a pencil on the ground on the way to take a test when you forgot one; or it could be something more… well, surprising, like finding a keychain in the street with your name on it, or entering an antique shop to find you have exactly the right amount of change in your pocket for the item you wanted.

This is magic.

Magic comes in many, many forms, some more well-known than others, but in all its forms, this one has to be my favorite – that small chance encounter that you almost missed. It makes you wonder, how many small, magical moments have you missed while not paying attention to the world around you?

For those of you about to put this novel down, the words 'magic doesn't exist' on the edge of your tongue, I would ask that you stop for a moment and consider – have you looked closely?

Have you felt the way the air feels just before and after it rains? Have you ever stood in the back of an empty antique shop, or in the woods in the early evening and sensed how differently the world felt?

There was a short time that my belief in magic died, when the world finally convinced me that everything was explained, known, and done with. That there was nothing left in the world to discover. And yet, here I am with a story of magic to tell, so, belief or not, I hope this story shows you that there might be a little more to the world.

My story begins with a rock. It was quite a cool rock, to be fair, but a rock nonetheless. It was laying a few inches into the snow, sunk there in front of a twelve-year-old girls house, waiting for someone to find it. Although, the person to pick it up was not the twelve-year-old girl of the house, but Molly Mihulka, the one approaching in flip flops despite the three-inch-thick snow, carrying a steaming pizza in a box in one hand, the other hand ready to knock.

It was early evening as Molly reached the door of the small house, surrounded by snowy woods and further on a small town tucked into the mountains, not far from the edge of the entire range. But before she could knock, her eye caught something hiding in the snow.

Despite her cold feet, she couldn't help but peek at what had been dropped. What she found was a crystalline object, two inches thick and five across, with five unequal sides shaping it. But calling it just a rock wouldn't nearly suffice to describe what Molly was actually looking at through the snow it'd fallen into.

She bent over and picked it up with eyes slightly widened with wonder, and what she now held in her hand made her bear the cold a moment longer, just staring. It was a see-through kind of blue, but within it, the universe seemed to unfold. An orange and red and brown cloud of what could only be described as space dust billowed from the bottom. Surrounding it, filling up the emptiness within the blue were small clouds of purple and green, and the effect was that this rock contained all of the cosmos.

Wow, Molly thought as she turned it in her hand, feeling it's unique shape and smooth sides, *this rock contains the cosmos.*

When the cold broke through to her once more and her feet began to burn with it, she tucked the rock in the pocket of her gray joggers and rang the doorbell of her friend's home.

Althea Achebe answered, her tightly coiled hair kept back in a French braid that stopped just a couple inches past her collarbone. She found her most observant and intelligent friend wearing flip flops in the snow. Well, I didn't say she had a lot of friends.

Althea let out a slow sigh, brown eyes giving away nothing but cold judgment for the condition of her friend.

"Molly," she stated, almost like a greeting.

"Yeah?"

Althea opened her mouth to say something exasperatedly, but instead just let out another sigh and waved her hand, taking the pizza. Any pretend tension in the air was alleviated.

"This better be the Thai Chicken pizza that I asked for."

Molly rolled her eyes with a smile, stepping into the much warmer house and closing the door behind her, shaking the snow off her bare feet and onto the rug.

"Well, hello to you too."

Althea smiled a little as she set the pizza on the counter.

"Yes, hello, glad you made it here alive with pizza," she said as she opened it to find it was, in fact, the pizza she had asked for. Molly slipped out of her wet flip flops and wiped her wet feet on the rug, avoiding the snow she'd just deposited onto it.

"I told you the roads weren't that bad," she said with a little grin she couldn't conceal even with her best attempt at a straight-faced joke. Her brown, roundish plastic glasses were fogging up with the transition into the warm air. Althea snorted.

"I mean, I still think you should have stayed home, but as long as there's pizza, I guess I'm not really complaining. Do you wanna pick a movie?"

Molly nodded and headed to the coffee table where some movies were laid out.

"Yeah, yeah, sure, but… Hey, did you drop like a cool rock in front of your house?" she asked, just a little nervous, but hiding it mostly as she picked up a movie and set it back down, going for a different one. Her other hand fingered the rock in her sweater pocket.

Althea raised an eyebrow at her as she grabbed the paper plates from the cabinets.

"A cool rock? I mean… There are a lot of rocks in my yard so…no? I don't think so?" Althea answered hesitantly, smirking a little at the end at the ridiculousness of her friend.

"Okay…um…can I keep it? It's like the coolest rock I've ever seen and I think it might be magic," Molly said all at once, nervous energy immediately revealing itself as she put the movie into the DVD player and wondered in the back of her head why they weren't just streaming a movie.

Althea chuckled lightly from the kitchen.

"Yeah, sure Molly, you go for it," she said easily, taking a slice of pizza for herself and then another for her friend. "Keep your cool rock."

Molly smiled a little to herself and touched the rock in her pocket, feeling relieved.

"Cool. *Moana* okay?" she asked, picking up the remote.

"Yeah, I guess."

And with that, Althea and Molly plopped onto the couch and ate their pizza as the iconic castle appeared on the screen and the snow began to fall again outside.

The snowy day was quiet and cozy from inside Althea's home, her family out for the evening and the heater effortlessly warming the small house. The quiet snowfall outside darkened the sky enough to make it sleepy, and by the end of the movie, the two were definitely feeling it. Althea took up more space on the couch, but Molly made up for it by making sure any free space was taken up by her legs, and when the movie ended, she was sleepily laying back against the couch's arm, legs across Althea's lap. Althea was falling asleep leaning on her own arm, but as the credits ended and the TV fell silent, something very out of place became noticeable in the quiet room. Quiet voices could be heard speaking in low tones just outside the windows behind them.

Althea found herself frowning and cocked her head toward the hushed voices, listening closer in the silence of the living room. Who was in her yard? She lightly shook her friend, who had drifted off next to her.

"What?" Molly said a bit too loudly, having been mostly asleep, straightening her sideways glasses, and although Althea immediately shushed her, it was too late. The voices were pausing, and then footsteps could be heard retreating toward the woods. Althea straightened immediately and jumped up, rushing to the window. She peeked through the curtains and saw the edge of two cloaked figures, what looked like a man and a woman, entering the woods through the snow-covered clearing.

"Cloaks…" she mumbled to herself with confusion as she followed them with her eyes.

"What?" Molly whispered from the couch where she was hiding, eyes already widened with fear, but Althea didn't respond; instead, getting up and quickly sliding her boots on. Molly straightened. "Hey!" she whisper-shouted. "What are you doing?!"

Althea didn't respond, waving her off as she pulled on her coat. Molly was jumping up to follow when Althea flew out the door. She quickly slipped into her flip flops and pulled her thin sweater around her, mumbling light curses as she followed her stupid and curious friend out into the snow.

"Althea!" Molly called softly when she got outside into the more-than-silent day, snow sucking up any ambiance there might have been. Althea was already moving through the clearing behind her house.

"…am I really doing this?" she groaned to herself as she did, in fact, do it. She followed Althea into the woods and away from the warmth and safety of the house.

Althea hid behind a tree as she watched the figures enter the woods together, and when Molly approached, Althea tugged her behind the tree with her, ignoring her protests.

"Shh! They went into the woods…" she updated her friend at a whisper, looking into the trees. Molly was shivering and pulled her sweater closer again, stepping from foot to foot lightly as her bare feet burned with the cold of the snow.

"Althea, if there are men in your yard, shouldn't we be hiding in your house and locking the doors, not going after them?" she whispered, concerned for their wellbeing, and wondering why Althea wasn't. "We're twelve." Althea ignored her.

"Come on," she said seriously, focused on the place where the figures had disappeared behind the trees.

"No, wait, Thea—" Molly tried, but it was too late as Althea was already jogging across the clearing. Molly hesitated a moment, before groaning again and following her friend across the clearing as quickly as she could with the limited traction her flip flops gave her.

By the time Molly caught up with Althea, she was stopped in front of where the figures had entered the woods. There was no one else there.

"Althea, seriously, this isn't safe, can we please—" Molly began with a shiver, but Althea didn't let her finish.

"There's a trail here."

Molly frowned, and her shoulders dropped a little as she stared at the back of Althea's head.

"W…what?"

"There's a trail." Althea, deadpan, was staring down the impossible trail, knowing there certainly shouldn't be one, not with markers and everything, not in her backyard. "I've lived here for years and there's never been a trail." As a kid, she'd played here a thousand times with her brother. They'd run through the mud, they'd played princess, capture the flag, Little Red Riding Hood, and there had never been a trail here.

Molly didn't know what to say, but as they stood there in the nearly deafening silence, with only the soft wind blowing and the crunch of the snow as she shifted from foot to foot to fill it, Molly couldn't worry about her friend's trail problem.

"O-okay, well, there's probably an explanation but let's go *inside* and discuss it and—hey, wait!" Althea was already making her way down the path as Molly spoke, not listening. "Althea!" Molly called, waiting. She glanced around the empty clearing, before sighing and reluctantly going after her, knowing she couldn't just let her best friend go after cloaked strangers in the snowy woods alone.

Althea moved quickly down the trail, watching for the cloaked figures. She stopped when she could only see more trees ahead, the path disappearing up a hill. There was no one in sight.

Althea sighed just as Molly caught up, slipping and falling into the snow behind her. Molly groaned as she slowly got up and brushed as much as she could off her sweater and pants.

"Thea, seriously, we should go back," she insisted in a more serious tone, shivering, cleaning the snow off her glasses with the dry side of her sweater.

"I don't get it! I know I saw them go this way, but now…" Althea rubbed her eyes, confused and frustrated. When she stopped rubbing and looked up, she saw two black cloaks disappearing over the edge of the hill.

"There!" she half-shouted and sprinted up the hill in her boots, with a dedication and skill that only adrenaline could have provided. She didn't stop to think about what she was doing, something incredibly rare for her, but something deep inside her was telling her that she had to catch those figures. She had to know what was going on.

"Thea!" Molly called after her urgently before sighing loudly in exasperation and sprinting after her in flip flops. She did, of course, slip and fall, so she angrily took off her flip flops and ran the rest of the way barefoot, shoes in her hand.

Both of them were chasing a fleeting form; one after the two mysterious cloaked figures, and the other after their idiot friend running through the snow after two mysterious cloaked figures.

Althea, as she ran, didn't notice the fading snow and ice around her, as if the winter in the woods were turning to spring with every step, but Molly behind her did. Molly didn't, however, notice the rock glowing in her pocket.

Molly's pace slowed a little, and she looked around with a combination of wonder and confusion as the snow beneath her feet thinned and vanished.

Althea finally had to stop and catch her breath when the cloaks had disappeared from sight and not reappeared. She was bent over with her hands on her knees, panting, when Molly finally caught up with her. Molly walked slowly, turning in a circle as she tried to take in the surroundings.

"I almost had them! I don't—"

"Shouldn't there be a house here?" Molly interrupted, her voice a little lower in tone than normal. Althea frowned and looked back at her.

"What?"

"A house, your neighbor. Shouldn't they be here? And why is there no more snow?" Molly continued, slowly turning in a circle, snow still covering one side of her sweater. Althea frowned again and looked around, noticing her surroundings for the first time since she started following the cloaked figures.

"Oh. Wow, I uh…I don't know. I didn't…notice that." Althea looked at the world around her for a moment, and Molly turned to look back down the way they came, where the winter seemed to pick back up down the trail a few feet.

"This seems like…like a magic thing," she said hesitantly as she slipped her flip flops back on. Althea sighed loudly, pinching the bridge of her nose.

"Molly, seriously, we've been over this—" She started, giving a speech she'd given a million times whenever Molly thought maybe something magical was happening, which was like at least once a week, but Molly cut her off rather aggressively.

"Look, I didn't get my Hogwarts letter when I was eleven, I wasn't brought to Camp Half Blood by a Satyr despite my obvious ADHD, no prince ever swept me off my feet, and Peter Pan never showed up to take me to Neverland, and now I've just chased you down a snow-covered trail in flip-flops that somehow turned to spring; you are giving me this!" Molly snapped in frustration, running a hand through her short hair.

"Look, I know what it looks like, but I'm sure there's some explanation; there always is. Maybe there's a lot of sunlight here. Maybe lots of deer hang out here and their body heat melted it; we don't know, but it's literally never magic!" Althea argued, an argument she'd given many times before. Molly took a deep breath.

"Look," she said and looked up at Althea. "I just chased you, barefoot, through the snowy woods—in flip flops—down a mystery path—that, I might add, shouldn't exist, you said so yourself—for what? So you could see who was creeping near your house?" Molly asked, putting her hands on her hips. "But the second it's what I want to do; the second magic comes up, I'm crazy and you won't do it?"

Althea stared at her for a moment before slowly gesturing to the path in front of her with a shrug and a defeated sigh that meant 'I can't really argue with that, I guess'. Molly let out a breath she didn't realize she'd been holding and nodded to her friend.

"Great. This way," she said with another nod, rolling her shoulders back and walking deeper into the forest with confidence she didn't really have. Althea felt crazy for feeding into this, indulging her friend in her incessant belief in magic, but she followed anyway.

As they made their way deeper into the woods, the evergreen trees began to shift to deciduous trees, and the cool mountain air began to shift to humid and warm summer air from somewhere at a slightly lower elevation. The two looked around themselves in wonder as they walked, the path going from rocky to dirt-covered, and soon the sun seemed to be setting and a warm evening began to form.

"What exactly are you expecting that we'll find here?" Althea asked after a while, looking at her friend.

"I don't know." Molly replied honestly, voice calm, looking around. "But it's gonna be something great," she smiled.

"This isn't gonna be like last time—" Althea began to ask only to have Molly cut her off with a huff, eyes squeezed shut to contain her frustration.

"No, Thea, it's not going to be like last time," she said sternly, and Althea gave her a look.

"Okay, 'cause last time you had me trudging around a 'magic forest' for hours looking for fairies because you read a fairy-catching book and were sure you'd find them," she said with a cocked eyebrow, arms crossed.

"That's because it had all the signs in the book! How was I supposed to know it was made up?" Molly huffed, kicking a rock.

"Because it was about a fictional creature?" Althea smirked.

"Magic is real, Thea," Molly insisted, looking at her. "I know it is."

"Okay. Sure," Althea said with a sigh and a bit of an eye roll.

"Explain this forest and the heat if you really think it isn't," Molly shot back at her, annoyed. Althea didn't reply for a while, which made Molly know she was right. Her heart began to pound a little with how excited she was that the magic was finally happening.

"Molly, we really should head back…" Althea said after a while, coat in her arms now. Molly rolled up her sleeves.

"No, not yet. Something is happening. Look where we are! It's summer, and I'm sure we'll run into something magical soon!" Molly said brightly, letting Althea walk in front of her as she imagined all the fun things they could find. Maybe there'd be a prince, or a dragon, or fairies or something. "It's definitely—"

Althea had stopped on the path in front of Molly, who bumped into her, having not seen her stop. Althea's eyes were wide as she stared at what was in front of them.

"—an Enchanted forest?" Althea finished Molly's sentence before she could.

"Yep," Molly's voice came out as a squeak as she saw what Althea saw. "It's an Enchanted Forest."

Chapter Two
Althea

I blinked, wide-eyed, at what floated in front of me. It was a group of small pink…humanoid things with wings. I will not accept that they are fairies. Not real.

"Fairies!" said Molly as she moved around me, toward them.

"Whoa, hold on there," I caught her arm. "We don't know what those are, but they are definitely not—"

"Fairies!" Molly filled in with a wide grin, bouncing up and down in her spot. She turned quickly and took another step toward them, but I caught her again.

"Molly, seriously, we don't know what those are or if they're safe, we cannot—" I started, when a glittery pink…fairy…thing…flew in front of my face.

"We can hear you, you know," came their tiny, offended voice. Up close, I could see that everything about them was pink. Hair, eyes, face, body—clothes? Or were those flower-petal-looking-things growing from its body?

"Oh. Uh. Sorry," I said, feeling the blood rush to my cheeks.

"So you are fairies!" Molly said with excitement I've only ever seen from her at theme parks. "Hi! My name's Molly and I'm a human!"

"Hi, Molly the Human," the tiny, pink fairy said, turning to her with an even tinier smile. Well, for them it was probably regular-sized. "You have very pretty eyes," it commented. Molly blushed.

"Oh, thank you! You have very pretty…everything! Pink is my favorite color," she said brightly. The fairies all giggled and…blushed? I don't know, they look darker pink somehow.

"What brings you to our land, Molly the Human?" Another fairy, hair seemingly made of glitter and light, asked. Molly smiled brightly. The fairies seemed to be making Molly a flower crown now.

"Oh, well, it's kind of a long story, but, well, my friend here saw some people in cloaks and we chased them into the woods and then all the snow disappeared and I told her it was magic, and then—well, we saw you guys and—" Suddenly, another fairy, this one a darker pink with sparkly lips and hands flew up to Molly, interrupting her.

"And then she said we weren't safe," it said, hands on its tiny hips as it looked me over. "Molly the Human, what are you doing with this prejudiced…Dark Elf?" The slightly more judgmental fairy asked, unsure, little pink eyebrows knit. I raised an eyebrow at them.

"I'm not an elf," I said with a frown, crossing my arms, still trying to figure out if I was dreaming. I was looking so closely at this little…person…that it would probably be considered rude. Is it glowing? How? Is it a boy or a girl or…well, neither? Is it a real, live being, or some kind of mirage? Did I slip and hit my head in the snow?

"Sorry, why are you with this rude Dark Human?" It decided instead and looked at Molly for an answer. Dark human? What did—Oh. I see now. This is…incredibly stupid.

"What, you've never seen a black person before? Do they not exist in 'magical fairy land'?" I asked, hands on my hips.

"No," the fairy replied coldly. "But you've never seen a fairy, have you, Black Human?" it snapped. I smiled tightly.

"No, I can't say I've had the displeasure. My *name* is Althea."

The fairies kind of glared and Molly hit my arm.

"Hey, be nice to the fairies!" she half-whispered.

"They aren't being nice to me!" I replied, looking at her.

"That's because we don't like you, Dark Human," the dark pink fairy replied, sticking out its tongue.

"*Althea*," I repeated, looking at the awful little creatures in front of me. "Okay, I'm done with fairies, I'm going home," I said, putting my hands in the air and turning back down the path. Molly caught the back of my shirt as a few more of them dropped a pink flower crown on her head.

"Nooooo, come on, we just got here," she whined and I sighed, reluctantly turning and crossing my arms.

"Molly, this is a dream or something. Fairies aren't real," I said, already pretty exasperated with this dream. Molly's eyes widened and she put her hands on my shoulders firmly.

"You can't say that! It'll kill them!" she insisted in a panic, putting herself between the fairies and me. With her hands still on my shoulders, she began to chant, "I do believe in fairies, I do, I do. I do believe in—Come on, Thea, do it with me—I do believe in fairies—" The dark pink fairy leaned around her shoulder.

"That's a myth, actually," said the fairy. Molly paused, then relaxed.

"Oh."

I sighed and stepped past her, facing the group of variously pink tiny people.

"Where are we? What is this place?" I demanded, crossing my arms defensively.

"This is the forest of Althalamist," the light pink one replied, crossing her arms to match mine. It was a standoff.

"And is there a *town* of Althalamist?" I asked, matching its glare. It looked me over.

"If I tell you, will you leave and not return?" Its tiny voice held more contempt than I'd ever imagined a fairy's voice could.

"Promise," I replied with a cocked eyebrow. The fairy rolled their eyes and pointed further down the path.

"Follow that path to the fork and go left."

"Thanks," I said with a roll of my eyes and grabbed Molly's wrist, dragging her down the path, through the fairies. She turned back toward them as they separated around us.

"What? But we just got here! Come ooooon!" she complained as I dragged her away. I looked back at her with a deadpan expression.

"Molly. They called me *Black Human*," I said and she sighed, before nodding in defeat and understanding, and waving goodbye.

"Bye fairies! It was nice to meet you!" As we walked through them, they dropped various other flower wear on her, waving goodbye. A few landed on me but I brushed them off with a grimace as we walked.

"Goodbye, Molly the Human!" They all called with waves and blown kisses. I rolled my eyes. Of course, this would happen to me. Why am I surprised?

By the time Molly started walking without having to be dragged, the snow on the path was long gone and the glow from the fairies had faded completely. And Molly had not once stopped gushing over them.

"They were so pretty! And were they girls or boys because I couldn't tell? But they were gorgeous and they looked so delicate! And you know, pink is my favorite color and—Agh, Althea, fairies exist!" She grinned at me with eyes wide with wonder and I sighed.

"Yes, they do, and they called me a dark human," I emphasized again with a raised eyebrow. She seemed to keep forgetting.

"Yeah, that wasn't great..." Molly admitted, glancing around. "Okay, maybe fairies weren't so great. But it does make me wonder what kind of place we're in, that they wouldn't know you were even human at first," she said with a frown.

"Early Medieval Europe?" I suggested jokingly, but then, ahead, I could see the fork in the road. "Finally," I mumbled to myself as we approached.

Molly glanced down each path.

"Which way did they say again?" she asked, and I frowned a little as I realized I didn't remember.

"Oh. I was so eager to get out of there, I don't think I even listened," I admitted a little sheepishly, and paused at the split, glancing between both trails. They curved off into the woods, so it wasn't really possible to see which one it was. "I guess we should just pick one?"

"Or we could go back?" Molly suggested with a little excited grin.

"No." I scowled. "I'm not going back there. Which way?" I asked, focusing back on the trail. She was pouting, I could tell even with my back to her, but she sighed after a minute and answered.

"Well... Left is always right?" she tried, and I knitted my eyebrows

"So...left then?" I frowned.

"Yeah, let's go left," she replied. I nodded and waited for her to go that way. When she didn't and I heard the sound of shuffling clothes, I glanced back to see her pulling off the sweater/cardigan thing she'd been wearing that was kind of soaked now that the snow on it had melted. She threw it over her arm.

I smiled at her a little mischievously while she fixed her shirt, waiting with my hands on my hips. She noticed my silence after a moment and looked up at me, blushing a little. "What?"

"You ready?" I teased with a little laugh and she shoved me lightly, walking up the left path.

"Yes, omg," she mumbled and I laughed at her a little as we walked.

"Just checking." I chuckled, the fork behind us getting further and further away.

After walking for what felt like hours, I glanced at Molly. "This magical destiny adventure is going on longer than I thought it would; we should go home, Molly." I was starting to worry about getting lost.

"No! It's just a little further," she said, looking forward. I sighed.

"Molly, we have to go home eventually," I insisted, turning to walk backward in front of her. "We're twelve, we shouldn't be out in the woods alone, fairies or not."

She looked me dead in the eyes the way she almost never did.

"Althea," she started seriously, "first of all, you're the reason we came into these woods at all, with your crazy need to be super dangerous and run after mysterious cloaked figures," she pointed out, and I couldn't exactly argue, but I'd try anyway.

"Molly, that was different, I wasn't planning on stayi—"

"Secondly," she interrupted, squeezing her eyes shut to contain her frustration with me, "this is what I've been waiting for my whole life. I finally get to go on an adventure, get to experience the magic everyone is starting to not believe in anymore. I don't care if it takes us a long time to get home, I want—no, I *need* this," she said seriously. I stopped in the path and she walked around me.

"What? Molly, listen to yourself!" I turned, watching as she walked away from me. "You said it yourself before—we're twelve. You want to spend the night in unfamiliar woods alone? What about your parents? What about your friends? Don't you think they'll worry if you don't come back?" I called as she kept walking. She threw her arms up in exasperation.

"Do you really want to miss out on our chance at an adventure novel because our family might worry?" she asked without turning. I thought about it for a moment.

What else was ahead, if fairies were behind us? If magic really did exist? I closed my eyes for a moment and took a deep breath.

"Fine. Fine, my mom will be back tomorrow morning, so you have a day, and then tomorrow morning I'm going back up that path and going home, whether we find a town or not," I said and jogged to catch up with her. It wasn't hard because suddenly, she was stopped in the path with a wide grin.

"I don't think you'll be waiting much longer," she said excitedly, pointing down to the town that had just broken through the trees. My eyes got a little wide.

"Wow…I guess not." I agreed in awe.

Chapter Three
Molly

If I had been wearing anything other than flip flops, I might have run down the hill and into the town; but not wanting to wipe out like I had in the snow, I stuck to walking quickly with Thea.

The town coming into view ahead of us was incredible because it was definitely not from our time period. It was a medieval-looking village, clothing and all, and I found myself grinning at just how cool this was. We must be in some kind of magical world, with princes and princesses and dragons and all that. I looked for a castle, but didn't see one yet.

Magic and adventure had been something I'd been deeply interested in for years, and I spent, like, all my free time reading books and watching movies that centered around that. I would give anything to be a wizard, or grow wings, or be a demigod, or manipulate the elements, or shapeshift, or…or anything! I just wanted to be special and magical and have an adventure instead of just going to school every day and learning and going home and eating dinner and going to school again the next day.

Everyone around us was starting to doubt magic… None of my friends believed in fairies or Santa, or anything else… Even the ones that had for years with me. But I knew that magic was out there waiting to be found. And now that we were in a world with magic, nothing would stop me from finding it! This is going to be an adventure!

"So which one of us do you think is the—" I started with a little grin.

"I am," Althea interrupted without looking at me. I frowned.

"But you don't know what I was going to—" I started again, getting in front of her a little.

"Who's the protagonist?" she asked and looked at me.

"Well, yeah," I said in surprise, then frowned more, "Wait but why is it you?"

"Because I want to be," she replied with a little playful smirk. I thought about it.

"I guess that's fair. Maybe we both are," I added thoughtfully, but to be honest, it didn't matter. "I wonder what our quest will be."

Althea sighed a little.

"Honestly, as long as we can get home quickly, I don't care. Magic is great and all but I don't want my family to worry, and school starts again in a couple of weeks, and I have all A's for once and I really don't want to lose that just to…I don't know, almost get killed by a dragon or something," she said as we strolled along, and I nodded mostly to myself, but still said:

"Nerd."

She made a face and smacked my arm with a laugh.

"Shut up. You're the nerd, fairy girl," she chuckled and I laughed too, and we made our final descent (down the hill) into town.

Night had almost fallen by the time we arrived, and the streets were starting to have less and less people. Which was good, because basically everyone we'd passed had stared at us like we were mutants.

"I don't think women wear pants here," I said in a hushed voice to Thea next to me.

"Oh, is that why they're staring? I just figured they'd never seen a black person either," she replied and I realized that was probably true as well.

"Both?" I shrugged, suddenly insecure on this magical adventure. "I think they don't wear their hair short either…" I touched my head nervously and glanced around. Fun 20's bob looking like less of a good idea. Oh, but that guy has the same haircut as me! Huh.

"It doesn't matter, we aren't from this world, we aren't meant to fit in. Let's just go back—" she said, pulling me by the arm back the way we came, but when we turned, an old and somewhat off-putting man grabbed my arm.

"Ye can't go back to thine woods at an hour such as this! The werewolves will surely get ye, if the ogres don't find ye first!" He howled, and I just kind of froze and looked at him. A moment passed, and then Althea carefully pulled his hand off my arm.

"Well then, thank you, Sir, we won't. Where, uh, where might we find shelter for the night?" she asked, as measured as she could, but I could tell she was freaked out too.

"There's a tavern over yonder, but they won't be accepting no women folk in pantaloons, and with no husbands to be seen. Where are ye husbands? Or parents?" he asked, stepping closer, and I took a step back, holding onto Althea's arm.

"Okay thank you sir have a lovely evening!" I said all at once and dragged Althea away from him. The later it got, the less nice and non-creepy folk there seemed to be out.

When we were far enough away, I whispered to Althea, "You were right and this was a bad idea. Should we go home now?" Althea, equally as panicked, shook her head.

"You heard the old guy, we can't, not until morning probably," she said, eyes on the ground as she did that thing she does when she focuses really hard, involving lip biting and hair twirling with just a sprinkle of pacing.

"Okay, then what do two twelve-year-olds with no money in a renaissance town do?" I asked, glancing around and hugging myself.

"I don't know, that's what I'm trying to figure out." Althea was quiet for a moment, before looking up and shrugging a little. "Tavern?"

I sighed slowly before nodding.

"Yeah. Yeah I guess," I said with a shrug. "As long as they accept 'pantaloons'."

"And no husbands," she snorted.

We walked into the Tavern a couple of minutes later, glad the street seemed mostly empty now. The tavern, however, was not. It was filled with loud men, laughing heartily and having a good time, eating and drinking. I saw a few women but given the fashion in which they were dressed, I knew enough to know that approaching them probably wouldn't do us much good.

Althea took the lead and took my hand, leading us through the crowd who mostly didn't notice two small, pants-wearing girls, but a few did and were staring in very confused or suspicious ways. Althea pulled us all the way to the bar and to the bartender behind it.

"Hello," Althea said, and the guy, a tall man with a long beard and a beer belly suited to a bartender, looked us up and down slowly. Althea cleared her throat nervously. "Um, we were looking for a room for the night and—" But the man interrupted her.

"More of you?" He sighed and grabbed a key off the wall behind him. "Room 7 is still open," he turned back to us with it. "You're the youngest I've seen yet," he paused, frowning a little. "How old are you?" he asked, and I glanced at Althea. *Lie, Thea. Tell him we're like, fifteen or something.*

"Uh, We're... We're twelve, sir," she said truthfully, like an idiot. *Noooooo.*

"Hmm," he hummed, looking at us again for a moment, holding the key to himself. "And I don't suppose you brought any gold? Or tradeable goods?" he asked, seeming just a little awkward. Althea looked at me, but neither of us had anything.

"N...no sir, we didn't," she said, but didn't back out yet, even though I was fairly certain we weren't going to be getting that room. My mind raced for solutions.

"Maybe we could help you get drinks? We learn quickly, and it's so busy here, and we're strong for twelve-year-olds..." I started, glancing around, willing to do whatever to not have to go back out there and face whatever lurked on the streets at night. Or that creepy old guy.

The man looked at us for another moment, thinking, before nodding slowly.

"Hmm, I suppose I could find you some work here... My name is Emory, what are yours?" he asked us, and I felt relief rush through me.

"I'm Molly," I said with a small smile.

"I'm Althea," said Althea with a polite nod.

"Nice to meet you, Althea and Molly. Let's...get you some aprons," he said with a little nod then walked out from behind the bar, through a doorway. He had kind eyes, and unlike the man earlier, I wasn't afraid of him. He seemed to have good vibes about him. I looked at Althea and she looked back with a little nod and shrug, and we followed him into the back.

The back had dirt floors, with assorted barrels around, some with nozzles, some without. It smelled very heavily of alcohol, but also of oak and pine, and it was warm and kind of nice. Emory picked up two brown-tan cloth aprons that were definitely going to be big for children and offered them to us.

"Althea, I'll have you serving drinks that go to tables first, and when they get too heavy, you'll fill them instead," he directed and she nodded, tying the apron behind her. It was a little big, but she was curvy and tall for a twelve-year-old so it was okay.

I, however, was not. I was tiny for a twelve-year-old. So when I pulled the apron over my head, it was gigantic. He frowned a little, then stepped toward me a bit awkwardly. "Here, let me fix that for you." His voice was this kind of warm, deep voice that reflected what the tavern's backroom felt like, and he spoke with the kind of softness that made him seem like he wouldn't harm a fly. A gentle giant. I turned so he could reach the ties, and he knotted the top of the apron to fit around my neck gently, then carefully tied the back. "Is that okay?" he asked. He seemed kind and awkward and like he was trying his best, which I relate to.

I found myself relaxing, feeling a lot better about the whole situation. "Yeah, thank you," I said, smiling at him. He didn't really smile back, but his eyes seemed to.

"Good. You will sweep and organize the backroom, and when you finish, you can help Althea," he said with a nod, handing me a broom and walked out the door again, passing Althea. "This way," he said stiffly to her.

Althea looked at me uncertainly, and I gave her a thumbs up.

"It's okay, I'll just be back here," I reassured. She nodded slowly, took a deep breath, steeling herself, and headed out to the bar.

I let out a breath slowly and then turned to the room. There was a lot of work to be done…but no one said magical destiny adventures would be easy.

It was probably like two hours later when I finished sweeping and organizing the backroom. I had a system and had even cleaned the shelves and the table and the beer-making instruments lying about, using a bucket of water Emory had given me.

The floor was dirt, but sweeping helped a lot, because now it was solid dirt and not covered in bits of trash and rat poop or whatever anymore. I straightened the beer mugs and shined them, and basically, I was proud of my work. I went to find Emory, stepping back into the tavern that was a little less lively now.

Emory was behind the bar, preparing a drink for a patron, so I looked for Althea in the meantime. She was carrying two mugs with laser focus, dodging men's elbows and the occasional drunken fight. She was doing pretty good, it seemed. I turned back to Emory as he handed out beer mugs and glanced back at me, wiping his hands on a rag.

"You're finished?" he asked, and I nodded. "Let's see it then," he gestured for me to lead the way.

He followed me back into the backroom, and I smiled proudly. "Tada!" I sang quietly in a joking way. He hummed an impressed sound, looking around.

"Wow. I'm sure it's never been this clean. Good job," he sounded surprised, and I felt my proud smile get prouder. He looked at me for a moment before nodding. "Well, you can help Althea for a little while and then we'll see about that room," he decided, and I smiled.

"Yessir," I said with a little salute and went back out into the bar. He followed me out and handed me two beer mugs, which were much heavier with liquid in them.

"Take those to that table with the three men and the boy," he said, pointing it out to me, and I nodded, tongue stuck out with the effort of not dropping them. I walked to the table and carefully set the two down in front of the awaiting men, barely managing. Too heavy. I glanced up to find the boy staring at me.

He was probably about my age, with long hair that fell in small braids and curly tendrils and dark brown eyes that stared me down curiously. I gave him an awkward smile and went back to the bar, pretending that that didn't happen. Partially because it made me nervous, but partially because he was kinda cute and I had to go and smile so awkwardly at him.

For another hour or so, Althea and I did our best to bring drinks to customers, but we quickly wore down. I didn't know what time it was, but it felt late, and we'd walked a lot today already. Soon I could feel my eyelids sagging and my smile fading. Althea wasn't fairing much better.

Emory seemed to notice, and the next time we came for more mugs, he instead offered me the room key.

"You two have worked enough for one night. You've earned your rest," he said seriously. I smiled sleepily at him and took it.

"Thank you," we both said, and he gestured up the stairs.

"Goodnight," he said and we trudged up the steps slowly.

I fell into the bed with relief, and even though I'm pretty sure it was made of hay covered in fabric, I swear it was the most comfortable bed I'd ever laid in. Althea collapsed next to me, letting out a breath, and honestly, the lack of tavern noise felt amazing. We could still hear it, down below the floorboards, but it was muffled and quiet and I already felt like falling asleep, but stopped to pull off my shoes.

"Okay. We did it. We got a room," I said with a little smile.

"That was rough," said Althea, staring at the ceiling.

"Thank god for Emory," I mumbled, closing my eyes for a moment. "I like him, he's nice. That was worth it not to sleep outside."

"I guess," she sighed and rubbed her eyes. "But we're going home tomorrow. Okay? I'm not doing that again. We were supposed to just watch a movie and eat pizza and go to bed, you know, relax. That was the opposite." My smile fell a little, but I nodded and set my flower crown and glasses aside, on the bedside table.

"Yeah, alright," I mumbled as fell asleep. "I guess that wasn't exactly what I was hoping for from a Magical Destiny Adventure (™). Goodnight Althea."

"Night Molly," she replied and I slipped into a heavy sleep.

Chapter Four
Althea

I woke up to the sun coming in the dirty panes of the window and hitting me in the face. I didn't know what time it was exactly but it felt kind of early. I guess this isn't a dream.

I felt gross in my clothes from yesterday, somewhat beer-stained now. I'd definitely spilled a few at the beginning... With Molly still soundly asleep, I decided to have a look around to see if I could find something a little cleaner to wear.

The room was small but had a full-sized bed that we both fit in, a dresser, and a vanity with a mirror. I looked at myself and frowned at all the tiny hairs that had come loose from my braid. I tucked them back in as well as I could, using saliva for lack of water, and then distracted myself from it by going through the drawers. There were clothes in all sorts of sizes, which confused me, given this was a tavern. What kind of tavern is this?

I pulled out a dress that looked about my size and a little canvas bag fell out with it. This...doesn't exactly look medieval... I frowned and picked it up, and found that it was a fabric that I definitely had never seen or felt before. Inside, I found only a pin. It was bronze with a symbol on it that consisted of two triangles, one on top of the other, points touching, with a circle around it. This definitely wasn't made in this time period. Maybe it was from our world? When I turned the bag over, it had the same symbol embroidered into it. Hmm.

The dress I'd pulled out was a tan-yellow, with a white underdress and a brown piece that went on top, kind of like an apron? I remember reading that people in the old days wore lots of layers, and when I went to the renaissance fair, it was kind of like this. The dress fit pretty well but was tight in areas.

It was meant for someone taller and thinner, but at least this way, my clearly-not-from-this-world snow boots were hidden.

I found men's clothes lower in the drawers, baggy shirts and pants. I looked at the dresses again, but thinking about how most of them were going to be absolute bags on Molly and would definitely drag on the ground and make her trip, I instead picked out a cream-colored shirt for her and the smallest pair of pants I could find.

I nudged her awake when I'd finished looking around, and she groaned, rolling over.

"Five more minutes…" she mumbled, pressing her face into a pillow. I smirked a little.

"Okay, I guess we can put off Magical Destiny Adventure…" I trailed, grinning at her a little.

"Mmm…yeah…wait…what?" She opened her eyes finally and looked around, squinting, before fumbling for her glasses on the bedside table. She put them on, and then sat straight up. "Oh!"

I laughed a little bit and nudged her the clothes.

"Yeah well, get dressed, we gotta get home before my mom gets home and notices we aren't just asleep in my room," I said with a little fond smile as my friend's hair stuck up in every direction.

She rubbed her eyes sleepily.

"Yeah yeah yeah, parents and boring things, got it," she said and got up, pulling on the clothes. I made the bed as she did. "These don't fit…" I turned to look at her and found her holding up the pants in one hand.

"The shirt fits," I pointed out. She stuck her tongue out at me.

"Yeah, but I can't just wear the shirt," she replied, and I sighed, glancing around the room for solutions.

"I mean…I don't know, can you just hold them up for now? Maybe we can find something," I said with a shrug. Then I saw her gray joggers from yesterday lying on the floor nearby. "You could try the string from that?" I suggested.

She shrugged and bent down, pulling on it. "No, it's sewn to the back." She frowned and straightened, one hand on her pants. "I guess this is fine… I'll just change back in the woods," she mumbled, looking in the mirror. She made a face similar to mine when I saw my reflection, and took the ponytail holder off her wrist to tie her hair back, and the moment she let go, her pants dropped. She tied back the top half of her hair, which kept the rest of it mostly in order. I frowned when I had a thought.

"Hey, Molly?" I asked as she finger combed the bottom of her hair.

"Yeah?" she said distractedly.

"What do you think Emory meant when he said 'more of you'?" I frowned. She frowned too and then shrugged a little.

"I don't know, maybe he deals with a lot of poor children asking for rooms?" she replied, pulling up her pants and straightening, looking herself over. I shrugged, thinking that that was probably as good an answer as any as she pulled her pants back on properly. "Alright, I'm ready. Let's roll."

We walked down the stairs into the deserted tavern and glanced around for Emory. I looked at Molly to see if she had any ideas and she shrugged, still holding her pants up with one hand, our old clothes shoved into the bag I had found. I opened my mouth to say something and then paused when I heard the clank of metal hitting other metal softly, coming from the backroom, and what sounded like frying eggs, probably.

We nodded to each other and walked into the backroom, where Emory was bent over the fire with a frying pan in one hand and a spatula in the other hand, making breakfast. He looked up at us when we came in, and smiled with mostly just his eyes.

"Good morning, girls," he nodded to us. He definitely seemed less threatening in the daylight, and he did have kind eyes, I suppose.

"Good morning, sir," I said, staying mostly in the doorway.

"Morning sir," Molly said too, stepping just ahead of me. "Thanks again for last night."

Emory waved his hand a little, dismissively, flipping the eggs he was working on carefully.

"It was nothing, you did good work and earned your room, and I appreciated the help. Are you hungry?" he asked us, and I didn't realize until that moment just how hungry I was. We hadn't eaten since the evening before, and we *had* worked pretty hard last night…I was starving. Molly nodded a lot.

"Very," she said honestly, and it caused Emory to smile, just a little. I smiled too.

"Figured you might be. Here," he said and slid a couple of eggs onto plates that already had big pieces of ham, offering them to us. "Thank you for all your help yesterday."

Molly grinned widely and took the plate from him, making her way out of the backroom quickly. I smiled and took the other plate.

"Thank you so much," I said genuinely, and he nodded a little to me.

Plate in hand, I made my way to a table where Molly was sitting now, digging in already. I sat and started to eat, and Emory came out with two glasses of water, setting them in front of us quietly and then sitting at the end of the table. After a moment, he frowned a little.

"Where are you two heading after this?" he asked, looking between us. Molly and I exchanged a look.

"Um…" I started and glanced at him after a second. "Home."

He nodded a little, considering that, and then walked behind the bar and started cleaning it. I looked at Molly, who seemed to be eating her ham a little more thoughtfully now. But we had to go home.

I set down my fork just a moment after Molly and finished off my water with a gulp.

"Okay, we'd better get going," I said to her, wiping my face on the apronish part of my dress. She nodded and grabbed our plates in one hand, pants in the other, and walked back to the bar.

"Here," she said, offering him the plates. "Thank you, it was really good."

Emory smiled kindly, a little smile, and took the plates and forks.

"I'm glad you liked them. Are you heading out then?" he asked and she nodded. He looked at her for a moment, and then put up a finger to indicate that she wait a moment and headed into the back again.

I frowned at her and raised an eyebrow, wondering what he was doing, and she shrugged in response. He came back a moment later with a long piece of thick twine.

"This might work a little better for you. May I?" he asked and Molly frowned in confusion but nodded a little.

Emory knelt in front of her and carefully weaved the twine through the belt loops of her pants, tying it securely in the front.

"Oh," Molly said, and smiled at him. "Thank you, that's a lot better." He nodded a little and stood again. There was an awkward moment, and then he patted her head.

"Have a good journey," he said, and she nodded, blushing a little, and headed back to me.

"Bye, sir," I said, with a smile.

"Bye, sir!" Molly said too, and he smiled.

"You can call me Emory," he replied as we got to the door.

"Bye, Emory," we corrected and waved, before heading into the bustling town.

The town was much busier this morning than it had been last night. People weren't looking at us nearly as much, but that turned out to be not great either. We found ourselves weaving through people and dodging carts of fruit and cheese and other goods. I pulled Molly out of the way of a very angry man carrying a fish just before he ran her over. We were very relieved when we reached the edge of the town and began making our way back into the woods.

"Finally. I felt like I couldn't breathe back there. Not that it wasn't *awesome*," Molly said from beside me as we made our way up the hill.

"I guess," I replied with a shrug, and Molly sneezed. "Bless you," I said, and we kept walking. A few steps later, she sneezed again. "Bless you, again," I said with a frown, and then the third sneeze made me glance over at her. "You okay?" I asked. "Allergies?"

She shook her head and wiped her nose on her sleeve.

"I don't know, man, I didn't feel great this morning. Maybe it's just weird old different world air?" she suggested as we trudged up the rest of the hill. She coughed a couple of times and then cleared her throat and seemed to be okay. "Maybe I'll get super powers like Superman."

"Maybe." I frowned, looking at her before focusing on the trail ahead of us again.

We made our way through the deep forest, and I looked up at the trees fluttering in the wind, hearing our breath, the sounds of the woods and our footsteps on the trail in the quiet of the morning.

Crack!

I turned my head to look behind us, stopping and holding my breath as I listened. Molly looked at me and then where I was looking, holding her breath too, staying as still as we could, and when nothing happened, we shrugged at each other and started walking again.

We passed where we had met the fairies without seeing any (which is what I was hoping for, to be honest) and Molly didn't even seem to notice really. Soon we were back to where we should have started to see snow, but… There was just more path. I frowned.

"Wait, what? Where's the snow?" I asked, looking down the path. Molly kinda just shrugged, eyes forward.

"I dunno, maybe we just need to walk further?" she suggested, pausing with me.

"I…" I was fairly certain that this had been where the snow picked up, but the woods were deep and I'd only been through them once, and I guess maybe I could be wrong about it. "I guess," I sighed, and we kept walking, but I was starting to feel like someone or something was watching us, and my family would be home soon, and I was really worried I'd get home late and have to come up with some kind of lie to explain our clothes and where we'd been, and then we'd get in serious trouble…

It was these thoughts that completely distracted me from the fact that we were walking straight into some kind of camp. It wasn't until I heard the crackle of the fire that I looked up and froze.

Molly kept walking and I couldn't make a sound to stop her when I saw what was just ahead. I reached out wordlessly, making some kind of choking noise, and she looked back at me with a frown.

"What?" she asked, and then a hand larger than her whole body swooped down and picked her up. My jaw dropped.

A giant…ogre-looking…thing, stood in front of me, over ten feet tall, holding Molly upside down by the leg. It looked…wrong. Gray-skinned, huge, disproportionate, with long skinny arms and incredibly bone-looking fingers. It held her closer to its yellow, glowing eyes, pupils tiny in a way that sent a shiver down my spine. It looked down at her, sniffing her. Large feet made loud footsteps as a couple more approached, looking at my terrified friend as I stayed completely frozen, mind racing. What do I do? How do I fix this? How do I not die???

"H-hello there," Molly said quietly from above, looking between them with a nervous smile. "Um… My name is Molly and—" She then sneezed on the monster's face and the monster froze, before growling at her angrily and wiping the spit off its face.

I was frozen far too long, because suddenly one of the creatures noticed me. Its face...it didn't look quite right. Places opened that shouldn't have. It was large and rough, almost scaly, and when it looked at me, every muscle in my body that had been frozen a moment ago now urged me to run. I turned and sprinted as fast as I could, but only got a few feet before I too was scooped off the ground. I screamed and its giant hand began to tighten around me painfully until I had to stop. It carried me back to the others as I panted, mind racing, failing at wriggling away.

Molly came to be eye level with me, and we looked at each other in panic. Molly started coughing and I watched the monster squeeze her tighter. Were we about to die? I struggled to think of solutions in the scariest situation I've ever been in.

The ogre holding Molly growled to the other three, who growled back some kind of agreement and carried us into their camp, toward the large fire. My heart pounded in my chest as I looked all around to try and find some solution out of this, finding none, and then we were being lowered toward the flames. Was this seriously the end already? I squeezed my eyes shut.

Something rushed through the air past me and hit the arm of the ogre holding me. He made a kind of yelping noise and pulled back, roaring as he looked at what he was hit with. It was an arrow, with green and black feathers sticking out the back. An arrow? The ogre and I both glanced back to where it had come from and just saw trees.

But I saw this moment as my chance and ripped the arrow from his arm, stabbing it into his fingers that were still closed around my middle.

The ogre roared and dropped me, which was a pretty long fall, but I did my best to roll up when I hit the grass; I was lucky to have just missed a very pointy rock. The ogre roared at me, and I scrambled back just as another arrow was loosed, hitting it directly in the tiny black pupil of its disgusting eye.

It roared so loudly I thought my eardrums were going to burst, and I covered my ears, falling back over away from him. The two ogres who weren't holding anyone but had begun building up the fire in preparation for their meal of us stopped what they were doing and straightened, looking for something to hit.

More arrows flew from the trees, hitting each ogre in multiple places, until they eventually dropped Molly too, her glasses falling off as they did. She scrambled to pick them up and put them back on, and I ran over to her as she managed to get them on her face. I grabbed her hand and dragged her toward the source of the arrows, knowing they could very well also kill us, but knowing at least it wasn't an ogre. I ran with fear and panic, heart pounding too quickly in my chest.

The ogre that had been holding Molly roared and ran after us, but after being assaulted with two or three arrows, whizzing right over our heads, it gave up and fell back with a whine. All four escaped into the woods at a run that shook the earth.

We didn't stop running though, until we completely crashed into the archer responsible for saving us. Molly tumbled down next to us mostly, but I landed directly on top of him.

Oh my god. Oh my god; we just almost died. We didn't die. We escaped.

I caught my breath and looked with wide eyes down at the boy below me, who was hugging onto his bow so it wouldn't break underneath the weight of Molly and I. My heart was pounding and my blood was rushing from panic still, so it took me a moment to fully realize what was going on and really notice the person under me.

The boy had tanned skin and dark eyes, as if he didn't come from here, but somewhere south of here. His hair that had to be shoulder length was tied back with various methods, involving braids and silver bits and string and finally a ponytail, but in a way that still looked elegant and badass. Like a Viking? A tan Viking.

And that's when I realized in all my panic and adrenaline, I was still on top of him, just staring at him, and all the blood already pumping through me from panic and adrenaline rushed to my cheeks. He was staring up at me with the smallest smirk, not exactly flirtatious, but definitely amused. Maybe a little shy. He didn't say anything and I scrambled off him.

"I'm so sorry!" I squeaked, falling backwards in my hasty attempt to run. He smirked a little and sat up, brushing himself off.

"Is that how you thank the person who just saved your life? By tackling them?" he asked, and Molly handed him his quiver, which was wooden and leather, and I guess had fallen off when we collided.

"Sorry. Thank you," I said, smiling awkwardly, still very aware of how hot my face was right now and how hard my heart was still pounding. I stood and offered my hand to help him up, but he didn't take it, standing on his own. "I-I'm Althea Achebe, what's your name?" I introduced awkwardly, feeling incredibly shy.

"Gaelen. No last name, never had one, don't ask," he replied, putting his quiver back on. Molly, who had been going about picking up spilled arrows, paused and frowned.

"Hey, you're that kid from the tavern last night," she said, and I frowned, not remembering. He nodded.

"I am. I could tell you weren't from here," he answered, slipping his bow over his head to wear across his body. "I knew you wouldn't last a day by yourselves out here, especially with no weapons," he said, gesturing at us.

"How do you know that we don't have any weapons?" Molly asked, crossing her arms and trying to look tough.

"Because ogres just attacked you, and I think if you had any weapons, that would have been a good time to use them," Gaelen said with one eyebrow raised sarcastically, amused smirk never dropping. Molly blushed red.

"Yeah, no, you're probably right."

I sighed, feeling awkward and wanting to move on from this conversation. Gaelen did that for me.

"What are you doing out here by yourselves anyway? What's down the path that's important enough to face ogres for?" he asked, crossing his arms and looking between us.

"Our home." I glanced down the path through the trees. "Or…that's where it was." I sighed, shoulders falling. How were we going to get home now?

Gaelen frowned for the first time basically since we'd met him.

"That way? There's nothing that way. The next kingdom in that direction is over thirty days' walk away. It's just dense forest and monsters," he said, looking down the path.

"And fairies," Molly pointed out helpfully.

"Well, yes, fairies and sprites and nymphs and other various forest creatures, of course, but also ogres and werewolves and regular wolves, and bears and dragons and—"

"Dragons???" Molly emphasized in amazement, and wiggled her eyebrows at me excitedly. I rolled my eyes, and he looked between us.

"You…really aren't from here, are you?" he asked, and suddenly his eyes got the kind of sparkle Molly's did when you brought up cake. "Are you from the Time Hub?"

"Time Hub? No, we're from Colorado. Where nothing magical happens," I said, shrugging. His eyes somehow got…more sparkly?

"And do you have the rock?" he asked excitedly, and I raised an eyebrow.

"Um, rock? No? What?" Molly began, but she had that suspicious face a kid makes when they steal candy, and my eyes narrowed. "Is it a cool rock?" I asked Gaelen while staring down Molly, whose face was red now, looking anywhere but me.

"Yes! It's a rock that's said to contain all the cosmos, to be the most beautiful Device in the history of time!" Gaelen said excitedly, and I raised an eyebrow at Molly. She shrank back a little more.

"Mhm," I said in her direction, and Gaelen looked between us.

"And do you possess this rock?" he asked brightly.

"W-why? What does it mean if we…IF we did have this 'cool rock' you speak of?" Molly said with a nervous laugh, hands in her pants pockets.

"It would mean one of you was the one the prophecy speaks of! The Time Walker that will save all of time and magic!" Gaelen said, and suddenly I was looking at him instead.

"A prophecy?" I asked, and Gaelen nodded, turning to me.

"It is said that the prophesied one will arrive to this realm with the Key to the Cosmos, and will have hair like the ground and eyes like the earth, and that the Prince of the Eras will fall in love with her upon sight! And that she will stop the Suppression of Magic that is destined to come!" Gaelen explained brightly, looking between us. "Have you arrived with the rock?"

I looked at Molly and she looked at me, and we both had the same idea.

"L-like…like this rock?" She raised the rock from her pocket and my eyes got a little wide. It almost glowed, it was so gorgeous. The colors were very clear and bright, and I almost thought the dust clouds within were moving.

"That *is* a cool rock…" I mumbled mostly to myself, and Molly smiled sheepishly at me.

Gaelen gasped and slowly approached, reaching out and gently touching the rock in her hand.

"The Key to the Cosmos…" he mumbled in amazement, and then looked up at Molly. "This is yours?" Molly opened her mouth and stuttered out a reply.

"W-well, I mean, I found it in Thea's front yard, so I guess technically it would be hers…" she admitted with a blush at all the attention she was suddenly getting from him. He looked at me and then I was the one blushing, because his gaze was intense and searching. He approached me and looked me over.

"Hair like the ground and eyes like the earth… Are you smart? And kind?" he asked, stepping closer.

"Very," Molly replied helpfully from behind him and I blushed more.

"I guess?" Was I prophesied to save people?

"It must be you then! The prophesied one! I've found the prophesied one!" he said excitedly, taking my hand and raising it like I just won some kind of championship or something. I found myself smiling sheepishly and blushing more.

"I guess we know who the protagonist is now," Molly said with a little smirk, still holding the Key to the Cosmos in her hand. "I guess you're gonna have to believe in magic if you're gonna be the one to save it."

Chapter Five
Althea

Gaelen, Molly, and I were now heading back down the path toward the village of Althalamist, and Gaelen was excitedly telling me about the prophecy in detail. Meanwhile, I could feel the bruises forming from being dropped.

"Okay, and that's all lovely, but how do we get home? Because any minute now, my family is going to be walking through the door and panicking, wondering where we've gone," I said, worried.

"No, if that Key didn't bring you back just now, it's not going to," Gaelen said, glancing at me. "But you have a destiny to fulfill here."

"Guys…" came Molly's voice softly from a couple feet behind us.

"I don't care about a destiny!" I said, throwing my hands up. "I had a whole life, a family, parents, they're going to be so worried and I just need to tell them I'm okay," I said, feeling for a moment like crying. This whole situation was incredibly frustrating.

Molly's voice rose very, very softly from behind us. "Guys, can we stop for a moment?" she mumbled, but honestly, I wasn't paying attention. I was focused on my own incredibly pressing issues.

"Is there a way to send a message at least? Or something?" I looked at Gaelen, but he was looking back at Molly with a frown.

"Your friend looks ill," he said, and I finally glanced back at her.

She was naturally pretty pale and living in the snowy mountains didn't help that, but this looked like she had no color at all. I frowned, stopping.

"Molly? Are you okay?" I asked. She stopped walking for a moment, and I could tell she was shivering a little.

"Um…I think I might be sick?" she said, putting a hand to her forehead. She sneezed, and it devolved into some coughing. I looked at her with concerned eyes.

"You *were* in flip flops in the snow yesterday…" I mumbled, playing with the ends of my hair as I wondered what to do.

Gaelen frowned, looking her over and then shifting closer to me, speaking quietly so that Molly wouldn't hear. "Your friend is sick? I don't know how that is where you're from, but that is a very serious thing here."

I frowned quietly, looking at her. A serious thing? He turned to Molly, speaking at a normal volume again. "Would you like a lift into town?" He turned his quiver and bow around so they were across his chest instead of on his back.

Molly gave a small thumbs up and climbed on his back without hesitation. She looked exhausted.

"What do we do now?" Molly asked from his back as we started walking again.

"I'm sure we could find someone to help… Maybe Emory?" I suggested as we walked. Gaelen looked at me with knit eyebrows.

"The barkeep? Why would he help a sick child that isn't his for no repayment?" he asked curiously.

"Well, he gave us a place to sleep last night in return for us working for him, maybe he'll let me work in return for letting her sleep or for soup or something…" I considered.

"Soup sounds nice…" Molly mumbled from Gaelen's back and I got a little worried. I wasn't strong enough to carry her, so I was glad that Gaelen seemed to be very strong for his a—

"Wait, Gaelen, how old are you again?" I asked abruptly when I realized I wasn't sure.

"Don't know. Somewhere between eleven and thirteen," he replied, which was concerning.

"You don't know?" I asked in surprise. He grimaced.

"This goes along with the last name thing, no asking," he said, looking forward.

"Hey, I'm Molly by the way," Molly mumbled sleepily from his shoulder. He smirked a little, in a kind of cute amused way, glancing at her.

43

"Nice to meet you, Molly. Do you also not have a last name?" he asked in a joking tone.

"Nah, I do, it's Mihulka, but don't bother spelling it cause no one can," she replied sleepily.

"Can you say it again?" he asked with a smile, eyebrows knit.

"It's like...Muh hull kuh. Or Mih hull kuh, it doesn't matter, I don't care. Does chicken noodle soup exist here?" she asked, eyes closed now.

"Yes, in fact it does," he said, almost a laugh.

"Good, good...I'm gonna take a nap till we get there, please don't drop me 'kay?" she said, trailing off at the end, eyes closed, chin on his shoulder. I chuckled a little and walked closer, patting her head.

"Get some rest, hun. We'll be there soon." I smiled at her.

"Mhm..." she mumbled and then fell asleep on Gaelen's shoulder.

We walked for a little while in silence, but questions were swirling through my head and I had to ask them after a while.

"Gaelen..." I started in a soft voice. He looked up at me. "What is 'The Time Hub'?" I asked, not sure I wanted to know but knowing it was probably pretty important. I didn't want to feed into this whole quest thing...I didn't really want to think about it at all. I just wanted to go home... But if I'm here and doing this...I'd better at least try, right? It might be...well, the only way home.

He thought for a moment before responding, voice low. "The Time Hub is a place for all the realm-travelers of the worlds to meet and be safe. I've also heard it called Time City and The City Outside of Time, and once it was called 6-1-2-1-2-7-5 by a person of indeterminate gender in a strange yellow and tan suit. They were a very...interesting one," he said with a frown.

I nodded a little and kept walking down the path.

He continued, "In any case, no one's entirely sure where the Time Hub is, or what it actually looks like, but having a Device is the first step to getting there, I've heard," Gaelen finished, glancing at me. I nodded a little but didn't respond, lost in my own thoughts now. I could ask more questions when my best friend wasn't asleep on the person answering them.

I glanced around at the trees, the forest air warm, a soft breeze coming up the path and rustling the leaves. It was cloudy now, like it might rain. The air felt nice... But I was mostly focused on my parents. My mom would be so worried… And I loved her, she was soft and gentle, and if I disappeared, she would think the worst and…

"Oh, uh…" Gaelen said, glancing at Molly on his shoulder, walking more carefully. Her glasses were just about to fall off her face, so I stepped over and gently removed them, tucking them into my bag. She didn't even stir, so I figured it'd be safe to ask one or two more questions.

"Gaelen, this magical destiny thing, how long do you think it'll take? Saving magic, or whatever?" I asked in a very quiet voice, looking up at him as we started walking again. He thought for a moment.

"Well, I suppose… The first step is to see the prince to know if that truly is your destiny, and if it isn't, he will be able to help you home, if anyone could," Gaelen answered, dropping between a soft voice and a whisper. We saw the town in the distance. "But finding him is more difficult than you'd imagine," he added grimly.

"Difficult how?" I frowned.

"You have to follow ancient clues to find ancient items that will lead you to the location of his kingdom," he explained as we walked, a couple of drops of rain falling. I nodded slowly.

"So… Magical destiny adventure then, I guess," I said with a sigh, looking out to the quickly nearing town.

"Magical destiny indeed," Gaelen agreed with a soft nod.

A little while later, we were approaching the door to the tavern, which I now saw was called *Celtic Knot Tavern and Inn* on a painted wood sign hanging above the door. It was nearly noon now, based on the sun and my growing hunger, so there were a few people in the tavern, but it was still mostly empty compared to last night.

Gaelen carried Molly in and we walked toward the empty bar. Emory came out of the backroom with a plate of food in each hand, heading for a table. When he saw us, Molly still asleep on Gaelen's back, he frowned deeply. I smiled sheepishly, waving just a little.

Emory set the plates at the correct table quickly, and then headed toward us. We stopped in front of the bar and Emory stopped in front of us.

"What happened? Did you run into trouble on the road home? Is she injured?" he asked with concern, cleaning his hands on a rag.

"No, she—we're okay. She's just a little sick," I said quietly to him. He frowned more and nodded, glancing at the patrons, who didn't seem to hear or be paying attention.

"I see," he said, setting down the rag. "Follow me," he nodded and walked up the stairs. We followed him up, and I smiled at Gaelen.

"I told you he'd help," I said brightly and he nodded with knit eyebrows.

"I guess," he replied, voice a little strained as he carried her up the stairs. We followed Emory into an empty bedroom, number 3 this time.

"Go ahead and lay her down," Emory said, pulling back the blankets. I set her glasses on the bedside table and Gaelen did as Emory said, dropping her a little at the end despite his best efforts. She stirred a little, her eyes fluttering open.

"Mm? We're here?" she asked sleepily, clearly a little out of it.

"Yes. Sleep now, I'll bring you soup later," Emory said in a soft, fatherly voice, pulling the blankets over her.

"That sounds nice…" she said sleepily and curled up, coughing a couple of times. Emory gestured that we step out and we did, waiting in the hall.

"Rest well, I will return soon," Emory said to her as he finished tucking her in.

"Okay. Thanks, dad," she mumbled the response, halfway back to sleep already. Emory paused, and a look that I couldn't quite distinguish crossed his face. He opened his mouth as if to reply, but decided against it and stepped out of the room, closing the door behind him.

He was quiet for a moment, looking at the floor, and then between us.

"You didn't reach home?" he guessed, and I shook my head.

"No, we never got that far." I sighed.

"Your key did not work?" he asked with a questioning look and my eyebrows knit.

"My key?" I asked in confusion.

"Your Device," he clarified.

"The rock," Gaelen explained softly to me.

"How did you know about that?" I asked in surprise.

"I thought you were Travelers," he asked with a frown.

"I-I mean, I guess we are, but it was an accident. And we couldn't get back," I explained and he paused before nodding slowly.

"Ah. Well, you are very young, after all," he said without much explanation and walked past us, back down the wooden hall. "I will watch over your friend while you figure out how to get home," he said as he walked, and Gaelen and I looked at each other with the same thought. For free? We followed him down the stairs.

"What are we doing in return?" I asked suspiciously as I caught up with him. He shook his head.

"Nothing, for this. Don't worry. When your friend is feeling better, we can figure something out," he said, stopping at his bar and glancing back at us. "Do you have an idea of how to start?" He looked between us both.

I shook my head a little but looked at Gaelen. He looked at Emory, straightening, but it didn't add a lot of height to him. He was still an inch or two shorter than me, and I wasn't very tall to begin with. Neither of us matched up to Emory.

"We will go to the Prophecy Wall and figure out from there where to go from the clues," Gaelen said confidently. Emory looked me over.

"You think Althea is the prophesied one?" he guessed with a bit of surprise. Gaelen looked at me, before nodding and looking back at Emory.

"Yes, sir," he said decisively, "I do."

Emory was quiet for a moment, considering. Then he nodded and put up a finger and walked to the backroom, and when he came back he had a silver sword that seemed to not be used very much and had intricate carvings up the blade to the brown leather handle. It was a simple sword, but also gorgeous and detailed. He looked at me for a moment before offering it to me cautiously. My eyes got a little wide.

"You're…you're giving me this?" I blushed a little. "I don't even know how to use it…" I said slowly, looking up at him.

"I am allowing you to borrow it, you will need it," Emory said, and offered it to me again. "You'll learn how to handle it."

I hesitated, looking at the real life sword, and slowly took it from his hands in wonder.

"Be careful, it is very, very sharp. Here," he took a leather scabbard from under the bar, holding it so I could slide the sword in. I did, slowly and carefully, and then gingerly took the sword from his hands.

"W-well… Thank you. That… Wow. Thank you," I said seriously and held the sword close to my chest. "I'll take really good care of it."

Emory smiled a little and nodded his head to me. Then he offered me a leather-bound journal, which I was somehow more excited about.

"Here, you'll want to write the prophecy down," he said, and I took the journal with my free hand. "And here," he added, offering a quill and little vial of ink. I put everything that wasn't the sword in my bag delicately, super excited to use them later. I'd always wanted to. I collected journals back home, but rarely actually used them. They were so pretty, they needed important information in them...

"Wow...I..." I didn't know how to say thanks for all of this. He was giving us so much and he didn't have to. He smiled and patted my head.

"I know. Don't worry about it," he said kindly, then pushed across a sandwich cut in half.

"You'll need your energy," he said, "Take food for the road as well," he gestured to a bowl with some fruit in it on the bar, and we didn't argue. I shoved an apple into my bag and took the half sandwich.

"Bye Emory!" I called behind me as I left. "Thank you for everything!"

He waved in response with a small smile, and I followed Gaelen outside, ready for whatever was to come. *I'm going to get home. I won't let my parents worry for too long.*

Chapter Six
Althea

We walked through the town eating our sandwich halves, the town a little emptier now that lunch time was winding down, and I let myself look at it a little better than I had before.

The sun was out again and there were clouds in the sky but they were small and white and fluffy for now. People were buying and selling things, and most had smiles on their faces. There were young children playing, and children my age working and helping their parents. I remembered a fact from history class.

"Gaelen, do people really get married at thirteen here?" I asked curiously as I looked around. He blushed red and looked at me and then the ground and smiled awkwardly.

"W-why do you ask?" he started and I couldn't help but laugh a little at seeing his reaction.

"No! Gaelen, no, I was just wondering because I think I read it in a history book." Gaelen nodded a little, still blushing a good amount.

"It's wonderful that you can read, as a woman and all," he said, glancing at me. "The man who looked after me when I was younger taught me how to read," he said proudly, and I blinked, remembering that people back then—now—couldn't read. I didn't know if it worked the same in this magical fairy land though. "What are things like where you're from?"

I smiled a little. "Everyone can read, well…" I thought. "Well, most of the world I think, but yeah, everyone over, like…five or six, I think," I said as we walked, looking at him. He looked shocked but like, the happy kind of shocked, and nodded. "And people don't get married until later. Like, you aren't legally allowed to at all until eighteen," I said, looking at him again. His jaw dropped. "Like, thirteen is so young! I'm still a child!"

"Eighteen?" he sputtered, "That's so OLD! That's like a third of someone's life!" he said, and I smiled.

"People live past one hundred sometimes where I'm from," I said brightly and he looked at me with wide eyes.

"Really? I think when this is over, I might come to this land with you," he said, looking forward with a distant smile. "It sounds…magical," he smiled at me.

I smiled back "Okay, but there's actually nothing magical. No ogres or fairies or 'sprites'," I tried the last one, not remembering if that was one that he had said that or not. He frowned.

"Only humans?" he asked and I thought for a moment before replying.

"No, there's animals and stuff, but nothing with like, magical powers or qualities. No giants or anything human-y. Except monkeys," I said with a little smile at the thought. I had seen a video of a monkey wearing a suit and drinking tea earlier this week and I couldn't help but think of it.

Gaelen turned to me. "You've seen monkeys? No one here has, just me," he said seriously. "On a boat, once." I shrugged.

"Yeah, I mean, but mostly just pictures, or at the zoo." When I saw his confused expression, I added, "The zoo is a place they keep a bunch of animals and take care of them and let people from all around come see them," I said and his eyes sparkled at the idea, nodding a little.

"Zoo. Yes, I think I'll come with you when we get you home," he decided, and I shrugged.

"I'm sure we can find a place for you…" I frowned as I thought about it though. Would my parents take him in, or Molly's?

As if he could read my mind, Gaelen spoke up.

"I hope your friend will be alright." His tone was concerned, maybe a little grave even. I shrugged.

"I'm sure she will be, she's had a cold before. This isn't new," I said easily and he looked at me in surprise.

"People here don't often survive sickness. It is good your friend is away from everyone and won't get them sick," he decided, and I frowned.

"What about Emory?" I asked, looking at him. Gaelen looked back and shrugged.

"I'm sure he'll be alright, he's big and strong." I nodded slowly when he finished, but interrupting the next sentence he'd been starting.

"What about you?" I added, remembering how much coughing she had done on his shoulder and he smiled a bit.

"I don't really get sick anymore," he replied and I felt a bit better. But I kept thinking about what we were talking about… It was crazy that people could get married so young!

Like he could read my mind, Gaelen looked at me. "Most people wait, you know," he said, and I looked up. He was smiling gently. "Most people here don't get married until sixteen or eighteen or more."

I blushed but let out a little laugh, relieved. "Good. I'm glad to hear it."

Gaelen smiled at me and we watched the road again. Soon, we reached the west edge of town, far from the woods we came in.

There were three paths going in different directions, the middle one dropping down the hill into a valley far off, the right one heading up into the edge of the woods behind the town, and the left one heading out into what looks like farms, with trees coming after it.

"Which one?" I asked, looking down each.

"Well, that one," he pointed left, "goes south into the next village in our kingdom, Vale, and that one," he pointed right, "goes north into the bandit camps and then toward the mountains, but this one," he pointed forward, "leads to the lake and then splits off toward the Prophecy rock, which is where we need to be," he said and I nodded, trying to remember all of that, and then deciding to quickly write it in my journal instead. Gaelen helped by holding the ink jar.

We headed down the path toward the lake, into the valley. It was a longer walk than I thought, but I've walked so much the last couple of days that I just don't care much anymore. The sun was beating down and this dress was hot with all its layers and honestly, this quest felt like it was going to take forever.

"I was going to mention earlier," Gaelen started after a while of silence. I looked up at him. "I think we should watch out for Emory."

I frowned, looking up at him. "What? Why?" I asked in surprise. Gaelen's face held a distrusting look, deep brown eyes looking out to the trail in front of us. His shoulders rose in a small shrug.

"No one…" he started, then changed his mind and instead began, "For him to willingly take a sick person he met yesterday into his care is very strange. He risks getting sick, even if he is tough, and he risks losing the business of his patrons if they found out. So why help if he has nothing to gain and everything to lose?" He looked at me for an answer, which he knew I probably wouldn't have.

"Huh," I said, thinking about it, messing with my braid. "I guess…I'm not sure. He was…kind of nicer to Molly yesterday, and I don't know…I get, as Molly would say, 'Dad vibes'," I said with a shrug. "He's nice, and I feel like he's nice enough to help out a sick kid while we try to get home," I said, looking down the road.

Gaelen shrugged. "I guess. But I haven't seen very much of that kind of kindness. I still think he wants something." I stopped in my tracks while he walked on.

"Well…do you think we should go back? Do you think we shouldn't have left her alone with him?" I asked, suddenly concerned. He paused on the path in front of me and then shook his head.

"No, we won't be gone long and he's got a tavern to run, I'm sure…" He rubbed the back of his neck. "I've known Emory since after the Great Sickness last year when I started doing work with the Men. He's always been a nice guy, never caused any trouble or anything." He looked at me. "I just don't trust that there's nothing he wants, you know? You don't take in a sick person for no reason…" He trailed off and I nodded a little, thinking.

"Okay. Then let's keep going. We can figure out Emory's reason when we get back," I decided, and he agreed to it with a shrug and we kept walking.

We reached the lake in about an hour, appearing over the edge of the hill we were climbing, and it was huge and sparkly and beautiful. My eyebrows rose.

"Wow…" It was absolutely gorgeous, and I couldn't help but smile. Gaelen smiled too, looking at me.

"It's one of my favorite places to visit. Should we take a break?" he asked and I grinned, nodding and running down the rest of the hill to the shimmering lake. When we reached it, it was one of the clearest lakes I'd ever seen. The rocks at the bottom were beautiful and colorful, and now that the sun had come back out, it was hot enough to need the cool break.

Gaelen followed me down with a laugh and watched as I set my sword and bag on the ground, doing the same with his bow and quiver.

I had pants and a tank top under the dress I was wearing, so when I neared the water, I pulled my layers of dress over my head, not wanting to walk around in a heavy, wet dress all day. I ran for the water with a grin, glancing back at Gaelen—who was staring at me with wide eyes and a face that was getting redder by the minute. I smirked at him teasingly.

"What? Come on!" I splashed water at him. He turned fully away from me.

"This…you…what if someone comes by???" He whisper-shouted. His face was really red and it was funny. I knew this was something to do with women having to wear full skirts and that whole omg-is-that-an-ankle-I-spy thing or whatever, but I'm not swimming in a dress.

"It took an hour to get here and we didn't run into anyone, I'm sure it's fine, come on!" I splashed him again, falling back in the water.

Face still very much red, Gaelen took a deep breath, squared his shoulders, and then slipped off his shoes and vest, walking into the water with his tan three quarter length pants and white puffy shirt, which was still super funny, but who cares. I splashed him with a laugh.

"Hey!" he protested, finally actually looking at me again. "I'm in the water now, no more splashing!" But I splashed him again.

"It's called a splash war, dummy. And I'm winning." I stuck my tongue out at him and he fake gasped, not hiding the grin that came with it. I was feeling good, in this moment, allowing myself to have a little fun.

"Not for long you're not!" And then he splashed me as hard as he could. I laughed, falling back and kicking the water at him. I felt like I was relaxing for the first time since I got here. He laughed and splashed back and soon it just kind of devolved into splashing aimlessly and laughing.

We were both soaked now, splashing and trying to turn away before the other could splash again, but this time when I giggled and splashed him again, I heard a plunk kind of noise and dared a look when I didn't get splashed. My laughing stopped slowly when I saw that Gaelen was nowhere to be seen.

"Gaelen?" I asked, and after a moment of complete silence, he suddenly popped out of the water a few yards further into the lake, eyes wide with panic, hair matted to his head with water. I couldn't see what was in the depths beneath him, even with how clear the water was.

"Run!" he shouted in a desperate tone that terrified me, swimming toward me and the shore as hard as he could.

He didn't need to tell me twice. I sprinted through the water, but suddenly something slimy had my ankle and I slipped, and before I knew it I was being dragged backward, over the rocks. I gasped in a breath just as the water went over my head, rushing past me and the smooth stones slipping by underneath me. I heard yelling from somewhere above the water and felt Gaelen try to grab my arm as I passed him, but I slipped right through.

I dug my fingers into the rocks but it wasn't helping and I was getting deeper fast. I pivoted my body in the water, which took a lot more effort than I thought it would, and worked on ripping the tentacle from my ankle. My hands slipped over it desperately as water rushed past me, and then, in the light beams falling through the deep water ahead of me, began to appear a very, very large squid with a very, very sharp-looking beak. I froze and my eyes went wide as it held me in the water in front of it, drawing me in a lot more slowly now, staring at me with its big, black eyes…

And then an arrow whizzed through the water past me and into one of the big, black eyes, leaving a trail of bubbles in its wake. The squid screamed a deafening screech, even under water, and yanked back its tentacles to cover its eye, releasing me.

I swam up as fast as I could and saw Gaelen standing on the shore, dripping and panting, another arrow notched and pointed at the monster. I swam as hard as I could, running when I touched the bottom, but the arrows zipping past me told me the squid was gaining. Gaelen was walking closer as he shot arrows, one after the other, and I felt the tentacle just behind me.

"JUMP!" Gaelen shouted and I dove for him, catching his hand just as the squid caught my ankle. We both clumsily fell into the water, being dragged back down.

I held tight to Gaelen's hand. He fumbled for an arrow as they all fell out of his quiver, the tentacle dragging us over the rocks in the shallow water, and when his hand finally closed around one, he used it to slice the tentacle around my ankle.

The squid screamed again and the water quaked, and Gaelen and I scrambled to get our footing and get back to shore. He pushed me forward and I ran, not looking back, toward the dry land. I jumped the last couple feet desperately. I stopped on the dry shore, catching my breath, and then spun around to make sure the squid wasn't about to take me again.

Gaelen was nowhere in sight.

"Gaelen? Crap!" I yelled, a hand going to my head. It had gotten him.

I watched the water closely, holding my breath. "Come on, Gaelen… Come on!" The water was still. *He isn't coming back up. What do I do?*

I looked around and saw my sword, and looked back at the water. Could I really swim down there and kill it with a sword I'd never used? I hesitated, looking back at the sword…and sighed angrily as I picked it up, running back into the water. Stupid fish!

I trudged as fast as I could through the water, swimming when I could, and when I felt the tentacle around my foot, I took the deepest breath I could and let it drag me down into the water.

I held tight to my sword as the water rushed past me, and once we were deep down and I could feel the pace slowing, I opened my eyes to see Gaelen struggling against the tentacle as it pulled him closer, wrapped around his waist. His bow was floating up to the surface above him and all of his arrows were back on the rocks.

I let the tentacle pull me all the way in, heart pounding as I got closer and closer to the slimy, monstrous creature. I waited until I was within reach, a foot or two away, and slashed at it.

Slashing underwater was surprisingly easy with how sharp the sword was, so the cut was pretty deep and the squid screamed, shaking me. I couldn't help but smirk a little at my success and glanced at Gaelen. My smile dropped when I watched the air escape Gaelen's mouth, a desperate look on his face as he looked toward the surface. I turned to the squid as it held me tighter, another tentacle wrapping around my waist and drawing me quickly toward its mouth, and hacked off both of them, near the base.

The tentacles around me released and the squid screamed violently, causing a ripple effect all around. I was still flying through the water toward the dark, gaping hole of the squid's mouth though, by momentum alone.

Remembering my swimming lessons, I flip-kicked off the top of the squid's beak once I reached it and shot myself toward Gaelen, who was squirming violently and reaching for the surface. The tightness in my chest made itself known and my face was getting very red; I needed to breathe, like, now. I glanced at the surface far above for just a moment, but I knew Gaelen needed air far more than I did right now.

I caught him, arm wrapped around his shoulder, and sliced the tentacle from around him as hard as I could. Gaelen couldn't do much to help, holding onto me as I finally got him free and swam hard for the surface. I needed to breathe desperately after all that, it didn't feel like we were going to make it.

I was mostly swimming for Gaelen now, and the surface felt so far away, I wondered if we'd ever reach it…a few more feet…and then suddenly we broke through and I gasped in a breath, head spinning. Gaelen was coughing up water as I paddled us away from the rumbling and screaming coming from the deep water, keeping a tight grip on my sword.

When we got to the shore we were basically crawling, and threw ourselves onto the rocks just out of the water, just trying to catch our breath. Gaelen rolled onto his side, coughing up more water and dragging in a couple breaths. His bow washed up next to him.

We sat there for a little while, trying to breathe and just kind of recovering, and the squid didn't try again. We laid quietly.

After a couple of minutes, Gaelen picked up his bow and stood, looking out at the water. I pushed myself up and carefully raised my sword, taking a calming breath, and together we silently entered the shallow water and began collecting his arrows. Anytime a tentacle came near us, I stabbed it with my sword as hard as I could with no reserve. Stupid squid.

We made our way down the path quietly in our dry clothes again, having dressed in silence. I started re-braiding my damp hair.

"Favorite spot, huh?" I asked softly, glancing at him with a raised eyebrow.

"Well, I'd never actually gone into the water before, beyond putting my feet in," he replied with a frown, fixing his hair as well, which had fallen out completely, but was starting to take the shape of damp curls again.

"If there's a lot more of that on this trip, I'm not sure we'll make it back," I admitted grimly, eyes on the trail.

"The wall is still quite away, and that's only the first step," he said quietly, and I nodded seriously, getting back down to business.

"Right. Destiny quest to get home," I agreed with a sigh, and we started down the path. "Let's get this over with."

We walked through grass and rocks for a while before entering some trees again, following a creek running down from the lake. It was beautiful and peaceful…and I took a deep breath.

"Okay," I said out loud, and Gaelen looked at me. "I want to get home. I want to sleep in my bed, and tell my mom I'm okay, and not have to worry about monsters when I swim in lakes, and not need to use a sword, and make sure everyone isn't super worried about me and Molly, but…I'm in a beautiful, magical world, and we're doing our best to get home, so I'm going to take a deep breath and enjoy it while I'm here because I almost just died and there's nothing else I can do anyway, right?" I asked, glancing at Gaelen. He nodded, thinking about it.

"Right, we're doing what we can. We'll get you home," he said with certainty, looking at me again. I nodded too.

"Right. So let's enjoy this adventure, and not stress," I decided aloud to myself. "That's what Molly's wanted the whole time anyway, right?"

"Right," Gaelen said, as certainly as he could. But in truth, neither of us were certain on anything.

"Because at this point," I continued, "my mother has already realized that I'm not at home and she probably is already super worried, and as much as I don't like that, there's nothing I can do about it at this point… And now that I've acknowledged this, I need to move on to the next logical step, which is completing this quest as quickly as possible and making it home," I said decisively and looked at Gaelen. He nodded slowly.

"Yes. That sounds like a good plan… I'm sorry you couldn't make it home to your parents in time." His voice was apologetic, and though I didn't really know him very well yet, I was beginning to feel like he was a good person. He did save us…and after that squid thing, I knew I could trust him.

"Don't worry. I…can't linger on unsolvable problems." I was still stressed about this whole thing and I think he could tell, but I was going to embrace Magical Destiny Adventure, because I didn't really have a choice and I guess I'm the protagonist after all. "So tell me about this Prince of the Eras."

We made our way through the trees, a hill making its way up next to us so that soon one side of the trail was just a solid wall of dirt and rock. As we walked deeper, the hill fell away and the path turned, and we found ourselves walking toward the drop off part of a cliff, the top hidden completely from our view because it was so high up. I watched it as we walked.

"We're here," Gaelen said quietly, leading me all the way up to the cliff wall. As we got closer, I saw the carved writing begin to appear. It was written in English, which I guess shouldn't have surprised me but I guess I was expecting Latin or Elven or something. Here is what it said:

Our world is magical and strange, but with certain events, that may change

The rulers wish to end our reign, but one can stop the ensuing pain

Hair like the ground and eyes like Earth, the savior will light the hearth

Kind of heart and a gentle soul, they will sustain magic for us all.

The Prince of Time will know upon sight, and a love for the ages will come to light

Only the Chosen One, strong of mind, can save our souls and with it, Time.

I frowned as I read it again. "Who rhymes soul with all?" I mumbled to myself. Gaelen stepped toward the edge of the wall.

"That's the prophecy, but there's more," he said, nodding toward where the wall slanted off out of sight. I leaned around the corner where he'd nodded to, seeing more words.

"Oh." These didn't rhyme. Hmm.

Go North to the Heaven's Spires, find the pin.

Use the Key to the Cosmos that brought you here to unlock the Shield.

To the south, find the Eye of Horus and the Staff of Loki, then trek to the forgotten kingdom for the last element.

To find the prince you must follow the signs and unlock the gate.

"Instructions?" I asked as I read them once more.

"Seems that way. Many have tried to follow them, but none have succeeded," Gaelen said, looking up at the words. "Many don't make it past the first step."

"'Heaven's spires'? 'The pin'? What could that be?" I asked, running a hand over my braid as I thought. Gaelen looked back down the path.

"Well, the Heaven spires are just inside the mountains, but no one's found whatever the pin is meant to be," he said, and replaced a metal ring that was falling out of his hair from the squid attack earlier. I pulled out the journal Emory had given me and offered Gaelen the ink.

"Would you hold this for me for a moment again?" I asked as I pulled out the quill.

"Oh, yeah, sure," he said awkwardly and popped the cork off, holding it up for me. I dipped the tip of the quill in carefully, and he frowned a little. I raised an eyebrow as it dripped.

"What?" I asked, and he looked up at me.

"Ah… Well, I think you're supposed to dip it in a little further, to fill the canal inside it with ink…" he said sheepishly, shifting feet to hold the ink at an easier position. I frowned.

"Huh. Alright." I did as he said and watched as tiny lines on the quill turned black with ink. "Thank you," I replied and he nodded. I quickly began to copy down the carvings, both visible from where we stood. This was definitely much easier than when I had tried writing earlier. I was glad he had said something.

I nodded as I finished. "I guess we'd better head to the spires then," I said determinedly, shaking what was left of the ink off the quill and tucking it and the journal back in my bag. Gaelen re-corked the ink and handed it to me. "Thanks." He nodded as I put it with the other things carefully. I headed back down the path with determination. "Let's do this, we got spires to find."

"Wait, that's going to be harder than you think," Gaelen called after me, catching up quickly. "We have to walk all the way back to town, and then make our way North through the bandit camp and into the mountains, all of those things take time and hold serious danger," he said seriously. I hesitated.

"Okay…well, we know where to go, we could start by going back to the town and getting some rest and supplies and then make a plan to get through this 'bandit camp'…" I thought, playing with the edge of my bag.

Gaelen looked at the prophecy one more time before nodding. "Okay. Yeah, that sounds like a good plan for now. Let's start heading back before it gets too late." I nodded in agreement and we headed back down the path quietly.

We didn't see the figure standing at the top of the cliff, watching us leave.

It took a couple of hours to get back and my feet were killing me by the time we arrived at the tavern. It was past dinner time and we'd eaten all of our snacks on the way back. We trudged up the steps and into the bustling tavern.

Emory saw us when we walked in and nodded to us, seeming a little relieved. As we walked in, Gaelen touched my arm.

"Hey, I'm gonna stop to talk to those men about supplies," he explained, nodding to a table of men drinking and laughing.

I nodded. "Okay, see you," I replied and he smiled and nodded back before splitting off. I approached Emory alone.

"Hey," I said when I got there. "How's she doing?"

Emory nodded a little. "Not well, but getting better. She's resting for now," he said and I nodded in response, not really sure what else to say. I…felt like I could trust him, despite what Gaelen said, but I also trusted Gaelen… So I wasn't sure for now.

"Thank you, again," I replied softly, smiling gently at him. He nodded and was quiet for a moment before he pulled out two bowls, filling them with steaming chicken noodle soup, setting them on the bar in front of me.

"Here," he said. "For you and your friend."

I smiled gently and sat down on the wooden bar stool in front of it, gesturing to the other when Gaelen approached.

"Thank you, Emory," I said and he nodded and slid me a key.

"This is for the room you stayed in last night." I took it and thanked him again. Gaelen pulled up another bar stool and started quietly on his soup. Emory paused as I took a spoonful. It was really good, I bet Molly had loved it. "How did…your journey go?" he asked a bit stiffly, awkwardly. "Did you find what you were looking for?"

I nodded with a little smile, lowering my spoon.

"Yes, we found the prophecy and stuff, and we're gonna get supplies tomorrow and try to follow the clues," I replied, and he nodded a little in response.

I glanced around the busy bar as I sipped another spoonful, Emory already going back to cleaning glasses. "Would you…like help again tonight?" I asked hesitantly. My feet ached and I really didn't want to move anymore. I just wanted to sleep. But Emory was doing a lot for us and he definitely didn't have to, and I was worried if I didn't help out, we'd have to leave, and then where would we go?

Emory smiled gently at me.

"Go to sleep, you can help me in the morning," he patted my shoulder and I yawned, rubbing my face.

"Yes sir," I replied and stood, glancing at Gaelen. He was finishing up his soup and stood when he was done, wiping his face on his sleeve.

"See you tomorrow, then?" he asked with a little smile and I smiled back.

"See you tomorrow. Thanks for helping me," I said seriously and he winked.

"Anything for the Savior," he teased and waved to Emory. "Thank you for the food, sir." Emory nodded to him.

"Thank you. Goodnight, Emory," I said as I stood and I headed up the stairs with a yawn,

"Althea?" Emory called from behind me, and I glanced back at him from a couple steps up.

"Yes?" I asked, eyebrows knit softly. He was frowning gently and gestured at my ankle.

"What happened?" he asked, and I glanced down with a frown. There was blood on my shoe and a cut on my ankle that was scabbed over.

"Oh," I said in surprise. "That…happened earlier. Gaelen and I ran into a lake monster," I said. "It…must have been when he sliced the tentacle off with his arrow."

Emory's eyebrows rose in surprise, but he nodded slowly. I blushed, feeling embarrassed even if I wasn't sure why. Emory nodded and I nodded and then turned, beginning up the stairs again.

"Goodnight Emory," I called, eyes already drooping.

"Goodnight Althea."

I got to our old room and saw that the bed was made. I collapsed into it and fell asleep the second my head hit the pillow without another thought, on top of the blankets.

Chapter Seven

Molly

I woke up mid-afternoon in a bed I didn't recognize. Oh, ugh, I feel awful. Where…am I? I listened for a moment, then sneezed into my arm, then listened again. Oh. The tavern. Right. I yawned and it turned into a cough, and then stretched slowly. I found that I was freezing and wrapped myself up more in the blanket. Isn't it supposed to be summer here? Why am I freezing?

I groped around for my glasses on the table, and then glanced around the room and realized I was alone. Where is Althea? And…that nice archer man who carried me here? Gae-something. Gaely? No, that sounds wrong and, well, not like a real name…

I shivered and pulled my legs close to me, propping myself up against the wall. I'm sick. And I hate being sick. And my mom isn't here to feed me soup and let me watch TV all day until I feel better. I coughed a couple more times and looked around for another blanket, or water, or…

"Oh." There was a glass of water next to me, I had touched that earlier looking for my glasses. I took it and quickly gulped down a lot of it. That seemed to help. Okay. Next, the blanket issue. None here…I'll have to get out of bed and go find one.

I was halfway out of bed when the door opened.

"Oh," Emory said in surprise when he saw me awake and getting up. He was holding a blanket in his arms.

"Oh," I said back in surprise and pulled my legs back into the bed. "That's what I was getting up for," I admitted sheepishly. Emory smiled at me a little, which made me smile a little.

"That's good then." He came in and gently placed the blanket over me. "You should get a little more rest," he said in a sort of comforting fatherly way, and I curled up again. But there was one thing on my mind…

"I was…wondering if maybe you had some soup I could have…" I asked slowly, feeling bad for asking but wanting it so much. Emory smiled at me, this time a full smile.

"It's almost done. Please rest until I bring it up," he answered as he carefully tucked the blanket around my feet and legs.

I blushed a little. "You were already making it?" He nodded with a soft smile and patted my head.

"Get some rest, please." He headed back out and gently closed the door behind him.

"Okay," I said, already sleepy, and rubbed my face, slipping back under the warmer blankets. "Thanks, Emory…" I mumbled but he was already gone.

I woke up again to the door opening quietly and I felt like time was jelly. How long had I been out? It felt like maybe a minute but it had to have been longer… Heavy footsteps approached and a weight sank into the right side of my bed.

"Molly," Emory's voice came gently, and I opened my eyes a little, waking up a little more.

"Mmm…soup's ready?" I said sleepily, making myself sit up despite how weak and tired I felt. Emory offered me the steaming bowl, a spoon sticking out of it, and I took it gently. "Thank you," I said with a yawn, but then started coughing and Emory took it back for a moment, before I spilled it all over myself.

I smiled sheepishly. "Thank you, again," I said, and this time instead of the bowl, he handed me a handkerchief first, which I blew my nose into. I kept that one, folding it up and setting it next to me for later. He gently handed back the bowl of soup.

It looked to me like chicken noodle, which honestly would be the best, and when I took a bite (and blew on it first, per Emory's request), I found that it was so much better than any soup packet I got when I was sick back home.

"Wow!" I said brightly between bites. Emory seemed pleased, smiling while I downed the rest, relishing the feeling of the warm liquid soothing my aching throat and warming my belly.

Emory stayed until I had finished, and then he took the bowl and patted my head as he left.

"Get some rest."

I fell asleep warm and happy and coughing less.

The rest of the day was spent sporadically sleeping, but in the early evening, I guess before the dinner/after dinner rush, Emory came up with a deck of cards and pulled a chair up to the side of my bed. I'd been awake for a while just lying there so seeing the cards made me sit up a little more, excited.

"Thought you might be getting bored," he said as he shuffled the cards, and I found myself smiling with relief.

"Yeah, I was super bored." I breathed in relief and he chuckled a little, beginning to deal the cards onto the bed. I sat against the back of the bed, pulling my legs up to sit crisscross and took the cards he handed me.

"What are we playing?" I asked as I straightened each card in my hand.

"A game I learned years ago from another traveler. It's called rummy, have you played?" he asked, setting down the deck and flipping a card.

"Mmm…I think with my grandpa, but I don't remember," I said, and he nodded.

"You are trying to make a set, that's three or more of one card number, or a run, that's cards of the same suit in order. Do you know what a suit is?" he asked and I nodded.

"Heart, spade, club, and diamond," I said proudly because I knew a thing. He nodded.

"So if you have the six, seven, and eight of hearts, that's a run, and you can put it down." He showed me by setting some cards down on the bed. "And then you can play cards on my cards if you have them, as in if you had the nine of hearts. Each card you put down is five points to you. Ten, jack, queen, and king are ten points, and the ace is fifteen," he explained and I nodded along. "Any cards left in your hand at the end take away points."

"Okay, I think I get it," I said, organizing my cards with laser focus. He smiled softly.

"Your turn first, then."

We played cards for an hour or two, and I beat him at a few rounds, but was mostly losing. When I lost another round, I sighed and he ruffled my hair with a smile.

"Don't worry, I have been playing for years, it takes time to get good at anything," he said and I stuck my tongue out at him, fixing my hair, but smiled a little.

"That's okay, it's still really fun," I said brightly, handing him my cards as he began to shuffle them again. I coughed a couple times into my arm, and then it was quiet. He looked off for a moment, eyes distant. I frowned, looking closer at him. "Emory?" I asked softly.

"This was my daughter's favorite game," he said, eyes distant. I was quiet, waiting for him to continue. He took a breath, still staring off, and spoke again. "When she was about your age, we would play cards all day when she was sick. More when she started beating me…" He laughed softly at the fond memory, but there was sadness behind it, and I noticed his eyes get a little shinier. He took a breath and blinked a couple times, almost like he had just become aware of where he was, and he picked up the cards.

"I'd better open the tavern for the evening," he decided, standing and putting his chair back. I watched him, not sure if I should ask but needing to know.

"What…what happened to your daughter?" My voice was soft. I knew she probably didn't just grow up and leave, but…

"She…she's gone," he said, and stood in the doorway for a moment before stepping out. "Get some rest."

The door closed and I was left staring at the back of it.

I woke up the next morning to find the light streaming through my window. It was pretty early and the air was chilly. I rubbed my face and sat up, pulling the top of my hair back again after it had come out in my sleep. I coughed a couple of times and wondered how Althea was, and if she got back last night safely. I walked to the door, keeping myself wrapped up in a blanket, and when I opened the door, I could tell there were only a couple of patrons in the tavern. The sun must have just come up. I stopped at the top of the stairs for a moment sleepily, and in that moment a door behind me opened and I could hear the voices of my friends.

"…the bandits, then won't it still take us hours or days to reach the Spires?" Althea said as she exited the room, Gaelen behind her, in full adventure gear. Her dark hair was freshly braided and she looked and sounded just as focused as she was when she had an English assignment to complete. Gaelen's hair was in a ponytail, which was honestly cute. Huh. What was he doing in her room? Where were they going now?

That's when Althea noticed me. "Molly! Hey! How are you feeling?" She approached. I looked between the two of them.

"Still sick… Where are you two going?" I asked suspiciously, raising an eyebrow. Althea seemed to understand what it looked like and blushed red.

"Molly!" she exclaimed in a reprimanding way, "Gaelen just got here, we have to leave to go find a shield north of here!" She smacked my arm lightly. Hmm…

"Sure, okay." I kinda half teased and she smacked my arm again, harder, face still red. Gaelen nodded quickly.

"That is what happened," he said with a defensive blush. I believed them, but I also thought their shyness was adorable. Hmm. I ship it.

"Fine alright, but I want to come with," I decided seriously. And then, sadly, I started coughing again. I cursed quietly. Althea smiled gently at me.

"Hun, I think you need to recover a while longer," she said, softly touching my shoulder. I pouted.

"I'm fineeee, I can just walk behind…you won't even notice I'm—" I coughed a couple times "—there," I finished. Gaelen shook his head.

"You should stay in your room until you are not sick. We do not have very good means of curing sickness here and it is very easily spread. You'll want to be very careful about coming in contact with anyone here until you're no longer sick," he insisted. My eyes went a little wide. Did that mean Emory was going to get sick? And Gaelen, because he had carried me?

Gaelen seemed to notice me worrying and smiled a little.

"Don't worry about me, I got sick last time everyone did and made it out fine, I'm unlikely to get sick again," he explained, and I felt a little better.

"But what about Emory?" I asked, and he shrugged a little, looking at Althea.

"I'm sure he knows what he's doing," he said with a nod, and I sighed, rubbing my face.

"Fine. Okay. How long will this 'adventure' take you, you think?" I asked, surrendering to the fact that I'm on a magical destiny adventure and I have to miss it because I'm sick. This is just like the field trip to Elitch

Gardens last year. Except this time, I'm missing riding dragons instead of riding roller coasters.

"It should take a couple of days or more, the mountains are a ways away, and once there we'll have to search for the shield, which no one has found," Gaelen said. "So maybe a week or two." My eyebrows shot up.

"A week or two? Where will you sleep? What will you eat? How will I know if you got kidnapped or killed by dragons or something?" I asked, running a hand through my hair.

"You won't," Gaelen said easily, "But we've gotten weapons and we're packing food, and I'm bringing rolled beds."

"Sleeping bags," Althea explained, patting my shoulder. "And we'll be back before you know it," she smiled at me reassuringly, but I was frowning a little now.

"Thea, what if you don't make it? What if you get hurt? There aren't ambulances and hospitals here," I asked her quietly, so maybe Gaelen couldn't quite hear. "Please don't forget, we're still twelve," She shook her head and looked at me.

"Molly, this is a magical destiny adventure, and I have a sword. We'll make it—"

"You have a sword???" I interrupted, eyes wide. She DID have a sword, it was attached to her hip. My mouth dropped open.

"Y-yeah, I do," she said awkwardly.

"When did you—a sword??? I want a sword!" I complained, and she put a hand up.

"Molly—"

"Seriously, where can I get one?" I asked incredulously, looking at Gaelen. "She just—she gets a sword?" He put his hands up like it was all out of his hands. "Seriously, When—"

"Molly," she stopped me, eyes closed in annoyance or frustration or both. "We'll both get through this and get home, okay? I promise," she said, and then paused for a moment, like she was going to say something else, face serious. She waved it off though, and smiled a little. "And you know how I get when I want something. I don't let anything stop me."

I rolled my eyes with a little smirk. "You are stubborn like that," I teased and nudged her. "Fine, go on your magical destiny adventure, but you'd better bring me something back! And it's gotta be as cool as a sword!"

Gaelen and Althea both smiled, but they weren't leaving yet and now they were looking at each other. I frowned, looking between them.

"What?"

Gaelen nudged Althea and she sighed, turning to me.

"Molly… We need the Cool Rock for the quest," she spoke gently like she knew exactly how much I didn't want to give it to her. My face fell.

"What? No! Not the Cool Rock! You said I could have it…" I complained and coughed a couple times.

"I know, I know, but that was before it was a magical destiny rock tied to my future and ability to get home. And I can give it back to you after the quest, but we reeeeally need it right now, please?" She begged, hands together, bottom lip out in an overdramatic pout. I couldn't resist the face.

"Fine! Here! You dork!" I said, a small smile slipping out over her antics despite the situation and took the rock from my pocket. I handed it to her. She grinned.

"Thank you!" she said and put it in her bag. She was wearing pants today, probably taken from that drawer. I couldn't imagine that skirts were great for adventures. "We'll be back as soon as we can," she said, closing her bag and pulling me into a hug. "Rest so you can get better and help us on the next quest," she said and I nodded.

"Yeah, I will. Go have fun. Don't get killed. Or maimed," I said, and gently let go. "I'll be here, eating soup and coughing."

She laughed a little and hugged me one more time.

"Feel better! Wish me luck on my adventure!" She was giddy with excitement. I hoped it really was fun for her, but also that the most fun stuff was to come so I could be a part of it.

"Good luck!" I called as they passed me. I caught Gaelen's arm as he passed. "Hey, don't let anything happen to her. You saved us, so I trust you, but if anything happens to my best friend and I find out you didn't even try to help?" My threat seemed to land despite the height difference, my eyes bearing into his soul. He gulped and nodded.

"Yes ma'am. I'll keep her safe," he said, and I nodded and let him go.

"And don't think I'm asking this 'cause you're a boy and she's a girl! It's because you know how to use weapons!" I called after him, and then suddenly, he stopped and paused, then turned, coming back up to me. His big nearly black eyes were serious.

"Molly, here," he said and quietly slipped me a little dagger, glancing around to make sure no one saw. I frowned but took it. "…Just in case."

"In case of what?" I asked at a whisper, tucking it into my pocket.

"In case of anything. Be safe, okay?" he said seriously, waiting for an answer from me. I was frowning but nodded a little.

"Yeah, I will. You too," I said and he nodded seriously and then patted my shoulder.

"Feel better. See you soon," he said, and began to leave again.

"Remember to bring me something!" I called after him softly and heard the quiet laugh from him before he headed down the stairs. I sighed softly, and then they were gone and I was coughing again and heading back to my room. This is the worst, but I guess I had to deal with it.

I crawled into bed and pulled the blanket around me, and then pulled the little knife from my sweater pocket. I wonder why he gave me this…but I guess I'm glad I at least get a weapon on this adventure, even if it's not a sword. I tucked the knife away in the drawer on the bedside table, and started thinking about Emory…I shouldn't play cards with him anymore, he's doing a lot for me and I can't risk his life or health…

I settled into bed, ready to tell him to go away for his own safety if he came back, and feeling pretty down. I'm missing everything that I've waited forever for…but there isn't anything I can do, so I guess I'm here, rockless and TV-less and I guess it doesn't matter… When I'm better, I'll adventure. For now…I need to focus on making sure I don't accidentally kill Emory.

I woke up an hour or two later when the door opened, jolting upright because I hadn't even realized I'd drifted off.

"Oh," Emory said with surprise when he walked in. "I didn't expect you'd be awake yet. I brought you some more soup from yesterday," he said as he came in, but I put a hand up gently.

"Emory, I think you shouldn't come in anymore," I said seriously and he paused, frowning softly.

"Oh. Why not?" he asked, holding the soup, staying awkwardly in the doorway.

"Because I'm sick and I don't want you to risk getting sick and dying trying to take care of me," I said, and relief washed over his face. He smiled softly in an amused way.

"Oh, you don't have to worry about that," he said as he walked in, letting the door close behind him. I frowned.

"I don't? Why?" I asked, and he came and sat on the edge of my bed again, next to me, setting the soup aside for the moment. He didn't answer right away, thinking.

"Do you...remember what I was saying about my daughter?" he asked me, speaking slowly. He looked at me now, waiting for a reply.

"Yes," I answered, listening quietly. His daughter that was gone.

"Yes, well...a year and a half ago, mid-winter, a sickness very much like the one you are fighting off swept through Althalamist. Except, unlike those back at your home, we aren't able to fight it off so easily. Many died. My wife got sick...I did too, but it was mild and gone within days.

"It took my wife very quickly, even as strong as she was. Alice was by her side every day, caring for her and stayed with her when she was gone... It was very hard on her," he said, eyes dropping to his hands in his lap. He was quiet for a moment.

"When everyone seemed to be past the sickness or dead, nearly a month after we lost her mom...Alice began to get sick." His voice was very soft now. "It started off slow and got worse with each day... It didn't help that it was the coldest week of the year," he sighed, and I could hear the break in his voice as he started again. "She spent weeks in bed, and I spent every moment with her, but there was nothing I could do. She—" He cut off suddenly, covering his mouth with his hand. When he spoke again his voice was high pitched and fragile, breaking with each word. "She left to be with her mother..."

My heart ached, seeing such a kind and gentle man break in front of me. Tears dripped from his eyes all at once. I reached out and gently put my hand on his shoulder in support. The moment was quiet. I didn't know if there was anything I could say. He wasn't ready to talk about this...

"I'm so sorry," I said softly after a moment, tears dripping from my own eyes now. It was...shocking to see this level of emotion from a man who didn't show much of any emotion up until this point. He squeezed his eyes shut for a moment, quiet. Then he took a deep breath and sat up a little straighter, wiping the tears from his eyes.

"But anyway, you don't have to worry about getting me sick. I'd better get back to the tavern. Please, eat your soup and rest," Emory said as he stood, gently patting my head without really looking at me and walking out the door.

Chapter Eight
Althea

"How'd this morning go?" Gaelen asked as we walked through the town center.

"Good. Emory woke me up a little before dawn and just had me help clean the tavern and set up for breakfast. It wasn't too bad," I explained with a shrug, and he nodded. "Did you give Molly the dagger?" I asked and he nodded again.

"Yes, she should be safer with it. I'm sure she'll be alright. Did Emory say anything about leaving Molly with him for a couple of weeks without you working for him as repayment?" he asked and I nodded.

"Yeah, I asked and he just said that when Molly was feeling better, he'd have her help out and it wasn't a problem." I paused. "But I'm glad you gave her the dagger just in case." Gaelen nodded in agreement.

The first stop on our destiny quest was to wherever Gaelen lived for food supplies. I figured it'd be like a little cottage or something, maybe shared between a few men, but what we walked up to was...well, maybe better described as a hovel. A very overfilled hovel.

We reached the outer part of town when Gaelen pointed it out, where the farms began and the village part faded out. The roof was made of mostly hay and the rest was wood, but it was kind of falling apart. There were men working outside of it, a few gardening in the yard near the hovel, a group out in the fields beginning their farming, a couple standing in groups and drinking and laughing...which felt early, given it couldn't be later than maybe seven a.m. and the air was only just starting to warm up.

I glanced at Gaelen uncertainly, but he just kind of smiled at me and led me toward the men. Okay. No judgement. This is where he lived...but lord, could it use a little cleaning... Okay, a lot of cleaning.

Gaelen led me around the corner of the hovel to a couple of guys hanging around a fire with a big flat piece of metal over it, lots of meat and eggs cooking on top of it, steam rising heavily into the chilly morning air. Overall, it felt very much like camping.

The man doing the cooking was tall and muscular with a short beard, almost like a five o'clock shadow, and long hair like Gaelen's, including pieces of metal and braids, but pulled back into a bun instead and clearly much longer than Gaelen's.

"Cecil!" Gaelen called happily and the man at the grill looked up from the food. He smiled in a warm, friendly way as Gaelen ran up and hugged him. Cecil, who I now was getting a better look at, laughed a little and hugged him back.

"Hey there, kid! Enjoying your quest?" he said in a voice that was deep and smooth, like molasses, and I couldn't help but notice the physical resemblance. That HAD to be his father. Their eyes were a very similar dark brown, and though Cecil had a slightly darker tan and darker hair, they had the same smile. They both looked somewhat Latino to me, especially compared to literally everyone else around.

Cecil had a sharp jawline and was basically just super ruggedly handsome, even though he had to be in his twenties or thirties, maybe. I don't know, it's hard to tell with the beard. I'm gonna guess thirties? He had tattoos down one arm, but they were kind of delicate and intricate looking… Oh man, am I staring? I blushed and looked down.

Gaelen let go of Cecil with a grin and gestured at me.

"Cecil, this is my friend Althea. She's the Prophesied One," he said proudly, and Cecil looked at me. His eyes sparkled similarly to Gaelen's as he looked over me carefully.

"The Prophesied One, huh?" he asked with interest, stroking his very short beard as he slowly circled me. I blushed a little more.

"Well, maybe…" I said shyly, and pulled out the Cool Rock. "I've got the Key to the—" Cecil interrupted me by quickly folding my hand back over the rock and putting it back in my bag, smile gone, eyes scanning the area around us quickly.

"That is a very important object, Althea," he said seriously, tone warning, eyes boring into mine now. "If someone stronger and greedier than you knows you have it, they might try to take it from you. Keep that safe and

73

hidden as much as you can," he warned me seriously, and I nodded a little, heart pounding.

"R-right, okay. I will. Thank you, sir," I said, tucking it away. He nodded seriously, and then the tension in the air released as he smiled at me.

"Don't worry about it too much. I'm sure you're a responsible kid, Prophesied One. And smart too." He winked playfully at me and I blushed a lot more.

"Aha, well, I try to be…" I said shyly, and he chuckled, patting my head.

"I'm sure you are. Gaelen told me a lot about you when he came back from your trip last night." Gaelen behind him blushed a little. I looked at him with a little smirk.

"Has he?" I asked, eyes on Gaelen. Gaelen blushed a little more.

"A-anyway! Cecil! We're here for supplies for our journey!" Gaelen interrupted, sweating a little and smiling nervously. Cecil chuckled and nodded.

"Of course. Have you two had breakfast yet? Eggs're just getting done." He went back to the grill, flipping eggs and taking some of the meat off the metal piece and onto a flat, smooth tree stump next to the fire. Random men from the hovel kind of filtered in and out, grabbing food.

"No," Gaelen replied, and was handed a thin piece of wood with some bread, two eggs and some bacon looking stuff on it. "Thanks Cecil!" Gaelen seemed calmer now that we weren't talking about him. Cecil offered me one too.

"Thanks," I said and sat on a log next to Gaelen. Cecil put the rest on the stump, and then took his own and sat on a log across from us.

I stared down at my plate for a moment, then glanced around for silverware. There didn't seem to be any. Then how do I eat this? Just stick my face in the plate? Hands to mouth?

"Like this," Cecil said with a soft smile, and tore off a piece of the bread stuff – now I'm guessing more a tortilla type thing – using it to scoop up some egg and sausage and eat it in bites, like mini tacos or something.

"Oh," I said and noticed Gaelen doing the same. I went and grabbed a few tortillas, trying it myself. It took me a couple of tries but I got it eventually. It tasted surprisingly good for something that definitely didn't have salt or pepper. Man, I miss seasonings.

"You don't really look like a 'Cecil'," I admitted to him between bites of eggs. Cecil's face got a little red.

"Yeah, you're right. I've gotten that a lot actually," he said sheepishly, rubbing the back of his neck.

Gaelen nodded.

"I said that too," he said to me and continued eating. Cecil smiled at him, taking another bite.

"Yeah, he did. But anyway, where are the two of you headed on your adventure?" He quickly diverted the conversation.

"The spires," I replied easily, focused on my food for a moment, trying to balance a bite on the tortilla bit that I tore a little too small.

"Oh, near the mountains? That makes sense. That's a pretty long and dangerous trip… I see you have a sword, do you know how to use it?" Cecil asked curiously, finishing off his food. I shook my head, chewing.

"No," I said, swallowing it. "I just got it." I picked up my last bite.

"Mm. Well, I can train you, if you'd like? I spent a while at a weapons academy," Cecil replied, offering to take my plate as I chewed the last bite. I gave it to him and swallowed before replying.

"Yeah! Maybe a little, before we leave. Do we have time for that?" I asked Gaelen who nodded.

"Yeah, we have a little time. You can learn while I collect supplies," he said, hopping up from the log we were on. "The men I talked to last night set out some things for us. I'll be back soon." I smiled at him as he left, and then turned to Cecil with a light blush.

He's…really cute. If Molly were here, we'd gush over every feature… But she's not so I'll have to do twice the work, mentally. Besides, Molly's normally the one to talk endlessly about guys. She had a type: actors/singers with shiny brown hair and blue eyes, on the skinny side, and usually somewhat nerdy. Usually the same height as her, or maybe barely taller than her, but she was tiny so that wouldn't happen for a while. Any actor or singer that fit that description.

Personally, I didn't really have a type…but I wasn't as passionate as Molly was about boys. I liked to read, and draw, and write, and honestly, I'm twelve. I gushed over cute guys for the fun of it, not because I thought anything would happen. Romance is great and all but I'm pretty sure Molly forgets we're twelve when she obsesses over 23-year-old actors.

"Althea?" came Cecil's voice to make me realize I hadn't heard a single word he's said for the last couple of minutes.

"Huh? Oh, sorry, yes, what were you saying?" I blushed, scolding myself for not paying attention and thinking of dumb things and crushes while he was trying to teach me.

"I just asked if I could see your sword," he said with an amused little grin, like he thought it was kind of adorable that I had zoned. I blushed more, embarrassed, and was glad it was hard to tell when I blushed. When Molly blushed, her whole face turned dark red up to her ears and it honestly was hilarious.

"Right. Sure," I said and offered him the handle, holding the sheath. I frowned when I noticed some letters carved into the handle. J.C.? but wasn't this supposed to be Emory's sword? Did he steal it? Or was Emory not his real name?

"Ah, this is a pretty nice sword," Cecil said, weighing it in his hand. "Steel, carved…" he said, turning it over, pulling it out of the sheath.

"Hand-carved?" I asked curiously, looking at the delicate lines. He frowned and looked at me.

"How else would it be carved?" he asked, and I thought about it. Oh yeah, they probably wouldn't have machines for carving here. Hmm.

"Right," I replied with a nod, awkwardly. He raised an eyebrow and quirked a smile in a really attractive amused way.

"Right, so, carved, a nice weight. Smaller, so definitely a woman's sword…" he said, and then looked up at me. "Not that some men don't have shorter swords, or that women can't have longer ones, that's just how it typically is here," he explained sheepishly, and I felt a little better about that, nodding.

"Right," I agreed from the log, listening.

"Right. So," he continued, swinging it once, "I'd say it's a good sword, especially for a twelve-year-old." He put it in the sheath again and then offered me the handle, which I took. "Now, stand here," he said, gesturing to space in front of him. I hopped off the log as he walked over to the hovel, knocking on part of the wall and leaning his head through one of the holes in it.

"Fendrel, can I borrow your sword? I gotta show this kid how to fight," he called through it, and there was some grumbling on the other side. "Thanks Fendrel!" He pulled out of the hovel with a sheathed sword in his hands, the leather of the sheath and handle black.

"Alright, so," he said, unsheathing his sword. It was solid black and the coolest thing I'd ever seen.

"Whoa," I said, stepping closer. "That's…wow! What kind of metal is that?" I asked, reaching out to touch it delicately.

"To be quite honest, I'm not sure," he admitted, looking over it. "Um…maybe some mix of steel and…obsidian, or something?" He weighed it in his hand. "I just borrowed it because I think it looks cool," he whispered with a wink "Anyway, shall we?" He smiled at me. I smiled back and nodded, raising my sword.

"Let's do this."

Chapter Nine
Gaelen

With sword fighting lessons picking up behind me, I headed to the small barn around the hovel, where we kept our food resources. I trusted Cecil would keep Althea safe because honestly, Cecil was the coolest guy I knew.

Our whole group was travelers and we bounced from town to town, working where we could and taking up residence in whatever was empty. We'd come to Althalamist right at the end of the Sickness, and there were a lot of jobs that needed to be filled and a lot of houses that were abandoned. Our group mostly stayed together at this abandoned farm at the edge of town, but a couple of men had split off and settled closer to the center of town once the danger of catching the sickness was over.

We picked up more young men, and more men left, finding wives and having kids and settling in town. This was kind of how it was everywhere we went, but especially here, given how much was available. We'd been in Althalamist much longer than anywhere else because of this, and now with the crops wc had planted that would be ready to harvest in just a few months, I figured we'd be here for a while.

I wasn't upset or anything – I liked Althalamist, it held the Prophecy Wall – but I kind of wondered if we'd ever end up leaving again. We'd left members in other towns, and while I knew it was their choice to settle down, I'd miss them…but I guess I was on a quest now of my own, so maybe I'll be able to see them again in my own travels.

Cecil had joined our group just a few weeks ago. He was traveling through town and we gave him shelter, which is pretty common among traveling groups like ours, and he clicked with us immediately. He was very funny and kind, and helpful around the group. He helped me carve designs into my bow, and taught me some things about cooking, and everyone said we looked alike.

The group had picked me up when I was just a baby, abandoned at a camp along the road to the port town to the south. I was raised by the group and never knew who my parents were, so it was kind of nice to have someone…kind of like a dad again. It was fun to pretend, at least…

I packed a shoulder bag with food that would last us at least two weeks if we conserved it, mostly crackers and dried meats, and a good supply of water. This would be my first quest alone, or at least outside of the group, and honestly, I was excited.

I stopped by the reflective piece of metal we put up near the cold stream that ran past our farm. I rubbed the dirt and grime off my face and arms with cold stream water and re-rolled up my sleeves, before setting everything down with a sigh and fixing my hair, which was falling out of place. The re-braiding took a couple of minutes, but then it was out of my face and looked nice, and I found myself grinning at my reflection. It was time for my quest. My quest to save magic and unite the prophesied one with the prince.

I'd never been very interested in girls, guys just seemed so much cooler. With their swords and their beards and their toughness. Girls with their dresses and poetry and babies… But Althea was something I hadn't ever seen before and I was intrigued. She was smart and tough and strong, and interested in so much more than just getting married one day. When I found out about the prophecy and realized the chosen one was a girl, I knew she would have to be someone like Althea.

When I turned the corner, Althea and Cecil were sword to sword, and then Cecil's sword was flying out of his hands and sticking in the ground. That prince wasn't going to know what hit him.

"Good!" Cecil said, grabbing his sword and going back to start again. Then he saw me. "Ah, looks like Gaelen's ready. Well, that's the basics pretty well down, just keep practicing that disarm and you'll be ready to take on any swordsman!" he said brightly, sheathing his sword. Althea was beaming as she did the same, nodding seriously to him.

"Thank you, sir!" she said. Cecil chuckled, waving her off.

"You don't need to call me sir, Althea, just…um, just Cecil is fine," he said with a nervous laugh, eyes flickering quickly to me, stopping himself before his name, like he might have forgotten it for a moment. Hmm…

"Okay, thanks Cecil," Althea said with a warm, almost dreamy smile at Cecil that made me…feel something. Something I didn't like.

Cecil smiled at her, and then glanced at me and smiled. He approached with a face that told me he wanted to say something important.

Stepping between me and Althea, Cecil bent down a little and gently put a hand on my shoulder.

"Listen…before you go on your first big quest, there are some things I need to make sure you know," he said seriously, and my eyebrows knit. Was…he about to say what I thought he was going to? He took a breath and then began to speak. "You're…stronger than you think. Even when things look tough or impossible, you'll find a way through them. Trust your friends, work together, and you'll get through it, but just… Never give up. Okay?" he said, looking at me seriously in the eyes.

I didn't know where this advice was coming from, but his tone was dire and his eyes were locked onto mine, so I gulped and nodded seriously. He seemed to relax and nodded, letting out a breath. "Great. Also…not everything is always what it seems okay? Just something to remember. Patience, forgiveness, and kindness. And…" He turned to Althea, ruffling my hair as he did. "Take good care of him on his first quest, Althea," he said in a kind of teasing tone, chuckling softly.

"I will. Thanks Cecil!" Althea said brightly with a laugh. I pushed his hand off with a blush and an eye roll.

"Yup, thanks Cecil! But we'd better get going!" I said with a tight smile, pushing a bag of supplies into Althea's arms and then pushing her back toward the road. "See you later!" I called behind me, eyes on the road.

"Oh, it was nice to meet you, Cecil! Bye!" Althea called behind us with a wave, and then to me, "Quit pushing!"

Cecil kind of chuckled and waved. Back on the road, I stopped pushing and Althea sighed and brushed herself off, pulling the bag I shoved into her arms earlier on properly.

"Well, that was just rude," she huffed, sheathing her sword properly.

"Sorry. Let's get going, it's a long trip," I said, walking down the road, avoiding eye contact. She huffed again and followed me.

"What was all that about?" she asked as she caught up and I shrugged, keeping my eyes on the road in front of us. She looked closer at my face, now walking backwards in front of me, but I kept my eyes on the road.

Suddenly she gasped with realization. "Were you...jealous?" she asked with a teasing tone I really didn't like.

"No!" I denied, looking at her now.

"Sure, uh huh, of course not," she said with a smirk I liked even less.

"No! I mean it! I just...was a little suspicious of why he said his name like that!" I said, quickly changing the subject, hoping my face was less red than it felt. Althea frowned then.

"Wait, what do you mean? ...Are you just trying to distract me?" she accused with a growing grin.

"No!" I argued, "When he said to call him Cecil, it sounded like he was going to say a different name. Who doesn't know their own name automatically?" I said, calming down when she seemed to actually listen to me, walking next to me now.

"Hmm. I guess, but I honestly didn't really notice. I guess Cecil could be a made-up name...but why would he lie about his name?" She asked me and I took a breath.

"I'm not sure, maybe to hide who he was?" I suggested with a shrug, thinking about it for real now. "Or maybe his real name would...give something away about him?" I shrugged, thinking maybe it was a royal name or the name of a famous criminal.

"Like...if he was your dad?" Althea asked from beside me and I spun my head to look at her.

"What?" I asked in shock, and she blushed.

"Well, you guys look so alike, I just thought..." she said shyly and I looked at the ground in front of us, mind racing.

"My dad? You think so?" I asked, running over it in my mind. "He...does look like he could be..." I admitted, thinking of the possibility. "But I was abandoned at birth! Why would he show up now? Nearly thirteen years later?" I asked, looking at her again. She shrugged slowly.

"You were..." She started softly, with a sad, sympathetic look I hated. When I glared, she thought better of it and didn't finish her question. "Maybe...he felt bad? Maybe he's been looking for you?" she suggested as we walked. I frowned, shaking my head.

"No, if that was the case, why not speak up sooner? Why would he need a fake name?" I asked, looking at her again for answers.

"Maybe he got scared? Or wasn't sure how you'd react, so he made up a name? Maybe he's been working up the nerve to say something?" she suggested with a little sympathetic smile, eyebrows knit like mine. I looked at the ground. "I mean, he looks just like you, but with like…sharper face angles. I don't know."

"I…I guess…" Cecil had been nice to me for weeks, since he got here. He taught me things and defended me from some of the jerks. I…secretly kind of hoped he was my dad. But why had he abandoned me then?

"Is that why you don't have a last name?" Althea asked suddenly. Oh, she figured it out, then…I let out a breath before nodding.

"Yeah. I only have a name at all because one of the Travelers, the leader kind of, had liked the name for a son one day and gave it to me," I explained as we entered the more populated part of town again. "But I'm not his son so it isn't my last name, so my name is just Gaelen," I replied with a little shrug. Althea frowned a little, as we walked into the town square.

"We could give you a last name. You know, make one up?" she suggested, smiling at me. Make me up a last name? I shrugged a little.

"I guess. Did you have something in mind?" I asked as we walked through the bustling market. She thought very hard for a couple of minutes, looked around the market, running her hand over things. I was honestly amused, but let her keep going.

"Mmmm…what about, like…Asterio? Or Calaway? Something cool," she said finally, looking at me. I shrugged a little. Now that she was throwing actual names my way, it wasn't so cute and amusing…

"I guess," I said, not really caring much about either of those. They sounded cool but it wasn't my real last name. "What was your last name again?" I asked, just to divert the attention from me.

"Achebe. It's cool because there's a famous author who has it too. And Molly's is Mihulka, which is cool because of how rare and hard to spell it is. You need like…your own last name. That no one else has," she insisted as we left the market and headed to the north side of the village. I shrugged again, not looking at her. I wanted this conversation to be over.

"Fitting," I mumbled, turning us onto a different path that would bring us back to the three-way fork that we started at yesterday.

"Why is that?" Althea asked with a little frown. I looked at her with dead eyes.

"Because I have no family to share it with anyway," I replied bluntly and kept walking, eyes on the path again. She stopped on the path for a moment. I heard her footsteps catching up a few seconds later.

"That...I'm sorry, I didn't mean—" she started to stutter out, but I stopped her.

"Don't worry about it. I don't have a last name, never have, never will," I said, fists clenched a little at my sides. "Making one up isn't going to change anything, so maybe it's better that we do what I said to begin with, and Stop. Talking. About. It." I was angry, and frustrated, and alone. I hated that I didn't know my last name. But making one up wouldn't help. It would never be real. And talking about emotions wasn't something that happened within my group of traveling men. Shoving it down and not showing your tears or letting yourself feel anything bad was what you did here. What I did. What strong adults were supposed to do.

I felt a hand on my shoulder suddenly and realized I had stopped in the path. I looked at Althea, who had shiny emotional eyes.

"You...you know it's okay to cry, right?" she asked in a soft voice and I immediately wiped my eyes, terrified they were giving me away.

"I'm not crying!" I defended, face getting red, and she held my shoulder a little tighter.

"I know, I just... This is really tough. I couldn't imagine what it'd be like to not have parents. Or siblings, or... They mean so much to me, and you're helping me get home to them, and... It's okay to be upset about those things, they're really hard," she said in this soft, sympathetic voice that I absolutely hated.

"I'm fine! Can we please just get on with this quest!" I pulled my shoulder away and walked ahead quickly, eyes on the ground, up the northern fork.

"But..." But Althea didn't continue, voice fading away behind me. I didn't want to face it. I wanted to pretend it didn't exist and go on an adventure.

I walked ahead by myself for a long time, but when we hit the trees, Althea caught up with me. We walked in silence for a while, and slowly I began to calm down. It was quiet here. I spoke up eventually.

"The woods here are beautiful," I mumbled softly as I looked around. Althea looked up at me wordlessly, so I went on. "The port has some beautiful forests, but the trees aren't nearly as big. And when we reach the mountains, the trees change and the forests smell amazing…" I said, looking down the path to see if maybe the mountains were visible yet, but it was just trees as far as the eye could see.

"That's what the forests are like where I'm from," Althea spoke quietly, with a little smile. "Pine trees and aspens."

"Are you from the mountains, then?" I asked curiously as we trudged up a small incline.

"Yeah, actually. It's really pretty there," she said, and then kind of looked off into the distance. "I live just inside the mountains a couple miles, in this really small town called Conifer. It's only got like, two fast food places, and the middle school is right near my house so I can walk to it, and it's gorgeous honestly," she said, smiling and continuing.

"There's a bunch of parks, and sometimes my friends and I go on hikes and bring lunch and pretend we're in a fairy tale land like this when we walk through. We used to pretend to fall in love with princes, but now we pretend to fight bandits and dragons and rescue princesses and princes, and it's just quiet and beautiful."

I smiled softly and let her continue. She spoke with a growing grin. "Once last summer, my mom dropped my little brother and I off and we sat in the gazebo and read and ate snacks for a couple of hours before my mom picked us up. When it gets warm again, we're gonna do it again." She looked at me with a proud little grin. "Last summer, I won the big prize at the library for the Summer Reading contest. It's really nice in the summer because it's quiet, but it's never very cold in the winter or very hot in the summer. And it's just so beautiful in the fall, when the aspen leaves turn orange…"

I listened to her as she continued to describe her home, and I could tell how much she loved it there. I wanted to go there now and experience the things she described. Playing pretend was something me and some of the younger boys of the group used to do sometimes, but it sounded more fun with her. Actually, everything she said sounded amazing. Maybe I just like the way she describes things.

Althea sighed pleasantly as she ended her description of the fall in her hometown, and then seemed to remember I was there and blushed.

"Sorry, I didn't mean to go on and on. You were probably really bored…" she said sheepishly, brushing loose hair behind her ear in a shy sort of way.

I smiled at her. "I wasn't bored. Conifer sounds wonderful," I said, and she brightened a little.

"Really?" she asked, eyes flickering to her feet and then back up at me as we walked.

"Yeah. Just one question," I replied. She frowned a little.

"Oh. What?" she asked.

"What's a fast food place?"

A half-hour later, I was grasping the concept of fast food. I nodded thoughtfully.

"Okay, I think I understand. So these…horseless carriages pull up to a hole in the wall and they're handed bags made of paper with very quickly prepared food in it and you…eat it in the horseless carriage?" I said, looking at her.

"Basically, yes," Althea replied with a nod.

"Hmm. Okay," I said with a nod. "Things must be very fast there compared to here," I decided.

"They are," she agreed. I felt calmer. I think we both did.

We walked for a couple of hours, stopping once for a quiet lunch on a couple of fallen logs. The sun had sunk below the horizon when we finally heard the bandit camp in the distance.

I put a finger to my lips and Althea and I stepped off the trail, into the trees, and sneaking closer. We ducked behind a patch of thick brush, observing the camp. Men sat around fires and tents were set up into the woods and all the way down the trail. Men drank, ate meat cooked over the fire, and laughed at the ridiculous stories they told each other. There were weapons everywhere.

"How do we get through?" Althea whispered, and I looked down the path. There was a tent close to us, away from the fire, that we could sneak around.

"We could stay here until most of them go to bed… Or we could try to sneak through, using the tents to hide," I guessed, looking at the path if we took that option. Althea nodded a little grimly.

"Hmm. Neither of those ideas are great… Let's just wait? See what happens?" she suggested and I nodded my agreement, sinking back into the bushes.

We sat there until night had completely fallen, listening to the men laugh and talk. It got very boring very fast and after a while, I silently pulled a bag of beef jerky from my bag and offered it to Althea. She took a handful and so did I, but time still passed very slowly. Althea began to fall asleep on my shoulder after a while, and my eyelids felt heavy too pretty quickly.

Just as I was wondering if it'd be bad to get out more jerky, we heard voices approaching from back down the path where we had come. Althea's eyes went wide and I looked up to see men coming through the darkness toward us with a dog on a rope.

"He smelled something this way. Look, he's still going." A guy with a very large beard and very short hair said to a couple of guys behind him, weapons drawn.

"Yeah, but he's leading us back to camp now, Alden. Sorry if I don't immediately trust the senses of Meat." One of the others, a younger man, said with a roll of his eyes.

"Hey! Meat's a great tracking dog! Just watch!" the bearded one, Alden, protested.

I knew that if we stayed here, Meat would find us and we'd be surrounded. When I looked at Althea, I knew she knew too. I grabbed her arm and pulled her to the right, back toward the road and through the bushes, staying low to the ground. Meat barked.

"What was that?" One of the guys with Meat the dog asked, and I pulled Althea as quickly as I could behind the tent near the edge of the woods. We slipped from tent to tent, the men still following but getting more distant.

A few tents later, I stopped and turned to listen behind us, backing up a couple of steps. We were backed against a gray cloth tent, in the darkness, a couple fires in each direction. I held my breath a moment, listening closely…

Meat barked again, much closer now, and my breath hitched. I grabbed Althea's arm and dragged her around the tent, but the second we rounded the corner, I ran directly into a man's back, stumbling back when I did. He turned, frowning, along with the five other men in his little group, most of them holding mugs of mead.

"Who goes there?" he asked uncertainly as he looked upon us, two unfamiliar kids, and reached for his dagger.

Cursing under my breath with wide eyes, heart pounding in my chest, I dragged Althea away, to the left, toward another tent, but they were following now. Shouts were echoing through the camp as everyone became aware of our presence, and I was starting to panic. We cannot get caught. Not only will they take everything we have, including our weapons, but they might not let us go. I'd heard of certain bandit gangs stealing children and forcing them to work for them. Or they could just kill us.

We made our way around the tent, but more men were coming and we were barely outrunning them. The whole camp was waking up now and we were right in the middle of it.

Okay, just another tent or two and we'll be on the other side and free. I ran around the side of a tent so quickly, Althea in tow, that I didn't have time to react when a man stepped out in front of me suddenly. I ran straight into his chest and fell back, landing on my butt on the ground. I dropped Althea's hand as I fell and she took a couple steps back, but then the men that were following us rounded the tent and blocked her escape, Meat the dog included. Meat barked viciously.

"Who do we have here?" the man before me asked in a gruff, angry voice.

I looked up in terror at the figure cloaked in darkness before me, the light from a fire burning behind him a few yards away, making his angered face hard to make out…and then my eyes adjusted. He was tall, over six feet, wearing deep green clothes, with red-brown hair and a grown-out goatee, mustache slightly curled up at each end, and a bow slung over his shoulder. My face lit up with a grin.

"Robin!" I said as I suddenly recognized the man who was standing before me. Robin cracked a grin, eyes sparkling mischievously, letting out a laugh as he offered me a hand up, which I took without hesitation.

"Young Gaelen, what are you doing sneaking into my camp? And with a girl no less?" he said in a jokingly scandalized way, chuckling, and pulled me into a hug the second I was standing. The rest of the camp was laughing too now, weapons lowered. I hugged him tightly. He still smelled like wood chips and leather.

"Robin?" Althea sputtered from behind me in disbelief. I grinned, turning back out of the hug to look at her.

"Althea, this is Robin Hood! He used to be with my group but split off a couple of years ago. He's the one who taught me how to use a bow!" I said brightly, dusting myself off. I looked back at Robin excitedly. "Robin, this is Althea! She's the girl from the prophecy!" I explained, and Robin's eyebrows rose in an impressed way.

"Is she?" he said, and smiled, ruffling my hair. "It would be you to find her, wouldn't it? Well, we'd be absolutely honored to welcome her into our humble party for the evening. How about you tell me all about this new destiny quest of yours over dinner?" he offered, gesturing to the biggest fire with a big roast cooking on top. I grinned.

"That sounds amazing, thank you!" I was so excited to see Robin again. He was the one who had basically raised me. He had taught me pretty much everything I know. When he left…

The men all clapped me on the shoulder or back as they passed, the search parties and attack dogs disbanding, giving passing words of welcome to me and Althea. I smiled at them, letting most of them pass before moving toward the fire. My pounding heart rate had slowed back down by now as I caught my breath and relaxed, no longer scared of dying. Althea caught my shoulder, walking next to me.

"Is that Robin Hood? Like *the* Robin Hood???" she asked at an excited whisper. I raised an eyebrow.

"*The* Robin Hood?" I asked. "What do you mean?"

"The famous thief? Steals from the rich and gives to the poor?" she asked with sparkling eyes, staring at him as he laughed with his friends around the fire, brandishing a newly filled wooden mug of mead.

"Thief?" I asked, and it dawned on me suddenly that that must have been why he was here with the bandits. He's a thief. I should have realized… "That's why he left me with the travelers…" I mumbled mostly to myself. Althea frowned.

"Left you? What do you mean?" I paused just before we hit the edge of the tents, still out of earshot of the bandits and Robin.

"Robin's the one who named me," I said, looking at Althea with a pained expression. "He left in the night three years ago and didn't take me with him… If I ever had a father, he's it," I said with a weak gesture toward Robin at the fire. But thinking about the reason he left me there, him being a thief… I felt the excited energy slowly leave my body. "If…there was a good reason to leave me behind without so much as a goodbye, this isn't it," I said softly, eyes grimly on Robin now as he laughed with his friends.

Althea shifted uncertainly, looking at the fire and then at me.

"Well…what are you gonna do?" she asked softly. I didn't know. I didn't know what I could do. I had so many questions, and at the same time I just wanted to yell at him for abandoning me, but I began to wonder if I had ever mattered to him in the first place.

"I guess…I don't know. It's been three years since I've seen him…" I sighed. "Let's just go sit, eat, and leave as soon as we can…" I decided, rubbing my face.

"Okay…" Althea agreed hesitantly. I took a deep breath, squared my shoulders, and we walked toward the fire.

Chapter Ten

Althea

We sat on the logs surrounding the fire, across from Robin Hood (did I really just say that???) who smiled at us as we sat. He had really pretty green eyes. An older man handed me and Gaelen plates of food, and I ate a couple of bites. It was quiet for a moment.

"So Althea, how long have you known Gaelen?" He asked conversationally and I still couldn't believe we just kind of ran into Robin Hood and he and Gaelen already knew each other.

"Oh, uh, just a couple of days. I just got here," I said with a little smile. He nodded, smiling at me with the sparkling mischievous eyes.

"Well, you're in luck. He's quite the brave warrior. He once saved my life from a wolf." Robin winked at Gaelen who rolled his eyes, but cracked a little smile.

"You were asleep. If you'd been awake, you would have been fine," he mumbled, and the men (merry men?) laughed.

"Well, that may be true, but asleep as I was, I was basically dog food." Robin chuckled and the men laughed again.

"You smell like it at least!" One of the men commented and another laugh rose. It felt really happy… But Gaelen wasn't really smiling.

"So, um, what made you join this…group?" I tried carefully, not wanting to directly call them anything that might be offensive. Gaelen sat up a little straighter, looking at Robin expectantly.

"You mean what made me want to be a thief?" Robin asked with a little smirk, which caused a couple men to laugh. I blushed a little but nodded. "Well, as a traveler, I saw a lot of people in need. People with nothing, doing everything they could just to keep food on the table, and I decided that just giving them the little I had wasn't enough," he explained with a fire in his eyes that reflected the fire in front of him.

"Why should the rich be rich? Why should the poor be poor? Why are the rich allowed to take even more from the people already struggling just to survive? So, I steal objects that half the time, the rich don't even miss, and I sell them for money that I give to the poor." Robin smiled at me. "To make this unfair world just a little more fair," he finished proudly.

Gaelen stood quickly, tossing his plate carelessly onto the log, staring down Robin with a look that silenced the men around us. The camp got so quiet that you could hear only the breeze rustling through the trees and the crackling fire.

"So, Robin," he basically spat across the fire, "if this is all so *noble*, then why'd you leave me behind, huh? Didn't think I had the makings of a thief? Didn't want the dead weight? Because obviously it wasn't to protect me from anything, if what you're doing is so *good* and heroic anyway!" He shouted with an anger and hurt that kind of shocked me to see, given how guarded he'd been about emotion earlier. My heart broke for him a little, and by Robin's expression, his did too.

"Gaelen…" he started gently, voice low in a kind of calming way.

Gaelen shook his head angrily. "Oh just save it!" he shouted, raising his hand to stop Robin and turning and stalking away from the fire, angrily disappeared into the darkness.

Robin watched for a moment, mouth opening and closing like he was trying to think of something to say. He seemed to remember me and the men then, and kind of awkwardly smiled and addressed me, standing and setting down his mug.

"We'll be fine, back in a moment," he said in a polite, fake-smile kind of way and quickly went into the darkness after Gaelen. I wondered if I should follow but I had a feeling that it wasn't my business, so instead I awkwardly glanced at the men around me, everyone silent now.

"…so, uh… Hi," I said awkwardly.

"Hello." One of the men said, the one with Meat the dog. Alden, I think. I smiled in a nervous way at the silent group of bandits looking at me now.

"I like your dog," I said, looking at it. "Is it an English Mastiff?" I asked conversationally, and the guy raised a confused eyebrow.

"It's a Meat," he replied and a couple guys chuckled.

"Is…Meat friendly?" I asked, and the dog barked happily at his name being said by a new person.

"He is if you give him food." Alden laughed, and I set my mostly empty plate aside and held up an uneaten drumstick. God, I miss vegetables. I never thought I'd say that.

"Meat! Want a drumstick?" The big, baggy dog barked and panted excitedly, and then ran over to me, jumping halfway into my lap and eating up the drumstick with an impressive amount of slobber. "Gross." I giggled, nose scrunched up, and more men laughed. Meat barked happily, finishing his amazing meal in my lap. I pet his head.

"So you're Miss Magic, are you?" One of the men, a middle aged guy with no hair on the top of his head, but a half-circle of it above his ears, asked. I smiled.

"I guess, yeah," I replied sheepishly.

"Well, she does have eyes like the earth." One of the younger men said with a laugh.

"And her hair is definitely like the ground." Another commented with a laugh. My smile fell a little. Ah. More of being the only Black person in a magical medieval world.

"Did you come from the south, then?" The middle-aged guy with the ring of hair asked. I looked up at him.

"The south?" I asked curiously.

"Well, hundreds of days' journey and a couple of boat rides to the south, there's a town I been to with lots of different types of people. Brown, black, white, tan –everyone. Some of them with no eyes," The man explained excitedly, and the rest of the men listened with interest. I cringed a little at the descriptions, but it wasn't hard to figure out what they meant. But…

"Where'd you come across such a diverse town?" I asked slowly, doing my best not to correct him on everything because I knew it wouldn't do much good.

"They called it the…the something Hub, I don't remember. One day, empty fields, and the next, hundreds of people and some magical things I've never seen before. A device, made of metal, that moved on its own! Told the time without the sun!" The men gasped and whispered among themselves. "A metal device that you talk into and someone far away hears it! A device that clicks at you and then makes an image of you without any painting or nothing!" he said and looked at me. My mind was racing.

"Oh, put a cork in it, Frank. We've all heard your nonsense stories before." A voice called from near the back, and some of the men laughed. Frank, which I guess was the middle-aged man's name, looking back toward where the voice came from.

"It's true! It was amazing. I stole this pin," he said and raised a small piece of metal above his head, and then offered it to me. "What do you say to that?"

I took the small pin, turning it over in my hands. It was a blooming rose with a triangle around it and looked like a lot of modern tattoos from my world. It was also an enamel pin... Which I knew didn't exist here. Probably.

"A town exists with modern things and diverse people...here?" I mumbled to myself, looking at the pin. "That must be my way back home!" I thought aloud, and all of the men looked at me. Meat hopped down off me to go find more food somewhere else.

"You're from a place with all those things?" the men asked in surprise, and I nodded.

"Yeah, I'm from a different world, in a different time I think. Clocks, telephones, cameras, those all exist in my world. And some of the people you described, they're what exist in other lands, far from here. Just like you didn't know people could look that way, some of them don't know people could have light skin or blue eyes," I explained as gently as I could, and the men kind of gasped and whispered to each other.

"You've explored the world?" Someone asked in shock and I frowned.

"Well, no, not exactly, but where I'm from there's videos—that's like, moving pictures—which I guess are like..." I laughed a little at the absurdity of all of this. "Well, like what he said, if you take just an image, like almost exactly what you see in front of us, but you can replay it whenever you want and show other people? And so I can see what other parts of the world look like." I could tell I was absolutely blowing their minds, and it was fun. I just hoped that at least some of it was making sense.

"How do they get this video? How do they share it with other parts of the world?" one man asked, and I thought.

"Oh, well, I'm not exactly sure about how video works, but I think it has to do with light? My little brother could tell you, he's super into engineering.

But well, for the sharing of it there's this thing called the Internet and—well, I'm not sure how to explain that either, but it's this big information thing that anyone can access around the world on phones and computers and—am I going too fast for you guys?" I paused to ask because they all looked super confused.

A few nodded. "Oh, sorry, well—a lot is different. I don't even know where to start…um… How about with cars?" I tried and they all nodded, leaning in with interest, absolutely silent. I grinned a little. This was going to be fun.

Chapter Eleven

Gaelen

I walked quickly away from the fire, absolutely livid. In the darkness, away from the heat and glare, I caught my breath, stopping between a couple of tents and the forest where no one was.

How could he do this to me? He raised me, he knew I'd follow anywhere he went, he knew how much I looked up to him, and he just left me? To be a thief?

I always thought he left to do something dangerous, save a princess or sail across the sea or something, but nearly this whole time he's been a days' walk away, stealing for the good of others? Why couldn't I do that?

If he was just going to be a thief, at least I could justify that he didn't want that life for me, but he was clearly proud of himself and what he was doing! And he couldn't take me with? He couldn't even stop by for a visit once in three years?

I had spent my entire life before he left following him around, hanging on every word... Before he'd left, I'd noticed him acting differently, but it was happy different, which was why I didn't see it coming. I thought maybe he'd gotten a quest or something...but no, he abandoned me for his own good. I didn't matter to him at all...

"Gaelen!" came his voice from not far away, catching up with me at a jog. I sighed angrily and closed my eyes for a moment, trying to collect my emotions, but when he caught up with me and I couldn't keep them down.

"How could you just leave me behind? For this?" I snapped, voice coming out angry and hurt, tears forming in my eyes even as I actively fought them. He stopped in front of me. "What, was I just some annoying kid that you didn't want following you around anymore? Were you just tired of dealing with me all the time?" I demanded. Robin let out a sigh, running a hand through his hair.

"Gaelen—" he started but I cut him off.

"Was I just not good enough for you?" I could feel the tears falling down my face now and I hated it. "Because if you just left to get away from me, you didn't have to go become a thief! You could have just told me to get lost—!" Robin stopped me.

"Gaelen, knock it off!" Robin said sternly and I shut up, jaw clenching as I looked at the ground. "You know that isn't true." His voice was softer now. "You're like a son to me. I didn't abandon you on purpose," he said, firm but caring. It was quiet for a moment, trying to calm down, trying to stop crying in front of the guy who had raised me and then abandoned me.

"Then why did you leave?" I asked softly into the silence, eyes still on the ground. Robin sighed again softly, and this time when he spoke his voice was lower. Sadder.

"I didn't want to. But I couldn't stay doing nothing with the travelers. We just…didn't see eye to eye on some very important things. I met some thieves in a bar, and they felt the same way I did. We needed to do something for the good of the people who needed the help, to defend the weak… I wanted to bring you, Gaelen, I really did." His voice was soft now.

"Why didn't you then?" I asked, looking up, face betraying my hurt and anger. Robin looked at me sadly for a moment.

"There…were a few reasons, but the most prominent being that the other travelers didn't want me dragging a nine-year-old into something that could easily get all of us jailed or hung. They said you were too young to choose your own path and it wasn't fair for me to pick it for you," he explained and I took a deep breath, calming myself back down a little more.

"But why didn't you say, Robin? Why didn't you tell me this then, instead of disappearing in the middle of the night? Why didn't you actually give me the choice?" I asked softly, looking up at him. He couldn't meet my eyes.

"I was…a coward. I didn't want to tell you that I was leaving you," he admitted. "I'm sorry…"

My eyes were hard as I looked up at him.

"I am too," I said, fists clenched at my sides, expression unforgiving.

I turned and walked away, knowing it was going to take me some time to forgive him, if I even could. He didn't follow.

I ended up back at the fire and paced just outside of earshot for a moment, calming myself down. That wasn't fun. The quest wasn't supposed to go like this. I let out a breath, stopping for a moment, when it occurred to me how much the men had quieted. What was going on over there? Was Althea okay?

I made my way back to the fire and saw Althea, eyes lit up with excitement, telling the group of very interested, starry-eyed men of all ages stories of her world.

"...and the engines run on flammable fuel, and the fuel makes these...well, they're called pistons but they move up and down and, well, basically the movement moves other parts of the engine and they connect down to the wheels, which propels the car forward..." She was explaining, moving her hands to try and further explain her point.

I couldn't help but smile a little as I watched the scene. She was...kind of adorable. With all the men hanging on her every word...I quietly slipped in and took a spot amongst the men, next to a younger man with short, wavy brown hair and a neatly trimmed beard, and the older man with hair only by his ears. I listened closely to her.

"Tell them about drive-thrus," I added with a little smile when she finished.

"Oh! Right!" she said brightly, smiling at me, having seemed to just notice my presence, and then explained those. And after that, telephones. And then washing machines. And then future hygiene. It got later.

"Wow..." the older man with not very much hair next to me breathed in amazement, sitting back. "And this is all destined to come? How the future world will be?" he asked and Althea frowned a little.

"Well, I...I guess I'm not sure. My world doesn't really have...magic. Or fairies or any of that, none of it existed there, so...I think you probably have a different future, in your own magical world here..." Althea said thoughtfully, and the men found themselves frowning, looking at each other unhappily.

"But I want that future." The younger man next to me said, looking up at Althea, and then at the other men. "I want carriages that pull themselves and telephones and...well, all of that. How do we get that here?" he asked, playing distractedly with the sleeve of his brown shirt, his big brown eyes wide with wonder.

"Oh," Althea said, and frowned a little, looking down. "Well...I suppose you could work on it," she looked up at him. "Advance yourselves and then your children. The more you change the world, the more change can happen for the future, right?" she said, thinking about it a little more and nodding. "If you teach your children to love and accept others, and to push for change and advancement, less wars of hate will happen and less time will be wasted, and more and more progress can happen," she said with a nod, looking around at everyone. The camp was absolutely silent.

I was kind of shocked at how smart she actually was. I knew she was supposed to be, based on what the prophecy said, but...for her to have all that knowledge about how things of the future worked, and on top of that be able to pose how to make a better future, sitting there, golden eyes sparkling in the firelight...I was kind of amazed by her. She really did seem like she was from another world.

"Yeah, I think that could work," the middle-aged man said with a nod, and another nodded too, laughing.

"She's right. Let's do that!" the young man said, and there was cheering and drinks lifting into the air. I grabbed a mug as well. "A toast to Althea, boys; and the future!" he said and raised his mug.

"To Althea and the future!" We all called and threw back our drinks. Althea was blushing red and smiling shyly. I grinned at her in this moment and she grinned back brightly, and I felt a lot better. For the moment at least.

With all the men again riled up, cheering and laughing and talking and shoving each other, Althea made her way over to me. She gently pushed the mug from my hand, making me set it on the table.

"Don't drink that, you're twelve," she said softly, but was still blushing from all the attention. I set it down and smiled.

"That was amazing. You're very good at explaining things," I complimented and she grinned shyly, lightly punching my arm.

"Shut up. I'm tired. Let's go to bed," she said and I laughed a little at her embarrassment.

"I think I'm going to sit here just a little longer, if that's okay," I said and she paused for a moment, but nodded, eyes beginning to look droopy.

"Sure. I'll just…go see if Robin has an extra tent," she said with a decisive nod and turned toward the tents.

"Okay. I'll join you soon," I said softly.

"Okay, no worries," she said and headed into the darkness.

When she was gone, I slowly let out a breath, looking at the ground, fingers intertwined in front of me. I knew I needed to calm down a while longer before I tried to go to bed. There was so much to think about and I knew if I tried to sleep like this I'd be up all night thinking. I needed to be well rested for tomorrow.

"So you're the famous Gaelen then?" The younger man beside me, the one with the short wavy hair and short beard asked, and I looked up at him, surprised to be talked to. All the other men were talking amongst themselves.

"Me? Uh, yeah, I am. Famous?" I asked him, eyebrows knit. He smiled kindly.

"Oh, yes, Robin talks constantly about you," he said brightly and I blushed a little, frowning.

"Really?" I asked in surprise.

"We've heard of all your adventures through the years, and all about how clever you are." The man, who I was noticing had very kind warm brown eyes, was smiling brightly as he spoke. "About how quickly you picked up the bow, and how talented a hunter and tracker you were, and…well, you come up a lot," he chuckled. "It's an honor to meet you, sir," he said in kind of a goofy way that made me smile.

"Well…I'm glad to hear he didn't completely forget about me…" I admitted, and he smiled gently, nudging my shoulder.

"Nah, we all know about the brave boy Gaelen who saved Robin's life time and time again." I could tell he was exaggerating to butter me up, but it made me feel better so I didn't say anything. I laughed softly.

"Well, thank you for saying so… What was your name?" I asked when I realized he hadn't said. He smiled a bright friendly smile and offered his hand to me to shake.

"Marian, at your service."

I talked to Marian for a little while longer before saying goodnight and heading to find if Althea had gotten a tent.

I found her sitting on the stump of a tree, in the darkness of the night, looking up at the stars. I smiled a little and sat in the grass next to her, looking up at the stars as well.

"Hey. Did you find Robin?" I asked, and she let out a breath and looked at me, smiling a little.

"Hey, yeah. It's that one. He already helped me set up the sleeping bags." She gestured at the small tent down the hill a bit. She shivered and hugged her arms against the cool evening. Now that we were away from the fire, it was quite a bit cooler. I pulled off my vest and wrapped it around her shoulders wordlessly, enjoying the cool a little after all the heat from the fire and men.

She looked down at me. "Are you two…okay now?" she asked gently, eyes full of concern. I blushed a little and looked away because people don't really look at me that way, and her eyes were sparkling under the starlight. It was hard to keep eye contact.

"I don't want to talk about it," I replied quietly, hugging my own arms, but more to keep myself together than to stay warm. It was quiet for a moment.

"Why not?" she asked eventually, very softly. I sighed, closing my eyes.

"Look, it just doesn't have to do with you. Why do you need to know so bad?" I asked and she scoffed quietly.

"I don't. I'm asking because clearly you're upset and hurt, and I'm your friend and I care about you," she said and I didn't look at her. She let out a sigh and touched my arm. Her hands were cold.

"Hey," she started gently, "I know how hard talking about your problems is if you've never done it before. But sometimes, talking about your problems helps," she said, and I rolled my eyes a little, to myself.

"Talking doesn't solve problems. Solving problems solves problems," I replied at a mumble and she crossed her arms.

"And…how do you find those solutions?" she asked and I was quiet for a moment, not knowing how to answer. "Right," she said and I sighed in frustration, getting ready to argue, but she spoke first. "Okay, look, I get that you don't believe me, but let me tell you a story. When Molly first moved to Conifer, we weren't really friends. She talks a lot, and seemed to think it was okay to tell me every thought in her brain from the first moment I said 'hi' to her.

"If she was excited about something as small as a photo of a cute dog, she had to tell me all about it. If someone looked at her weird in one of her classes, she was going on and on about how they hated her and how that upset her and how she didn't know what she did to make them mad.

"I thought, for a while, that she was really, really annoying, but then one day my mom came home and told me that she and my dad weren't going to be together anymore. We had always been a tightly knit family, we always had each other's backs. I spent ninety percent of my time with them, doing family things," she said, a little softer now, looking at the ground. I was quiet, listening closely now. I could tell it wasn't easy for her to talk about all this.

"So my dad..." she began again, "he moved out. Not far, but he didn't live with us anymore. I...had to be there for my little brother and my mom, who really wanted us to be happy. She and my dad weren't, but..." She was quiet for a moment, squeezing her eyes shut. She let out a breath. "But I realized that I wasn't handling it well. I didn't know how to handle it. But you know what happened?" She looked up at me finally, and I met her eyes, listening. "I went to school, and Molly sat down, and started her same old telling me everything she thought of on the way to school, and suddenly, I just couldn't do it anymore.

"I yelled at her; told her to shut up. Told her I didn't care about every thought she had every day. Told her to stop talking for once in her life. And by the time I stopped yelling, she was silent, staring at me.

"You know what she said?" Althea asked me with a soft smirk. "She asked me if I was okay. She asked me if I wanted to talk about it. I was...well, I thought she'd hate me," she admitted, rubbing the back of her neck with a little laugh. "I thought she'd cry, or tell me I was a horrible friend or something, but instead she was there, worried about me."

Althea laughed a little, shaking her head. And I realized that, yeah, I did want to talk. So I pulled her into the hall and I told everything that happened. With my mom, with my dad leaving, with trying to be strong for my brother. I told her how scared I was, and how betrayed I felt... And suddenly, it was like...like I was me again. Like I didn't have to pretend to be this strong, perfect kid for my mom and brother, like...like I could be upset. Like I was allowed to be.

"And after that, I started to tell Molly when I was upset, or mad, or when something was bothering me, and it was like a huge weight lifted, and..."

She looked at me directly now. "And Gaelen, you're smart and strong and going through something, and I know how much of a relief letting it out could be for you. You've…never really had someone to do that with, and I just…I want to be that person for you, if I can. Like Molly was for me…" She trailed off a little, rubbing her arm gently and looking down.

I watched her for a moment, quietly. This person, who didn't have any responsibility toward me and wouldn't get anything out of me telling her how I felt, was asking me out of genuine care about my emotional state. She just wanted to make sure I was okay. And besides maybe Robin, that had never been something I'd had before.

I let out a slow breath, eyes on the grass beneath my legs, and then on the starry sky, and then on her.

"Alright," I said, and paused again, taking a breath. "Fine." I rubbed my face for a moment, trying to form words to explain. "I…I don't know how to feel about parents. I just…I wish I had some, but mine abandoned me and I'll never know why, and the travelers take care of me and all, but I'm not, like, their kid exactly, so I feel like a burden a lot, a guess…" I mumbled, looking at the ground for a moment.

"That makes sense…" Althea said softly from her stump above me. "And Robin?" she asked. I looked up at her, but couldn't really sustain eye contact, embarrassed that I was even telling her how I felt at all. But I was aware of the fact that she had just told me all about something very difficult for her…

"Robin was…well, he was the closest thing to a father I ever had. He took care of me and joked with me and took me with him wherever he went, to learn and help… He always checked in on me and helped me when I needed it and whenever he needed someone to go with him on a quest or to assist him with a job, he chose me. When I got sick, he stayed with me and cared for me and made me laugh all the way through it.

"I…felt like he and I were family, you know? Even if no one else cared what I thought, he was patient and would listen, and…" My voice broke a little and I realized all at once that I was crying. I felt like I'd done that a lot lately. I wiped my eyes quietly and took a moment to breathe.

"And then, I woke up one day to find he wasn't at the camp. I looked around for him, and thought maybe he'd be back later, maybe he just went out for supplies or something, but then night was falling, and he wasn't anywhere to be found, and finally someone in the camp told me he was gone;

had left in the night to join some other traveling group. I thought they were lying for a long time…"

I knew I was crying again, and I couldn't see the ground anymore, but I didn't care right now. "But he didn't come back. He didn't even leave a note… And then we moved on, to the next town, and I knew I probably wouldn't see him again. And I…I just couldn't understand what I'd done to deserve being left. I thought maybe he was dead for a while, and then I thought maybe he hadn't ever really cared about me or liked me, but that I was some kind of entertainment for the short amount of time he was here…"

I sighed and rubbed my face again, feeling my heart pound in my chest. "And when we got here and ran into him, I was ecstatic, because it was like I was seeing my dad again for the first time in years, but then I saw what exactly he'd been up to…and I remembered how he'd abandoned me, and… Well, it hurt to find out that the reason he abandoned me was to come here and be a thief." I sighed, shrugging.

"Like, why couldn't I be a part of that? Why did he have to leave me behind completely?" I asked, gripping the cloth on my knees in my hands. "I…always thought if he was okay, somewhere out there, he was doing something he couldn't take me to, like he was going to kill the king, or something…" I shrugged a little, rubbing my face.

"And you talked to him about this?" Althea asked very softly, voice gentle. I let out a sigh and shrugged again, looking down.

"He said he didn't want a nine-year-old kid to drag along. He said he didn't tell me where he was going because he was too much of a coward to hurt me to my face," I mumbled, teeth grit. Althea was silent for a moment.

"That…sucks," she said after a moment. I frowned and looked up.

"What?" I asked, and she looked up at me.

"That he abandoned you. That he couldn't even give a real reason. It sucks!" She looked up at me with righteous anger in her eyes. I was surprised, but found myself nodding.

"Yeah, it does." I paused for a moment. "Sucks, is that a term from your world?" I asked.

"Oh. Yeah. It means like, that it's stupid, or bad," she explained. I nodded.

"Oh. Then, yeah. It does suck," I tried out. But then I looked down a little. "But now I don't know what to do. I...I mean...I still..." I didn't exactly know how to phrase it.

"You still love him," she said with a nod. I blushed.

"Well, I mean..." I awkwardly rubbing my arm, trying to phrase it differently but not knowing how. "Yeah, I guess. I still care about him. I...I still...I still miss him. I still want...I don't want to go back to never talking to him, and I don't want him to think I hate him. I...I'm really mad but it's just because I did care so much, and he just left. And I don't want him to ever do that again..." I was thinking out loud now, about things I'd never let myself think about. "But I don't know what to say. I'm still mad. I want him to know that," I said with a serious nod.

"Then maybe you should explain that," Althea said, and I frowned, glancing up at her.

"What do you mean?" I asked quietly. She shrugged.

"I mean, if you could tell him you're still mad for what he did but you miss him and you still want a relationship with him, maybe your problem would be solved. You could be done with it, you know?"

"Huh," I said, thinking about it. "I guess you're right..."

We were both quiet for a while, listening to the crickets and the breeze and the distant voices. I felt my heart rate calm, and took in a deep breath of the cold night air.

"Okay. I...feel a lot better," I admitted with a soft chuckle. "I think it's probably time for bed."

"I think so, yeah," she chuckled, looking down at me with a fond smile. "And I'm glad you feel better," her smile was genuine. She stood and stretched and offered me a hand. I smiled back softly and took it, letting her pull me up, and we headed into our tent for the night.

We both slipped into our bed rolls, the tent just a little quieter than the outside world. The bed roll was cold when I got in, but warmed up quickly as I settled into it.

"Goodnight, Gaelen," came Althea's voice from somewhere above my head, on the other side of the small, quiet tent.

"Goodnight, Althea," I replied softly, letting my eyes close and the tiredness take me.

Chapter Twelve

Gaelen

The sun and the smell of bacon woke me up. I was tangled in a bed roll and the heat of the bright morning sun bearing down on the tent was intense. I wrestled my way out of my hot prison, and pulled my pants back on, which I guess I must have pulled off some time during the night.

The tent we slept in must have been a supply tent, because in the daylight, I could see boxes of food and weapons piled around the sides. I stepped desperately out of the tent, the heat becoming overwhelming, the air thick and hard to breathe. The cool morning air hit my skin and felt amazing, and I breathed a sigh of relief. No wonder the thieves get up so early. I tied my hair back up quietly.

The camp in the daylight looked a lot friendlier, the deep green tents standing tall on the road between the trees. Birds were singing, and the air was light. From here I could see a few sleepy men just leaving their tents, stretching. I could smell the coffee brewing already.

I looked up to see Marian leave his tent, hair standing up in every direction from sleeping. I couldn't help but smirk a little, stifling a laugh. And then Robin stepped out of the same tent after him, and with an affectionate smile, he put Marian's hair back into place. I frowned. Wait…

Robin and Marian walked toward the fire we sat at last night, and I wondered if maybe Althea was right. Maybe we did need to talk…

I heard a loud yawn from behind me and saw Althea stretching as she stepped out of the tent, still wearing my vest.

"Morning sunshine," she said through the yawn. "How'd you sleep? Because I slept like a baby after all that walking," she said, rubbing her face now to wake herself up. I smiled a little at her antics.

"Yeah, pretty well. But I hope you're ready for a lot more walking," I said, catching her yawn involuntarily. Althea stretched now, more athletically and less sleepily.

"Yup. Destiny quest. Gotta get home," she said determinedly. I nodded with a soft smirk.

"Right, destiny quest," I repeated, glancing back to where Marian and Robin disappeared, smile fading. "So... Breakfast and then pack up and leave?" I asked, tucking a piece of hair that fell loose back in its place.

"Sounds good. That bacon smells really good," she sighed and I smiled a little.

We headed through tents of newly awoken men to the fire, which was burning much lower than last night, a big cast iron bowl sitting on top of it and bubbling with a see-through brown liquid. On a sheet of metal next to it, Marian was making what looked like a giant veggie omelet. I guess the thieves had chickens hiding somewhere. Robin was standing behind Marian and just kind of watching Marian cook as he sipped his coffee, still waking up it seemed.

Marian saw us approach and smiled.

"Good morning, Gaelen and Althea! Breakfast?" he asked. Robin looked up and smiled at me, somewhat sheepishly after last night. I didn't really smile back.

We ate in mostly silence, all of us still not fully awake yet. It was just the four of us for now. It seemed like the rest of the camp was still working on waking up, or had settled at different fires. The camp was pretty big...

"So...headed out today, then?" Robin asked after a while, and I nodded, taking another bite of the omelet. "Ah, I suppose destiny waits for no one, hmm?" he said, but his smile fell a little. I looked up at him.

"We'll be through this way on the way back, though I'm not sure how long it'll take us," I said, and Marian offered me a canteen of water. "Thanks." I took a drink.

"Right. Well, we might have moved by then, but we don't have any plans to at the moment," Robin said with a nod, and things got quiet again. "Is there anything you'll need for your quest? Perhaps some more provisions?" he added eventually. I glanced at Althea and shrugged.

"I think we're alright," I said, looking at Robin.

"Perhaps some fresh fruit?" Marian chimed in.

"A wonderful idea, dear," Robin said brightly. "Some fresh fruit for your trip, and vegetables." I felt awkward.

"Okay," I said with a little shrug, finishing off my breakfast. I looked at Thea. "Ready?" I asked and she nodded as she chewed her last bite. I set the plates back near Marian. "Thanks again."

"Of course. Have a good quest, Gaelen, it was wonderful to finally meet you," he said warmly, and I nodded awkwardly, not knowing what to say really.

"Um, you too." I guess. I turned to Robin, who smiled a little. The moment was tense.

"Ah, Althea, why don't you let me show you to the fresh produce?" Marian said quickly, looking between us.

"Oh uh, sure, lead the way," she said, standing, and they were off. "That was delicious, by the way." I heard her say to him happily as they walked.

"Oh, thank you! I've always loved cooking," he replied, and then they were out of earshot, into the tents. I rubbed the back of my neck, looking down, feeling the awkwardness from before more intensely in the silence left behind. Robin spoke up after a moment.

"Well, um… It was wonderful to see you again, Gaelen. And you know you're welcome in my camp anytime," he said with an awkward smile. I nodded a little.

"Right," I said quietly. Robin was quiet for a minute.

"Right," he said, and was quiet for a moment, looking into his coffee, "And I'm very glad you met Marian, I was meaning to introduce you two," he was smiling softly, before it became nervous as he glanced up at me. "What was your first impression?"

"Of Marian?" I frowned.

"Yes, what do you…think of him?" he asked, swirling his coffee anxiously. I shrugged a little, not sure what he wanted from me.

"I, I don't know, I guess he seems nice. Has a nice smile. Seems very…caring?" I replied awkwardly, looking around instead of at him. He seemed pleased with my answer.

"Oh, well, wonderful. He is very caring. And a great cook, he's been teaching me." His smile grew to be kind of sheepish and warm. I raised an eyebrow.

"Teaching *you* to cook?" The tension lessened a little. "You, who's burned everything you've ever cooked?" Robin chuckled a little and I could feel some of the tension lifting.

"Yes, me. I haven't burned a thing in weeks." Robin put his hands up in his own defense and I smirked.

"Where was Marian when I was eating burnt sausage and eggs every morning?" I asked and Robin laughed a little more. Things got quiet then, as the laughing faded. I didn't know what to say. I don't think Robin did either.

"Right. Well… Have a wonderful first quest. I know you'll do amazingly. The prophesied one is lucky to have such a strong warrior with her," he said with a little nudge and a small smile. I returned the very small smile.

"Thanks, Robin…" I said softly, eyes on the ground.

"Of course," he replied, and the conversation ended awkwardly. Robin cleared his throat. "Well, I suppose you'd better get packed up before those two get done," he said and I nodded.

"Yeah," I said, not sure if I should hug him or not. I went with no and awkwardly turned and walked toward the tent I'd slept in. "Bye."

"Bye," Robin called from behind me.

I finished rolling the bed rolls by the time Althea met me outside the tent with a new bag added to her things.

"Ready?" she asked with a smile and I pulled the two rolls onto my back with my bag.

"Yeah, let's go."

We headed down the road around mid-morning, walking down the hill for a while before it started heading back up.

We walked all day without any problems, mostly quiet, stopping for a lunch of fresh raspberries and jerky, and then hours later a dinner of cauliflower and more jerky.

I thought about talking to her about last night but I just… I didn't know how I felt about it yet. And I wasn't used to talking about these things yet. Besides, I think we were both pretty tired today. By the time night was falling, our legs were aching.

"How much further from here?" Althea asked as we set up our little camp, consisting of bed rolls and our bags in between us. We tucked ourselves into the trees off the road, just in case someone came by. The sun had gone down but the sky was still light.

"Two days?" I guessed. "I've never really traveled all the way there, but I've heard that it's around four days of walking," I said, slipping into my bed roll. Althea groaned.

"Well…I'll be very fit after this quest," she sighed positively. "Oh, here's your vest," she shrugged it off and offered it to me.

"Thanks." I put it in my bag before laying down. After the high emotions and then a day full of walking, I was exhausted, even if the day wasn't actually that eventful. "Night."

"Night," she mumbled, laying down as well with a sigh and the light went away slowly, but I fell asleep before then.

Chapter Thirteen
Molly

I woke up slowly, a few days having passed since Althea and Gaelen had left, and found that I wasn't coughing. I didn't feel quite as tired. Or cold. For once, there wasn't stuff in my throat. I sat up slowly and stretched, which I hadn't done in a couple days and felt amazing. So did being able to fully swallow and breathe through my nose. God, I took that for granted.

I got up slowly and, still in the loose fitting sleeping clothes Emory gave me, I made my way down the hall and down the steps to see the usual early morning patrons eating their breakfasts in the quiet tavern. I got a wave or two and waved back. Emory wasn't here, so I stepped into the backroom and found him starting on breakfast, slicing pieces of bacon from a big piece of meat.

"Morning, Emory," I said with a little smile and he looked up in surprise.

"Oh, you're out of bed. Feeling better, then?" he asked and I nodded.

"Yeah, a lot better." I sat in the little chair near the door. "Do you need any help?" I yawned. He nodded.

"Sure, why don't you bring me the box of eggs from the cabinet and I'll show you how to fry eggs," he nodded toward a shelf with a basket on it, slicing another piece of bacon.

"Okay," I said, and got up again to get it.

He showed me how to crack the egg, and when to flip it, and that if you cooked the bacon first, the eggs would taste better, which pretty much blew my mind. My mom would be so impressed with me when I got home.

Eating our eggs in the early morning air, surrounded by the smell of the bacon, I looked up at Emory.

"Um…" I started, which made him look up from his plate. "Emory, are you…okay?" I asked softly, rubbing the back of my neck shyly. After the other day, we hadn't really talked and… Well, I knew he was an adult and that he could probably handle himself, but the last couple of days, I'd just been thinking about all this and I kind of realized he didn't really have anyone to ask him if he was okay. If I'd died, and my mom died, and my brothers, and my dad was left alone in the world… Well, I'd want someone to check on him.

Emory seemed to blush almost, but raised an eyebrow at me questioningly.

"I am, yes…why?" he replied, looking at me with a curious expression. I thought he might tease me for worrying about him, but he seemed genuinely surprised and concerned as to why I'd asked at all. My eyes were mostly focused on the eggs left on my plate as I spoke.

"Well, uh…just…checking after the other day. It's hard to…well, to lose someone you love, and especially when it's…well, everyone, and…yeah." I shot a quick glance up at him. "Are you…okay?" I asked again, hoping I'd explained alright.

Emory seemed surprised by what I'd said. I was a little nervous he'd get mad or stop talking to me or something, but instead he let out a slow breath and looked at his folded hands for a moment.

"You know, not many people around here ask those kinds of questions, but…I think I'm alright. It's been long enough that, while I'll never forget, I think I'm ready to move on," he said, punctuated with a little nod, almost to reassure himself he really was ready, and I nodded as well.

"Well…good. That can't be easy," I said, looking up at him again.

"No," he replied, looking up at me now too.

"So…good job. And…I'm glad. And…" I didn't know what else to say. I'm 12; I'm not equipped for this.

"And you'd better finish your eggs," he replied with a little smile.

"Right," I breathed as the tension fell away, smiling a little and finishing my eggs.

When the food was gone and the dishes were clean, Emory turned to me, drying his hands on a small cloth while I put the last dish in its place.

"Well. How are you feeling today? Well enough to go out?" he asked, looking me over. I gave a thumbs up and he nodded. "Good to hear. I think some fresh air would do you some good. Would you mind, then, running a few errands for me in town? There's no rush, so feel free to look around and take your time," he said, paused, and then added, "And take breaks if you don't feel well."

I grinned a little at his concern.

"Yeah, I think I can handle that." I giggled a little. He nodded.

"Great. I'll write you a list."

Soon I was on my way into town with a list of veggies and meats and other assorted ingredients. Some of them I didn't know, like 'hops'. But I had time. And if I'm good at anything, it's asking questions.

I wandered through the village, feeling my legs wake back up. I'd been in bed for days... The village was bustling as ever, but still so much quieter than the towns back home. I...kind of missed them.

I thought destiny adventure would have been fun, but now that I'm thinking about home... Will we ever be able to get back? I...tried not to think about my mom. Or my dad...

Feeling pretty down and not paying much attention to what was going on around me, I ran directly into a small child who had run out in front of me, carrying a little basket.

Everything in the basket scattered across the dirt, and the little blonde girl, maybe four, was knocked onto her backside and began to cry.

"Oh no! Oh, I'm so sorry, let me help you," I said and dropped to my hands and knees, collecting miscellaneous fruits and veggies, and also a doll with a missing button eye and a bottle of milk. She stayed sitting on the ground for now as she cried. She reached for her doll when I picked it up and I handed it to her.

"Hey, hey, it's okay, everything's back and—"

"Her eye!" she cried, hugging her doll, basket forgotten. "Daisy's eye is gone!"

"Oh." I looked at the doll and then around in the dirt. "I...I don't see it, but—" That triggered more crying. "Okay, that's okay, we'll just...here, we'll get her a new one, okay? Um..." I looked down at my shirt. The buttons were brown instead of black like the doll's eyes, but... I pulled the top button off carefully.

"Okay, so the doll's name is Daisy, what's yours?" I asked, trying to distract her and calm her down. She took a little breath and her sobbing stopped, but the tears were still flowing.

"My name's Aveline," she mumbled, hiccupping, rubbing her eye with the hand not clutching her doll to her. I nodded.

"Right, Aveline, that's a pretty name. I'm Molly," I said in a soothing voice, and noticed some loose thread hanging off her sleeve. "Mind if I borrow this?" I asked, pointing to the thread on her arm. She nodded quietly, hugging Daisy close to her, and held out her arm, hand in a little fist. I gently held her sleeve and snapped off the loose piece.

"May I see Daisy now?" I asked, holding my hand out. She looked uncertain. "I promise I'll give her back," I said with a reassuring smile. She looked up at me with her big brown eyes, which were extra adorable and glittery from crying, judging whether she could trust me or not. I smiled again, patiently holding out my hand until she gave it to me.

"Okay..." she said hesitantly as she held her out. I gingerly took her, smiling.

"Thank you, Aveline. Okay, let's see if I can fix this..." I said, mostly to myself as I held up the little thread. I noticed already it was a lot stiffer than thread from back home. It was a little thicker too... It made it easier to poke through the hole that the other button had been sewn on. I carefully pushed the thread through and then through the button's holes, until I had secured the button on. I tied a knot and tucked it under the button as Aveline watched, and then when I'd finished, I looked at my work. The new brown button was a little smaller than the doll's right eye, but it had kind of a quirky cute look to it.

"There," I said with a smile, offering it to her. "Good as new." Well, kinda.

Aveline absolutely grinned as she took it, tears forgotten, and hugged Daisy to her. I smiled because honestly, she was adorable.

"Now, here's your basket...are you getting groceries too?" I asked and she nodded a lot, carefully tucking Daisy back into her basket and picking it up. I nodded as well, standing again. "We can go together?" I offered.

"Okay!" she said brightly with a giggle. "Mama said I needed basil, and apples, and potatoes, and, and..." She began excitedly, in a dedicated sort of way. I followed her as she went on, leading me into town, and was honestly impressed a four-year-old could remember all that. I was just glad I could read, because without Emory's list, there was no way I would have remembered most of it.

I spent most of my day with Aveline and by the end, I was exhausted. It was a nice day, getting to explore town and barter with the people in the market, but all the walking and talking to a four-year-old wore me out by the end.

I made sure Aveline got home alright before I made my way back ho—I mean, back to Emory's tavern. It was a lovely summer evening, warm, with a soft breeze. I smiled as I looked around.

While I was looking, my eye caught a boy's, maybe 14 or 15, with longish blond hair and striking blue eyes. I blushed a lot as it happened, and he smiled at me. My arms were full or I would have waved awkwardly, but instead I just kind of nodded and hurried off to the tavern.

I arrived to find Emory passing out plates of fish and potato, and he smiled as he saw me. He met me halfway across the tavern and took some of what I was carrying, helping me carry it to the back.

"You found everything alright?" he asked as he looked through it quickly. I nodded.

"Yup, wasn't too hard." I smiled proudly. "A little girl in town brought me around."

Emory smiled and nodded. "Good, thank you…would you like some dinner?" he offered, walking back over to where the fish and potatoes were cooking. I nodded.

"Yes please."

Emory nodded, sitting at the little table in the back and setting both plates down. I sat across from him and then noticed the mischievous glint in his eyes. I knit my eyebrows and smiled suspiciously.

"What?"

Emory smiled a little, and then pulled out a deck of cards, passing me seven. I groaned playfully. Rummy.

"Alright, fine, but I swear I'll beat you this time." I laughed.

"We'll see, little girl, we'll see," he joked, and to the sounds of people eating in the bar behind us and the little fire crackling next to us, we began to play cards and eat dinner. It was a good moment.

Chapter Fourteen

Althea

I was really glad that I was used to higher altitudes, because there was no way I would have made it this far otherwise. Even then, I was pretty winded as we made it up another slope. I was definitely not in shape. Ugh.

I'd never been particularly interested in physical pursuits… That is to say, I preferred reading, and writing, and watching movies much more than running, or basketball, or dance or anything like that. Molly and I were very similar this way, which was partially why we were friends.

When there was a big basketball game at our school, we'd get together and watch movies and make bracelets or something. Or we'd play pretend, but those days were kind of winding down for me. Instead, I'd read, or Molly and I would write fanfiction, or…

Well, bottom line, I'm not in very good shape for this.

"Gaelen…" I started and he sighed.

"I'm not sure how much further. Probably at least one more day," he said, and I felt bad for asking a lot, but this is so much walking.

"Okay… Sorry," I said and he sighed again.

"Want to take a break at the top?" he offered with a tired little smile, and I shook my head.

"No, we need to keep going. Can I have some more water though?" I looked up at him. He took one of the canteens out of his bag and offered it to me. We stopped just before the top of the hill and each took drinks. The forest was quiet around us, and the air had been getting colder the further we walked. We were definitely going up in elevation.

While I was taking my turn with the water, Gaelen headed up the hill a ways, stopping at the top.

"Oh." I heard Gaelen say suddenly, looking down the path. "Maybe less than a day."

I frowned and climbed up to see a gorgeous mountain range appear over the crest of the hill, a distance off, but visible from as high up as we were. So I was right, it was quite a hike.

"Wow. Yeah. Wow," I said in surprise, taking it in. They were sharper, pointier looking than the mountains back home, but they were honestly gorgeous.

"See those points just barely sticking out over there?" Gaelen pointed and I followed his gaze. "Those are the Heaven Spires."

I nodded, looking out. "They seem pretty far away still…" I said and he nodded.

"We'll most likely reach them tomorrow. Let's keep going though, we only have a couple of hours of daylight left and we'll want to reach the spires early tomorrow," he said and started walking again. I tucked away the canteen as we started making our way down the hill.

"Why?" I asked with a frown.

"Because there are wraiths in the mountains," he said casually, like that wasn't a terrifying thing to say. "And they're dangerous at night."

"Oh. Great. Wraiths. Like *Lord of the Rings*. Not terrifying at all," I said sarcastically. Gaelen frowned and looked at me.

"Actually, they're very terrifying. That's why we don't want to be there once the sun sets," he said and I sighed.

"I was just—whatever, let's just hurry up and get there," I said, giving up and walking a little faster.

"Right." Gaelen's voice came from behind me and we continued on our incredibly long walk.

We ended up camping in the trees just outside the mountains. And despite sleeping with the hilt of a sword in my hand all night, I still didn't feel safe. I woke up in the morning feeling exhausted.

The morning was cool, the sun having just risen, and it was quiet here. It was quiet everywhere here, with no roads or people to fill the silence.

I took a deep breath, looking around the quiet world for a moment. I…kind of loved this. A world before cars and people taking it over. I bet this is what my home felt like before the town and highway were built…

I slipped out of the bed roll and stretched, listening to the wind blowing through the trees and the soft chirping of birds. I heard breathing too, in all the silence, and glanced over at Gaelen.

He was asleep, his hair falling all around his peaceful face. It was dark and shiny and beautiful…with little braids running through it…I couldn't help but smile a little.

Gaelen was such an interesting person. He was kind, and smart, and all that, but he was also just… Well, basically the most interesting person I'd ever met. I was lucky to have him helping me. And he thought I was some kind of Chosen One…

Though I wouldn't admit it, I was a pretty big nerd at school, and Molly was one of my very few friends. I spent most of my time reading or doing homework, and dreaming about the future. But here I was, in a beautiful, magical world, the Chosen One, with a boy who fully believed I was destined for greatness, and I was complaining and worrying about how to get home.

I took another deep breath, breathing in the beautiful morning, and then nudged Gaelen gently with my foot.

"Mm…" he hummed, stirring, and I nudged him again. "What?" he mumbled.

"Hey. It's morning," I said with a little warm smile, nudging his shoulder one more time. "It's time for some spires."

"Mm…breakfast first," he mumbled, bringing a hand up to rub his face.

"Right, then spires," I sat on the grass, opening one of our bags. Gaelen sat up and pushed all the hair out of his face with a yawn, barely catching the apple I tossed his way. I ate a couple pieces of jerky and then handed him the bag, eating an apple myself.

"Okay," I said as we ate. "So, we're gonna head into the mountains, find the spires and the 'pin', and then…uh…was it a shield?" I opened my journal to glance back at the prophecy. "Yeah, a shield. We'll find it with the Cool Rock and then… Yeah, I guess we'll head back?" I asked, looking up from the journal. He nodded, eating another piece of jerky.

"Sounds right. How are we gonna know what the 'pin' is?" he asked, and I shrugged.

"Not sure. But…I suppose we'll figure it out when we get there," I tucked my things away in my bag, when I felt something in a pocket of my dress. I frowned and reached in, pulling out—"Oh!"

Gaelen looked up at me as I pulled the purple enamel pin Frank had shown me yesterday. "What's that?"

"The pin...Frank's, that he showed me yesterday. Shoot! I must have gotten too caught up in talking about stuff from my world and forgotten to give it back..." I turned it in my hands. "But... What if this is the pin?" I looked up at Gaelen. He frowned.

"Could it be...that easy?" he asked and I shrugged a little, glancing at him.

"I mean, if it's really my 'destiny'...I guess we'll find out..." I tucked away the pin and we packed up camp, heading into the mountains.

By mid-morning, we were approaching the spires, the cool mountain air around me making me miss home. This kind of weather in the mountains always put me in the mood for an ice cream cone.

It was gorgeous here and we saw a couple of larger white-blue fairies floating around, but thankfully, they just sort of waved and continued on their way.

We eventually reached the spires, which opened up in front of us suddenly as we stepped out of the trees.

I thought they'd be a bunch of...well, rock spires, just kind of sticking out of the ground, and yesterday when we saw them atop the hill, that's what they looked like, because we could only see the tops. But up close, they were towering spires that made almost walls, stuck into the mountains surrounding them. They were almost pure white, made out of what looked like mostly quartz, with jets of colored rock of different types all the way through.

"Wow," I breathed, for what felt like the hundredth time. "They're huge."

"They are," Gaelen agreed in amazement, and then stepped closer. "But now we have to look for the 'pin'."

"Man, I wish I'd brought my camera..." I mumbled as we walked closer.

"We should split up and look for the pin, whatever that ends up being," Gaelen said as he looked around, adjusting his bags on his back. I nodded.

"Good plan. I'll go this way..." I pointed left, and he nodded in reply.

"Call if you see anything," he said and headed off to the right.

"Good luck," I called back to him and then headed into the spires.

I looked over the rocks for some kind of...pin, or even like a flower or something, but I wasn't finding anything. Just rocks on rocks. It was quiet enough here that I found myself humming very softly to myself as I walked, just to not be freaked out by the silence. The song was *September* by Earth, Wind & Fire, and it was only stuck there because my mom had played it over and over in the car when we were getting groceries a couple of days ago, and it felt ridiculous to sing here in this beautiful place on my destiny adventure, but it was stuck endlessly in my head so it's what I sang.

By the time I was singing it over again, I reached the back wall of the spires, and started to turn to walk around the other way, when I heard footsteps and my heart jumped into my throat. Wraiths? I tucked myself back into a gap between two spires and put a hand on my sword, listening. They were getting closer...walking slower now.

My heart was pounding and I looked down at my sword. Would it be loud, taking it out of its sheath? I took the chance, slowly pulling it out, holding my breath...and then the sword, dragging against the leather, became very audible.

I cursed in my head as I pulled the sword the rest of the way out as fast as I could and stepped out to attack, but found the tip of an arrow to my throat.

I immediately raised to swing, but the second we made eye contact and realized who we were facing, we both started laughing in relief.

Gaelen was standing in front of me with an arrow notched and aimed at me, panting with the intensity of the moment. "Althea," Gaelen laughed, lowering his bow. "You scared me!"

"You scared me! I thought you were a wraith!" I giggled, putting away my sword. "Oh my god, my heart is pounding," I breathed, stepping out of my hiding spot.

"Mine too. I guess the path circled," he laughed and put his arrow away, replacing his bow over his shoulder.

"I guess." I giggled, catching my breath now. "Did you find anything?" I asked and he shook his head.

"Nothing. Only rocks," I frowned.

"Me too. Huh. Well, it's gotta be here somewhere," I glanced behind me, running a hand through my hair, replacing what fell loose. That's when my eye caught it.

"What…" I stepped closer, touching the symbol, hidden where I'd been hiding, in the gap in the rock. It was…I frowned and reached into my bag, touching the symbol gently. "How could?"

"What?" Gaelen asked with a frown, stepping closer. I pulled the pin from my bag, but not the flower one from Frank, no, the one I had found when I first got here.

The symbol was small, two triangles, points touching, one on top of the other, with a circle surrounding them. I looked at Gaelen, showing him the pin.

"I…found this at Emory's when I first arrived, in a drawer filled with clothing," I explained, looking closer at the metal pin and then at the carving, frowning. "You don't think…"

"Try it," Gaelen answered with interest, stepping closer. I carefully lifted the pin to the symbol and gently pressed it into place. It fit, and the wall next to me, in the back of the space, creaked open inwardly. Whoa. I gently took the pin back and it stayed open. I looked at Gaelen and he nodded, urging me on. I took a breath and pushed the door in slowly, letting it swing open.

Chapter Fifteen
Gaelen

Dusty, stale air met us as we stepped into the dark room before us. We couldn't see much past the door as we walked in, and I felt Althea grab onto my sleeve and then my hand as we fumbled our way through the dark. I blushed a little despite the serious moment, but got over it fast, holding her hand tighter.

"What now?" I asked, given it was far too dark to see now.

"I'm not sure, maybe there's a torch or something," Althea replied, reaching around in the dark, when suddenly the light was fading. We both looked up quickly to see a dark figure in the doorway, and the door swinging shut. My eyes got wide.

"No!" I yelled, running for it desperately.

"Wait! Stop!" Althea yelled, running after me, but by the time we made it to the door, it was completely shut and sealed. I banged on it, trying to get it open, but it wouldn't budge.

I cursed and backed up, trying to look around and see anything, but it was completely dark.

"Who was that?" Althea asked, "Who would lock us in here?" I could hear her turning in a circle but it was so dark in here that I couldn't even see the hand in front of my face.

"I don't know," I said grimly, running a hand through my hair as I tried to fathom the situation we were in.

"Gaelen?" came her voice softly, from somewhere nearby, tinged with fear. Okay. I'm the one who's used to being in this world. I'm the one prepared for quests. I took a breath and gently reached out for her.

"It's okay, we'll make it out of here," I said and found her elbow, stepping closer. She quickly hugged onto my arm.

"How? We can't see anything. We don't know where we are or what's around us or what we're supposed to be doing! How exactly are we getting out of this?" I could hear the panic in her voice. I held onto her arm a little tighter.

"I don't know, Althea," I said honestly, even though I knew it wasn't what she wanted to hear. "But we will, because we have to," she sighed in frustration, and sank slowly to the floor. I followed her down, sitting next to her while she continued to hold onto my arm.

For a moment, it was quiet. Like, I mean fully silent. with the cave-room sealed off, all of the sounds of nature outside were gone. I waited to see if my eyes would adjust to the darkness when Althea spoke up.

"Gaelen, this wasn't supposed to go like this," she said, leaning against me a little.

"I know," I replied softly.

"We were supposed to find the pin, grab the shield, and head back," she added, shifting us so she was leaning back against my back, electing to hold my hand instead. In the pure darkness like this, the contact helped to orient yourself and to feel like you weren't lost in the darkness. I was quiet.

"Even this wasn't supposed to happen. I never should have followed those cloaked people into the woods…" she breathed, and I felt her put a hand to her face. I frowned.

"Cloaked people?" I asked in surprise.

"Yeah," she said with a bitter laugh. "We were just watching movies when I heard them behind my house, and then my stupid curious self went into the woods after them."

She was quiet for a moment, and I could hear the rueful smile in her voice when she spoke again.

"They were on a trail I'd never seen before and I just…I needed to know where it led. And Molly followed me in, because she's cool like that, and then everything turned to summer, and then Molly insisted we walk further and explore…I knew we should have gone back! If we'd just gone back, we could have relaxed inside and gone to bed and I wouldn't be trapped inside this stupid pitch-black cave with you!" she ended, letting go of my hand and throwing her arms up in anger and kicking a rock before putting her head in her hands.

I was quiet for a moment. I guess I didn't know that was how she had arrived. But if she'd gone back…

"You never would have met me," I commented quietly.

"What?" she asked, raising her head. I glanced back at her a little, even though it was dark.

"You wouldn't have met me. If you had gone back right at the beginning," I said. "I mean, you also wouldn't have been attacked by ogres, but…" I looked down at where my lap would have been. "If you had gone back, I wouldn't have followed you that day. I wouldn't have gone on a quest, or had someone to talk to Robin about. Actually, I wouldn't have even seen him again, or known where he was," I said, and looked back at her again, even though I couldn't actually see her. "You wouldn't be stuck in this cave with me. You wouldn't have known I ever existed."

"Oh," she said quietly, thinking about it. "I…guess I wouldn't have," she said, even softer.

"And who would save our magic, if not you?" I added.

"I…I guess you're right…" she mumbled, and I smiled just a little, eyes half closed.

"So… We're trapped in a very dark cave. But that's okay, we're on a quest, and you haven't saved magic yet, so we'll make it out. It's foretold," I said with a shrug and she snorted a little.

"Alright, dork, I get it…" she mumbled, and shifted a little against my back which was very audible in the silence of the cave, still leaning against me.

"So, why don't we take a little break, take a nap while it's nice and dark, and when we wake up, maybe our eyes will have adjusted a little more and we'll have a better idea of what to do?" I asked and she sighed.

"Alright…but only because all this darkness and walking is making me sleepy. And that's not a terrible idea." We shifted so we were laying back on the floor instead, shoulders touching, feet going the opposite way. "I just hope this cave isn't full of monsters waiting to kill us," she joked and I smiled a little.

"Me too," I admitted, and we both got quiet. Althea leaned her head against my arm, which I assume felt like a comfort to her just as much as it did me.

We fell asleep to the sound of water dripping somewhere, surrounded by the pure blackness of the room.

It was hours later when I woke up, on the cold rocky floor of wherever we were, next to Althea, whose breathing was still deep enough to let me know she was asleep. I looked around the quiet room, still not able to see anything. How were we going to get out of here? Just blindly fumble around in the dark until we find an exit?

I was getting kind of hungry and assumed it was around lunch time, so I leaned over and opened Althea's bag carefully, looking for fruit, when light hit my eyes. Strange, soft, greenish light, seemingly emulating from Frank's pin. I carefully took it out, testing that it wouldn't burn me before picking it up. I gently shook Althea as I stared at it.

"Althea," I said softly, shaking her shoulder, which I could see now, even if the light was still pretty dim.

"Mm... What?" she mumbled sleepily, before her eyes fluttered open to see light, and my grin as I held it up. She gasped and sat up. "Frank's enamel pin! It's glow-in-the-dark!" She grinned, taking it gently.

"Ah, Frank, you've saved us," I said as I stood, helping her stand as well. She held the pin up, looking around the room.

It was small and mostly empty, with a pillar in the middle holding up the ceiling. I looked for some way to make a fire, or torch, but everything here was kind of damp and I doubted a fire would even light in here.

By the dim light of the pin, we walked around the room, which we found was completely empty.

"There!" she said, pointing to a narrow hall at the back and pulled me by the hand down it.

We followed the hall deeper and deeper until we were stepping into a vast room that our little pin couldn't light all of. Althea and I looked at each other uncertainly, before stepping into the room and walking deeper.

The deeper we went, the less we could see, the walls getting further and further away, and I was just starting to think that maybe we should have gone around one of the sides when we saw something shimmer in the center of the room.

"There!" Althea exclaimed again and made her way toward it, dropping my hand. I caught her again, stopping her.

"Careful. We don't know what will happen," I reminded, but she just kind of smiled.

"Don't worry, it's the shield, I'll just grab it and we'll find our way out of here," she said positively, and let go of my hand again, walking closer to the shiny object.

I followed as close as I could, and what we found in the green glow was a silver metal shield with three points on top and one on the bottom that the shield curved down to. There was an empty place in the middle, a circle surrounded by lines that made it look like an eye of sorts.

Althea stepped up onto the podium, pulling herself up onto it when the shield was out of reach.

That was when we heard the unearthly screech.

I was reaching for an arrow by the time Althea looked at me in terror, and before she could ask the question or I could notch the arrow, a white figure scooped her off the ground and the pin fell from her hands.

I cursed as I rolled to grab the pin, currently our only source of light. I stumbled up and tried to follow the screaming happening to my right.

I nocked an arrow but I couldn't see well enough to actually hit anything, following the screams. "Althea!" I shouted, trying to find a shot.

"Gaelen!" Althea shouted. "*HELP!*" But I couldn't, listening to them go from one side, hit the wall, and then go to the other side.

"I can't! I can't get a clear shot!" I shouted back desperately, following them as the screams moved toward the high ceiling.

"*GAELEN*," she screamed demandingly, and I climbed onto the pillar.

"I'm trying!" I called back, struggling to aim at such a low light. I lined up the shot as best as I could, and the second I could see the horrifying, white ghost-demon looking thing, I shot my arrow.

It struck the arm of the monster, which gave Althea the space to draw her sword and slash wildly at the thing. It screeched and clawed back before throwing her into the wall, which she hit hard and then fell to the ground.

"Althea!" I called, arrow notched and aimed at the thing as it flew wildly around in the darkness. "Are you okay?"

I couldn't see or hear her at this point and the screeching stopped all at once. Suddenly, I was being thrown into a dark, silent room, where a monster and my possibly injured friend were.

"Althea?" I called softly into the darkness, heart pounding. And then a grunt and a screech came from behind me, and I spun to see the mutilated face of a wraith, inches away from me, but not moving any closer. I glanced down to see she'd already been run through with Althea's sword. She had a hard glare as she drove the sword into it, the thing's jaw unhinging further as it screeched, before entirely blowing up into dust that faded on its own.

"Holy—" I started but she lowered her sword, looking at me, and I saw how she was holding her side. "Are you okay?" I asked instead.

"We're even now," she said, catching her breath and carefully tucking her sword away. "It's your turn to save my life again."

I couldn't help but laugh a little, despite the situation, putting away my arrow and bow. "Wow, yeah, thank you. That was close." I was catching my breath now too, but I could tell she just wanted to get out of here, so I looked at the shield in its holder. "Let's get this shield and get out of here," I said and helped her up onto the podium of rock.

She pulled the Cool Rock out of her bag and as she did, it began to glow, and the shield began to glow, and when she reached out and took it, the glow between the two was so intense it lit up the whole room, so bright we had to squeeze our eyes shut.

When our eyes opened, Althea had the shield and the rock, and the wall to the left of us was beginning to open. We winced as the bright light hit, but as my eyes adjusted, my jaw dropped.

Chapter Sixteen
Molly

Fall. Or autumn, as you'd call it here. I'd been working with Emory all through the summer and had actually gotten a little taller and definitely was stronger now.

Two weeks had turned into four weeks, which turned into eight weeks, and soon it'd have been twelve weeks and the leaves on the trees were turning orange and yellow and falling.

I didn't know where my friends were, but I knew that magical destiny adventures take time and I knew they'd come back for me. Emory reassured me that he was pretty sure they'd come back, and that any number of things could have meant they couldn't come back yet, like if they hadn't yet found it (whatever it was), or if they were following the next clue or something. I was still worried…but I knew I couldn't do anything about it, so I helped Emory around the tavern.

Today, I was cleaning a table where some beer had spilled, when someone walked through the doors.

It wasn't like the tavern was empty; there were a couple patrons around, eating or drinking, but this guy looked like he was on a mission. Emory was in the back, preparing one of the guests' meals…

"Can I help you, sir?" I asked the man, straightening and tucking away my rag. He looked over me uncertainly, but nodded.

"Perhaps. I'm looking for some people who might have come through here," he said, looking around the tavern. People? I shrugged.

"I might know; I could try at least. What were their names?" I asked in a friendly manner, and he looked at me.

"Gaelen and Althea," he said, and my eyebrows shot up.

"You know them??? I've been waiting for them to come back for weeks! How do you know them?" I asked with a frown. He looked at me with a frown.

"Yes, they came through my camp and stayed on their way to the mountains. How do you know them?" he asked, looking over me.

"Oh, I'm Molly, I came here with Althea," I explained, but he still looked confused.

"They didn't mention you." My smile fell, as did my shoulders a little.

"They…didn't?" I asked softly. Althea didn't even mention me to this cool adventurer guy who had housed her for a night? "Oh… Well, Althea and I aren't from here and I just stayed behind because I was sick," I said, and he nodded a little.

"Uh, so, why are you looking for them?" I asked with a curious frown. He stroked his goatee beard thing.

"They never came back through my camp and I was getting worried… I thought maybe they'd made their way past when we were asleep, or gone a different route… They'd mentioned staying here, so I thought perhaps they'd stopped in here on their way back…" he explained, and I frowned a little more.

"No, they never did… Do you think…something happened?" I asked, eyes getting a little wide. What…what if they were captured? Or hurt??? Or died???

The man frowned, expression grim. "I don't know," he said, "but I'm going to find out."

He turned to leave and I caught his sleeve.

"Wait, take me with you," I said seriously, and he turned and looked at me, raising an eyebrow.

"You? Why?" he asked and I frowned.

"Because I'm their friend and I haven't been able to take part in any of this magical destiny adventure and I'm tired of it. Please?" I begged, doing the pouty lip, and he sighed.

"Well…I suppose, but hurry and grab whatever you're bringing, it's four days' walk and we'll be doing it as quickly as we can," he said and I lit up and nodded, running back toward the stairs, but popping my head into the backroom.

"Emory! I'm going on an adventure to find my friends! Be back soon!" I called and ran up the stairs to my room.

Emory

I frowned heavily as Molly ran up the stairs. An adventure to find her friends that hadn't returned? We've talked about this a few times, and each time I've convinced her to stay, that going after her friends alone wouldn't help. What if they had gone somewhere else? What if something happens to her? She agreed with me every time before. What changed now?

I stepped out of the backroom to find Robin Hood standing in my tavern. I knew who he was, because I'd once watched his old traveling friends kick him out of here and tell him never to return. They'd called him some nasty names…

"Hood," I said, setting the completed meal on the patron's table and approaching the thief.

"Claypool," Hood answered with a nod. "Good to see you." I frowned.

"What are you doing here?" I asked.

"I was trying to see if Gaelen and Althea ever came back. Apparently not," he said grimly.

"And so, you're going to go look for them?" I asked, crossing my arms.

"Yes," he replied, looking me up and down. "They never came back, it's been much longer than they needed, and their food supplies have definitely run out at this point," he explained, crossing his arms to match mine. I wasn't intentionally trying to be standoffish, but here we were.

"Okay. And why are you bringing Molly?" I asked slowly. He frowned at me.

"Because she asked to come. She's worried about her friends," he replied easily.

"Yes, but she's a child. She doesn't know how to use a single weapon, and you'd be bringing her into a dangerous situation," I explained. He raised an eyebrow.

"I'm bringing a twelve-year-old from a different world into the mountains to look for her friends, surrounded by a band of men able to fight and win against anything they come across," he defended. "Why are you so worried about this?"

"Molly has been under my care for nearly three months. I don't think it's in her best interest to be running off with a band of thieves to save her friends from an unknown danger," I said a little more firmly. "I'm not stopping you from going, but I am stopping you from taking her."

Hood let out a sigh and shrugged, putting his hands on his hips.

"I guess I don't blame you for feeling that way, and I won't take her if you really don't think she can handle herself, but I do know that she will be pretty unhappy with your choice," he turned for the door, waving behind him as he left. "See you some other time, old friend,". I frowned deeply as the door swung shut, wondering if I had made the right choice.

Just as I was turning away from the door, Molly ran down the stairs in a black cloak with a white long-sleeved shirt that tied up in the front and the tan pants I'd sewn to actually fit her, a bag slung over her shoulder and her hair tied back.

"Okay, I'm read—!" She started, but stopped when she saw Hood was gone, smile falling. "Where...where'd he go? Did he leave without me?" Her shoulders sank a little, before she moved quickly for the door.

I approached with a sympathetic expression and put a hand lightly on her shoulder.

"Molly, he left," I began to explain softly, but she stopped me before I could continue, looking up at me with big, sad eyes.

"What? Why?" she asked, and I gently squeezed her shoulder.

"Well, we agreed it would be better if he went alone," I explained carefully, gently moving her to sit at the table, sitting as well. I knew the conversation wouldn't be great, but hopefully she'd understand... Her eyebrows knit.

"Why? He was going to take me." Her eyes scanned my face intensely. "Did...did you tell him not to?" She looked at me with a heartbroken look I very much did not like.

"Molly—" I started, but she pulled away from my hand on her shoulder.

"You did! Why? You let Gaelen and Althea go without stopping them!" she argued, voice getting louder. Mine got softer by comparison.

"Molly, they had weapons, and training—" I started.

"Althea didn't! She just had a sword! What is this about really? Is it because I'm a girl? Because I'm small? I'm the same age as Althea!" She had tears streaming down her face now, and when I reached out to wipe them

130

away, she pulled back. "You don't think I'm strong enough, do you? That I couldn't do it on my own?"

"Molly—" I tried again, but she stood and pushed past me, toward the door.

"I don't care what you say! They're my friends, this is my adventure too, and I'm going to help! I should have left weeks ago!" she insisted, and I wanted to follow her, but I knew it wouldn't help, and I couldn't force her to say here...

"Molly, please. I just don't want you to get hurt," I called after her, and she stopped in the doorway, silent. When she turned back, her eyes were full of tears.

"What if they're dead? What if they died because no one came for them? Because you kept telling me they'd come back?" Her voice broke as she spoke and I found I couldn't answer. She turned back to the door. "Goodbye, Emory. I've been stuck here long enough," she said and walked out. For the second time today, I found myself staring at the back of the tavern door.

The patrons in the tavern had gone silent, and I looked up when I realized.

"Excuse me," I mumbled and stood, walking into the backroom, wiping the tears from my eyes. I couldn't stop her. But I prayed she was safe.

Molly

I stormed down the road with tears in my eyes, gripping my bag close to me. I'm going to find my friends. No one's going to stop me. Because...because despite what *some* people think...I'm strong, and capable, and this is my quest too.

I wasn't sure exactly where the goatee guy went, and I didn't know what his name was either, but I was sure I'd catch up with him quickly. And if I didn't, I'd find them myself.

I made my way through town, determined, and my face must have showed it because people weren't bothering me today.

"Molly!" came a soft, happy voice from behind, and I looked back to see Aveline following me. She smiled brightly. "Where're you goin'?" she said and followed. "I wanna come!"

I smiled a little, because she's sweet, but gently patted her head.

"Sorry Aveline, not today. I've got to save my friends," I said with a nod, and she frowned.

"Oh… Well, I'll help save your friends too!" she decided and followed brightly. "I'm smart!"

I chuckled softly because ahh, she's cute, but no, I've got to do this alone.

"I'm sorry, Aveline, but it's gonna be pretty scary and I don't want you to get hurt. But when you're…when you're a little older and stronger, I'm sure you'll go on all your own quests!" I tried not to make the connections between what I'd just told her to what Emory had said earlier. This was different. I'm not four.

"Oh…okay…you promise?" she whined, sticking out her bottom lip. I ruffled her hair again.

"I promise, Aveline. You'll save princes and dragons and be a hero," I said brightly and she nodded.

"Yeah! Dragons! I'm gonna go save a dragon!" She giggled and ran off.

"Oh, no, I meant fight—" I started to correct, but she was already in her own world, running to the other side of the market, saving herself a dragon. I smiled softly, shook my head, and then headed back on my way. I got people to save.

Without really knowing where to go, I wandered through town and it didn't take me long to reach the edge of town. There was a barn-type building here with a bunch of men in it.

"Hey! Boy!" One called as I walked by. I looked up when I realized he meant me. I guess I do look like a boy here, in these clothes and with this hair. It was just touching my shoulders now, having grown over the last couple of weeks, and there were multiple dudes I'd met with this same haircut.

"Oh, hey, what's up?" I asked, stopping. The guy frowned and slowly looked up a little, before looking back at me, confused. Dang it, I keep forgetting. "Oh, sorry… Hail fellow! Well met," I corrected, and the man smiled, confusion cleared.

"Ah, yes, right, well met! You are headed off on a journey, are you not?" he asked, gesturing to my clothing and bags.

"Oh, yeah I am. My friends went missing," I explained, and he nodded a little.

"Are those friends Gaelen and the girl from the prophecy?" he asked hopefully, and I nodded. Man, everyone knows them, it seems.

"Yeah, that's them! Do you know where they went exactly? I don't think they told me," I admitted sheepishly, rubbing the back of my neck. The man shook his head.

"No, not specifically. I know they were going after the prophecy's instructions," he said, leaning on the fence. "Missing, you say?"

I nodded. "Yeah… They were supposed to be back weeks ago, so I'm going to look for them," I said, and he nodded.

"Yes, we've been quite worried about Gaelen… Well, My best guess is that they would have gone south, to the trading town for the Staff of Loki, so I suggest taking the road there…" He gestured to the road crossing the one I'd been following, just past their barn. "And following it a couple of days south, until you reach the fork to the Old Ruins, then take the road to the right and you'll reach Vale in a day or two," he said helpfully, and I smiled.

"Awesome, thank you for your help!" I said brightly, and waved. "I'll let you know if I find them!" He nodded and waved me off.

"Good luck, traveler!" I smiled brightly as he did, waving back until it got weird, and then turning and making my way down the path. Right at the fork to the ruins, right at the fork to the ruins… I've totally got this. Yeah.

Chapter Seventeen
Althea

"It's Fall?"

I climbed off the platform, leaving the shield in its place for now, and walked toward the opening. I winced against the bright light, having spent the last couple hours in the pure darkness. The leaves had all turned orange and red and were starting to fall.

"How is it Fall already? It was just summer!" I exclaimed, glancing back at Gaelen.

"I…I'm not sure. I know we weren't in there that long… We didn't have food to last that long," he said incredulously, climbing off the podium and taking the shield with him. I looked down at the rock in my hand.

"Huh," I said, looking out again and took a couple steps out into the dying grass. It was chilly now…I pulled my rolled up sleeves back down, hugging myself. "Maybe…maybe we're back in my world now? Maybe we…jumped again, or whatever you call it?" I suggested. Gaelen stepped out after me.

"Jumping sounds like a good term for it. But I guess we can't be sure; this still looks like my world to me," he said, looking around with a shrug.

We weren't where we'd been; we were deeper in the mountains, it seemed. The spires were nowhere to be found. I could hear water flowing somewhere off to the right.

"Where do we go now?" I asked, looking around. There were no paths, just dense forest in front of us and a huge rock wall behind us.

Gaelen walked back in and pulled the shield from the rock platform.

"Let's go toward the water. Maybe it flows down and out of the mountains?" Gaelen shrugged, tying the shield's handle into the strap of one of his bags and slinging it over his shoulder. "We could find our way back to Althalamist from there."

"I don't have any better ideas. Lead the way?" I asked, gesturing as he walked back up to me. He nodded and headed off, following the rock wall we'd exited toward the sound of rushing water.

It took about twenty minutes to get to the stream, but it wasn't too hard from there to tell which way was downhill. We began heading down, following close to the water. Honestly, it was gorgeous, but I was just looking for signs we were back in our world. I really hoped we were…

As 'fun' as this destiny quest was, I don't really think I'm cut out for it… I just wanted to go home, and see my mom, and go back to school, and write, and read stupid fanfiction online and…

My attention was caught by Gaelen in front of me, who was smiling serenely, looking around at the fluttering leaves around us. There were a surprising number of deciduous trees up here, which made me think we might be near the edge of the mountains, but that wasn't what caught my attention.

The reflection of red and orange leaves in Gaelen's brown eyes was a sight, his long hair, though tied back, flowing gently in the breeze, the easy smile on his face as he walked…I found myself blushing softly. Maybe…I didn't mind being here as much as I thought.

Molly would so make fun of me for this, but I think I—"Molly!" I suddenly exclaimed, and Gaelen looked back at me.

"Hmm?"

"Molly! Oh my gosh, if it's fall now, we left Molly alone with Emory for weeks! Months, even! Oh my god, she must think we're dead…" I said, stopping for a moment, covering my mouth.

What would she be thinking? Would she think we had abandoned her? Would Emory have kicked her out when she was better? Or after a month or two? Were we even in the same world as her anymore? Was she—

"Althea, I'm sure she's fine," Gaelen comforted, putting a hand on my arm. I looked up at him. "I'm sure she's just back working for Emory and waiting for us to return," he reassured me, and I rubbed my face, looking around.

"You really think so?" I asked, playing with my braid now, mind running through everything that could have happened to her.

"I do. Where else would she go?" he asked, and I began to nod slowly. He's right. It's not like she could just go home, right? She was probably having the time of her life in the medieval town, learning how to…brew alcohol or sew or something.

"But…but what if we're back to my world? What if she's trapped in Althalamist all alone?" I asked urgently, a hand to my head as I felt my heartbeat rise.

"We aren't sure where we are yet, but if she's in my world, and we're back in yours, then we'll find a way to get back. We have the device, we'll figure it out, okay?" he said, voice calm and sure, like he knew what he was doing. "But for now, shouldn't we just focus on getting out of the mountains and back to the tavern?"

"Right…right, you're right. Okay. Let's just…get back quick, okay?" I said, and he nodded.

"Okay. Let's go," he agreed, and we began walking again.

By the time the ground started leveling out again, it was starting to get dark. I could tell Gaelen was starting to get nervous, glancing around us as we walked, his hand resting on his bow. I had my hand on my sword similarly.

"Do you think—" I started to ask, but he shushed me quietly. I knit my eyebrows.

"Wraiths," he explained in a breath, not even daring to whisper. He didn't have to explain; I could infer that they were attracted to sound.

We should have been out of the mountains by now. I was getting really cold, the fall air dropping dramatically in temperature the darker it got. We didn't have any clothing for this type of weather, because we hadn't expected to time-travel straight into Halloween. We both were getting nervous. What if we were stuck in the mountains overnight? What if we were going the wrong way and never got out of the mountains?

Snap.

Gaelen and I froze as we heard a twig break up ahead. My heart rate jumped to my throat and I reached for my sword, but Gaelen put a hand out in front of me, stopping me. I froze, sword part ways out, but didn't dare move as I watched Gaelen for what to do next.

His hand slowly moved, inch by inch, for his bow. I could see his breath in the cold air as he slowly pulled his bow from his shoulders, with a level of silence I didn't think possible given everything he was carrying.

Slowly, bow in one hand, listening to the silence, he began to draw an arrow, but I saw what was going to happen before it did. The arrow's tip was about to hit the edge of the shield and I moved to try to stop or warn him, but wasn't fast enough, and the metal tip clanked again metal shield.

I watched Gaelen cringe, but something was moving with terrifying speed through the leaves now. I drew my sword, and he tried to notch the arrow, but whatever was coming for us jumped out of the shadows and tackled him. I stumbled back, pulling out my sword.

Gaelen

Before I could get the arrow nocked, or even near the bow, something tackled me to the ground, and then I felt the cold metal of a blade pressed to my throat. I froze, knowing the smallest movement could mean the end of me, until I heard the voice of the thing pinning me to the ground.

"Gaelen?" came the surprised voice, and I looked up to see-

"Marian?"

The knife came off my throat in an instant, and the face above me, Marian, grinned.

"Gaelen!" he exclaimed, standing and pulling me up by the hand. "Oh my god, we've been looking everywhere for you! Are you okay? I didn't hurt you, did I?" he asked, looking over me. I touched my throat and rolled my arm.

"Ah, besides bruises, no." I laughed a little, with relief.

"Marian?" Althea asked, from somewhere in the darkness to our right Marian looked over at her.

"Oh good, you're both okay. When you never came back through the camp, we got pretty worried. We've been out searching for a couple days now," he explained, touching Althea's shoulder as if to reassure himself she was real and there. It was pretty dark. "Oh, you're freezing! Here," he said, and pulled off his cloak, wrapping it around her shoulders. "What have you two been doing out here for weeks on end? How did you last this long without proper clothing?" he asked, looking between us.

"We didn't, we entered a cave yesterday, three days after we left, and we got out a couple of hours ago and it was autumn," I explained.

"The rock glowed," Althea added with a frown.

"The Key rock?" he asked, eyebrows raising.

"Yeah," I answered, glancing around. "Where's Robin? And the rest of the Thieves?" I asked, looking up at Marian.

"He went back to town to see if maybe you took a different way back, or passed through when we were sleeping or something. The rest of the men are off searching elsewhere." Marian explained, removing his coat and offering it to me. "Here, you'll freeze in that thin summer shirt," he said and I took it, leaving him in a puffy long-sleeved white shirt. It was cold enough out here that I wasn't going to argue.

"Why would he think I would sneak through?" I asked with a frown.

"Oh, well…" Marian seemed to blush a little, rubbing the back of his neck. Or maybe he was just cold. "After your talk last time…and after meeting me and all…I think he wasn't sure what to think," he admitted.

Robin thought I was mad enough at him to completely skip past him without saying anything, or take a different route just to avoid him? I mean, don't get me wrong, I was mad, and hurt, but I didn't hate him. I shook my head a little and looked up at him.

"I'm not…I'm just…" I glanced at Althea, because, well…admitting feelings is hard. She nodded, encouraging me on. "I'm just hurt he left me behind. I'm not—I'm glad to have met you, Marian." I hope that came out right.

Marian smiled a little and nodded, seeming to relax a little. "Oh, well, I'm glad for that. I know that Robin cares a lot about y—"

SCREECH!

A horrible, high-pitched scream echoed through the woods, and we all froze in place.

Chapter Eighteen
Gaelen

Marian swore under his breath, pulling his knives back out. "Forgot about the wraiths…" he mumbled. "Get close to me."

I had an arrow ready in three seconds flat and Althea had never really put her sword down, so we backed together into a circle and watched the woods around us, waiting for any signs of movement. I could hear Althea's nervous breathing behind me as we waited for an attack.

For another moment, everything around was silent. I could clearly hear the stream trickling past a couple yards away, I could hear the trees rustle in the wind. My heart began to pound, waiting for the attack to come. It felt like forever.

SCREEEECH!

The hideous noise was much closer now and seemed to be surrounding us, echoing through the woods. We had to have attracted quite a few… The temperature had dropped and I could see my breath clearly in front of me despite the lack of light. I held my breath, listening closely, scanning the darkness around me a mile a minute, waiting for my shot.

Suddenly, Althea screamed and began to slash at the air with her sword, and I spun toward her, spotting the distorted face in front of her immediately. I fired my arrow into the center of it. It disintegrated, but another was coming in from behind.

I notched another arrow as fast as I could, but with a battle cry and an angry swing of her sword, Althea turned that one to dust as well.

"Watch out!" came Marian's voice behind me and I heard the dying screech of a wraith an inch from my ear. When I turned, it was disintegrating around Marian's knife. That was very close.

The wraiths began to swoop at our heads, moving in all at once now.

"How many are there?!" I heard Althea yell over the wraiths, swinging her sword over her head as one dropped toward her.

"Too many to count!" Marian replied, slicing one after another with impressive skill.

I focused on shooting as many down as I could, firing off arrow after arrow into the moving mass of ghostly figures. It wasn't long until I reached back for another arrow and found I had none left. The dread set in as I looked up and saw one coming for me, dead eyes boring into mine.

"Back off!" Althea yelled as her sword came swinging around me, slicing into the incoming wraith. She was naturally better at swordplay than I would have expected.

I let out a breath of relief and looked at her in amazement. "Thanks."

She nodded, swinging at another, jaw set and face hard and focused.

I turned back just in time for one to grab my wrist and drag me away from the others.

"Gaelen!" Marian called, trying to catch my arm but only succeeding in grabbing my bag strap, which tore quickly, throwing the shield that was attached to it to the ground at Althea's feet.

As I was pulled into the darkness, I gripped my bow, my only weapon, and began beating the wraith with it as hard as I could. I could feel the wraiths around me, surrounding me as I was dragged through the dirt and grass.

With a final hit, I got it off me and quickly rolled, stumbling up and into a run. I scanned the ground for one of my arrows, just for something sharp to swing at them as they dropped toward me from above.

From here, I could see just how many wraiths were here. The sky was filled with them, swarming the three of us and outnumbering us ten to one easily. I froze for a moment, watching in horror and amazement.

"Althea!" I heard Marian's voice yell, followed by a high-pitched scream, rising higher into the air, snapping me out of it. Oh no. I turned, running that way as fast as I could.

"Let go!" she screamed from somewhere off the ground, and I broke through the trees to see her eight feet off the ground in the clutches of a wraith. More were surrounding her as she struggled, sword falling to the ground.

I dodged a diving wraith and looked to Marian to find him fighting off three or four of his own, unable to help anyone.

"Help!" Althea yelled and I began searching desperately again for arrows. Come on, come on, there's got to be at least one somewhere…

I heard a gasping sound from above and watched in horror as the eight or nine wraiths around her began to pull a silvery essence from her. I could only guess at what it was, but I knew it wasn't good.

The silvery light caused something in the grass to glint, and I dove for it. An arrow.

I got to my feet quickly and aimed at the one holding her, firing as quickly as I trusted myself to, and hit the wraith squarely in the head.

It disintegrated, but another one caught her and they kept pulling the light from her. I cursed and looked for another arrow, finding one a few feet away. I fired it, but there were still so many wraiths… Althea wasn't making a lot of noise anymore.

I searched desperately but only found one more arrow… And I knew I had to make this one worthwhile.

The sword glinted underneath her…

"Thea!" I yelled. "I have an idea!" She didn't respond. I frowned, taking a couple steps closer, preparing the arrow. "Thea?" I shouted, but her eyes were fluttering closed.

"Thea, please, I need you to wake up!" I called desperately, panicking a little as she stopped moving. Okay. Okay, this was risky. But I couldn't think of any other way.

I raised my bow, and aimed…I took an extra moment, knowing I couldn't be off by even a centimeter, as I aimed directly at her head.

The arrow shot from my bow and toward Althea's face and I held my breath as the moment felt like an eternity…and then the arrow brushed across her cheek, leaving a small line of blood.

Althea cried out, eyes opening, and glanced down at me just as I rolled under her, grabbing her sword and loading it into my bow, aiming at the wraith holding her in place.

The second I saw her nod, just barely, I released the bowstring and the sword went spinning toward her. I hoped she knew where I was going with this…

The small sword sunk itself into the wraith's chest and Althea grabbed the hilt, driving it further into its chest. It exploded into dust around her.

Another wraith grabbed her and she swung at it, dusting it and the next one before it even had a chance to touch her.

I dove to catch her and she crashed into me, sending us both tumbling to the ground. I felt the sharp side of the sword on my arm at some point, but had too much adrenaline to know if it cut me or not.

We scrambled to our feet, Althea with a little help from me, and turned back to the wraiths.

There weren't nearly as many now, but I still didn't have much of a weapon.

"Gaelen!" I heard Marian shout from somewhere off to our left and turned just in time to dodge a knife, watching as it sliced through the air past me and lodged itself into a tree. I looked at Marian in shock.

"You were supposed to—go get it! Watch out!" he shouted and a wraith sliced him right across the chest with its claws. He cried out and stumbled back, pulling out another knife.

I ran for it, pulling it, but it didn't come out of the tree. Oh no. I glanced back as I yanked at the knife, and saw a wraith notice me, alone and weaponless. It floated closer, mouth opening far more than it should have been able to. I tore desperately at the knife.

"Come on, come on…" I mumbled through gritted teeth, putting my foot up on the tree as I pulled at it. I felt a sharp pain at the back of my neck that seemed to pull through my whole body, and then it felt like my energy was draining from my body. No, no!

I turned to see the wraith, inches away from me, pulling that silvery light from me into the chasm of blackness that was its mouth.

I turned, and gave one last desperate tug at the dagger as I felt my body getting weaker by the second. With a soft pop, it gave way.

In one movement, I had the dagger in the thing's face, sinking into its white, ashy cheek, and it stared at me blankly before doing something the others didn't. Instead of crumbling to dust, it simply faded away around my dagger and was gone, leaving only a cold feeling that seemed to sink all the way into me.

I shivered and caught my breath, wondering for a moment what had just happened, before Althea's voice broke through to me.

"Gaelen! Help!" she demanded, and I snapped out of it, jogging back over to her. She'd taken out quite a few wraiths, each one blowing up into dust and silver light. Each time, she seemed to get stronger.

The rest of the fight seemed to go quickly as we took out the remaining wraiths one by one. When the last one had exploded with a final screech, I dropped my hands onto my legs, breathing heavily.

"Oh my god…" Althea breathed, in a similar stance. Marian was on one knee off to our left, winded.

"I can't believe we won that," he said incredulously, dropping his head for a second as he breathed. "Not to be morbid or anything but that was incredibly dangerous," he said with a little laugh. "Wow."

I let out a little laugh as well, relief washing over me now that the fight was over. "Wow," I said back, looking at Althea.

"Why are you laughing? We just almost died!" she argued, still out of breath, looking between us.

"But we didn't," Marian replied with a little grin that was peeking out of his hair, which had fallen over his face. I couldn't help but laugh a little. She looked at me, but couldn't help but crack a smile either after all the tension was released.

"You're both crazy," she laughed, and between all the laughs, we managed to catch our breath.

Marian made his way over to Althea and I, and we quickly took inventory of our injuries, sitting in the grass. Althea had quite a few cuts and bruises (including the one on her face I had caused and apologized for), and had rolled her ankle when she landed on me, but was okay overall.

Marian had a big cut across his chest, but it wasn't deep enough to worry too much about. He definitely was the worst of all of us but still smiling. I didn't know how he did that.

"Gaelen, your arm!" Althea said suddenly as Marian was wrapping her ankle for the walk back to camp. I frowned and glanced down to see that her sword had in fact cut me, and had cut me much deeper than I thought. The blood was flowing out of it pretty steadily now, staining my white shirt and seeping into Marian's coat.

"Oh," I replied, pulling the sliced jacket sleeve around so I could see it.

"Gaelen, let me see that," Marian said gently as he tied the wrap on Althea's ankle, pulling more bandage from his bag. I frowned.

"Why do you have that much bandage with you?" I asked curiously as he looked at my arm. He looked up at me.

"Oh. Well, you'd been gone so long, we feared maybe one of you had been injured and unable to get back because of it, so I brought supplies just in case. Seems like they were a good idea in the end, huh?" he said with a soft smile, and I nodded a little. They were that worried about us?

"You're going to have to take off the coat for a moment," Marian said apologetically, and I nodded, carefully shrugging it off.

"Sorry," I said, realizing I'd basically ruined it.

"Don't be sorry about getting hurt; I'm sorry you got hurt on my watch," he said, waving me off. He carefully rolled up my sleeve, so it was over the cut, and then began wrapping it.

"So what now?" Althea asked, pulling her feet under the skirt of her dress and hugging her legs. "Do we camp here? Or keep walking out of the mountains?"

"Well, while I'm pretty sure we just killed every wraith for miles around, we'd still better head toward camp. We aren't too far, maybe an hour's walk," he said, and I winced as he pulled the bandages tight. His face was apologetic when he looked back at me. "Sorry, it has to be tight to stop the bleeding," he explained in a soft voice, and I nodded a little even though the pain was radiating up and down my arm now.

He tied the bandage and carefully rolled down my sleeve, offering me the coat again.

"There we are, let's get walking before we all freeze, eh?" he said with a goofy little smile as he stowed the bandages and stood, offering me a hand. I took it with my undamaged arm and stood, waiting as he helped Althea up as well. "We're almost out of the woods."

Chapter Nineteen
Althea

It took an hour of walking through the dark woods to get back to Marian's camp. I took out the glow-in-the-dark pin about halfway through to light our way a little better but out here, it didn't help too much.

My ankle hurt to walk on, and when I saw the light of the campfire in the distance, I let out a sigh of relief. Gaelen looked at me, holding his bandaged arm as we trekked the rest of the way down the mountain.

"Is it hurting a lot?" he asked quietly, Marian just ahead of us. "Your ankle, I mean."

"Oh, yeah, I'll be fine though." I gestured at the fire, "Not much further." He nodded a little, adjusting the bags on his shoulder and looking forward again. Marian had taken up carrying most of my bags and my bedroll, and had attached the shield to his back, but Gaelen, carrying some of his own things, still insisted on taking my final bag so I didn't have the weight of it on my rolled ankle.

That was...insane. I couldn't believe...I was so scared, and there were so many, and we were overwhelmed, and...and I was pretty sure for a while there that we were going to die. But...we didn't. Somehow. And it felt incredibly lucky.

As we approached camp, we could see Robin pacing back and forth in front of the fire, a black silhouette. Men milled around and sat around the fire, clearly not the entire band of merry men, but still quite a few.

"Robin!" Marian called as we entered, catching his attention. Robin stopped pacing and looked at us, and his deeply concerned expression broke into a grin.

"Marian!" he breathed in relief and quickly approached, pulling him into a hug. "God, you're freezing! Here," he said, quickly wrapping Marian up in his own deep green cloak and rubbing his arms up and down to warm him up. Marian smiled softly and pulled it close.

Robin seemed to notice us then. "Gaelen! Althea!" he exclaimed, letting go of Marian and not hesitating in pulling Gaelen into a tight hug, which only lasted about half a second as Gaelen cried out softly and Robin let go with a concerned frown.

"What's going on, are you alright?" he asked, looking over him. He found where the coat was sliced and seemed to notice the bandages underneath. "Where were you? What happened?" he asked, holding Gaelen carefully at arm's length.

"I'm fine, it isn't too deep," he explained softly, seeming to be embarrassed by it. Which was stupid because it was a battle wound but I didn't think saying that would change Gaelen's mind.

"We were attacked by an army of wraiths," Marian explained, rubbing the back of his neck.

Robin glanced back at him with a frown, but didn't let go of Gaelen just yet. "I arrived just after nightfall and was surprised to find you hadn't returned to camp yet, for that very reason," he explained, and Marian nodded, shrugging a little.

"Yes, well, I was on my way back when I…I don't know, something told me not to yet, so I walked a little deeper and thought I heard footsteps, and…well, it turns out to be a very good thing I stayed, because I found these two and then about forty wraiths or so found the three of us," he explained with a gesture toward us. Robin nodded a little but he was still frowning.

"Right… That's good, though, well done, Marian," he said, but still seemed a little upset. He looked back at Gaelen, leaving one hand on his good shoulder. "Where have you been for the last few months? We were getting worried."

Gaelen blushed and shrugged a little, looking down.

"It…well, it's kind of complicated—" he started and Marian interjected.

"Why don't we go warm up by the fire and they can tell us what happened?" he suggested, and Robin nodded a little, squeezing Gaelen's shoulder before letting go of him.

"You're right," he said to Marian, and then to Gaelen, "Let's go warm up."

By the fire, we were given warm cups of what appeared to be milk by the men, but didn't taste exactly like it. Maybe they had goats, but I hadn't seen any. Either way, it wasn't bad and it definitely helped me warm up. I huddled closer to the fire.

Marian dropped the bags and shield carefully, lowering himself onto a log. Robin sat next to him, looking him over quickly.

"I'm fine, Rob," he said with a little smile, taking his own cup of milk from where it'd been warming over the fire.

"Forty wraiths, you said?" he asked in amazement. Marian nodded.

"Yes, the fight wasn't pretty. I've never fought more than two at a time before," he admitted, and I started to wonder how we actually got through that alive, staring blankly at my lap.

I'd never been in a situation that stressful before, but honestly? I'd never felt that powerful either. And we won. Even if we almost didn't. I shivered as I remembered what it had felt like when they had me. I was fairly certain they'd been sucking out my soul, or my life force, or something...I had felt like I was dying.

"What... are wraiths, exactly?" I asked slowly, looking up at the three others gathered around the fire with me. Marian spoke up first, face more grim than I'd seen him be. Well, except for in the wraith fight, I suppose.

"Wraiths are... Well, they're said to be lost souls, the souls of those who died in life with unfinished business."

"Like a ghost?" I asked, and Marian nodded.

"Yes, like a ghost, but... Well, when a directionless soul is stuck for long enough, it... changes. It's as if, the longer it stays in the land of the living, the more it loses of itself," Marian's dark eyes reflected in the fire as he continued. "Eventually, nothing is left but its grief, and its desire to be whole again. So it seeks out those with souls, hoping to... well, to be complete again."

I slowly nodded, but the mood was somber now.

I touched my cheek subconsciously, where Gaelen's arrow had grazed me and snapped me out of, well, losing my soul, it seems. It would take a little while to heal—

"So, tell me everything. Where have you two been?" Robin's voice cut through my thoughts and I blinked and looked up. Gaelen glanced at me, but I didn't know how to explain what happened any better than he did. He still had my bag, which, now that I'm thinking of it, I really hope still has the Cool Rock…

"We…well…" Gaelen looked at me. "We left your camp, and got to the mountains…" He glanced at me again, struggling to really explain it all.

"We camped at the edge and went up early in the morning." I took over when he trailed off, looking at Robin and Marian across the fire. "We got to the spires at a good time, and found the 'pin', which ended up just being the pin on my bag that I had found at Emory's." I shrugged because I didn't really know how to explain that. "And it opened a hidden door. When we went through it, we couldn't see a thing, and then someone shut the door on us and we couldn't get back out," I explained and Robin frowned deeply.

"Someone shut you in there? Who?" he asked, leaning toward us with interest, and I shrugged.

"I don't know, we didn't see," I answered, and he nodded a little.

"Someone had to be following us," Gaelen commented, and I frowned a little, remembering something.

"I did feel like someone was following us back at the prophecy rock, and back when Molly and I tried to go home the same way we came, but… Well, I figured the first one was you," I said, looking at Gaelen. He nodded a little, smiling softly.

"Yeah, that one was me," he said and sipped his probably-goat's milk. "But I felt that at the prophecy wall as well…" he added, glancing up at Robin.

"Well, no one else came through my camp behind you, that I know of…" he said thoughtfully. "But anyway, what happened next?"

"Well, it was too dark to see, so we took a break and fell asleep for a couple of hours and when we woke up, Gaelen found the pin I had accidentally borrowed from Frank," I explained, removing the green-glowing purple pin on my dress and holding it up. It wasn't glowing too much now. I set it down next to me. Frank's eyebrows rose. "Sorry Frank," I commented and he smiled and waved me off. Robin frowned.

"Frank's pin is magic?" he asked, and I shook my head.

"No, it's glow-in-the-dark," I explained and he raised an eyebrow. Right, not a thing here. "It's, like, a chemical reaction thing that collects light during the day and then keeps it…" Everyone looked confused. I waved my hand, shaking my head. "Never mind, it's…it's a my-world thing, but it helped us find a really long tunnel that led us to the shield…" I gestured toward the shining metal shield by Marian's feet. "And also a wraith," I sighed.

"And we fought it," Gaelen said. "But it was still nearly impossible to see so it wasn't a great fight. But she used the Cool Rock…" Gaelen said, fishing for it in the bag. Robin frowned.

"What's the Cool Rock?" he asked, and Gaelen stopped.

"Oh, it's…sorry, it's the Key to the Cosmos," he explained sheepishly. "From the Prophecy." Out of the bag, he pulled the rock. Still there. Still gorgeous. I felt a little of the weight of everything happening lift from my shoulders.

Marian's and Robin's eyes lit up in wonder, along with quite a few of the men's. "Wow," Robin breathed in amazement.

"It really does hold the cosmos…" Marian mumbled, and Gaelen nodded, looking at it.

"Well, when she held it up, it glowed, and the shield could be removed, and then part of the wall opened and it was autumn," he explained before tucking it away. Robin blinked and then frowned.

"Wait, that's it? It was just, suddenly autumn?" he asked in surprise.

"Yes," Gaelen replied.

"I think we might have 'jumped' or…something," I interjected, and the eyes turned to me now. "I don't know how…'devices' work, but if that's one of them, and it glowed…I don't know why but maybe it took us to fall." I glanced at Gaelen, unsure if that made sense. He frowned.

"I can't say I know too much about Devices or Jumping or any of that, but that may be," Robin spoke up, and Marian touched his arm.

"I do," he said, and we all looked at him. He blushed a little, and then sighed. "Before I was a thief, I lived in Althalamist…" He glanced at Gaelen. "That's where I met Robin actually, before we decided to…well, start all this," he gestured around at the camp vaguely. Robin looked at him with interest.

"But what does that have to do with your knowledge of how devices work?" he asked curiously and Marian smiled at him a little.

"Well, lots of travelers come through Althalamist, for the prophecy I'm sure, but before I was a thief, I was a clothes maker, and I had many an out-of-place traveler walk in and ask for clothes fitting to the era for tradeable goods like gold and peppercorn, but I also got a lot of good stories out of it," he said with a little proud smile, "like, for instance, I found out that using their devices mostly has to do with feelings, and wants." He looked at me now. "What were you thinking about when you picked up the shield?"

I frowned a little as I thought about it. "I guess…" What was I thinking about? "Well…the shield kind of reminded me of a tin-foil one I made when I was like, nine for my little brother when we went as a knight and a princess for Halloween." I looked up at them, and then my eyebrows rose a little. "You think that me thinking about Halloween made it Halloween?" I asked in surprise, and Marian shrugged a little.

"Maybe. I don't really know for sure, I've never seen it done, but it sounds likely," he said, then frowned and looked at Robin. "Is today the thirty-first?"

Robin frowned and then nodded a little. "I…think it might be," he looked up at me. "That would explain the number of wraiths, anyway."

If I successfully used the rock, just by being nostalgic… This meant everything. This meant we could go home! I looked up at Gaelen, grin forming, but his eyes were on the ground. I frowned a little.

"That's great then! You got the shield, and figured out how to use your device! Now you just have to find the last few things in the prophecy and magic will be saved! Right?" Marian asked with a grin, which faded when he looked at us. "Right?"

"No, it means Althea will go home and we'll lose magic forever," Gaelen said, setting aside his cup and standing. I sighed.

"Gaelen—" I started, but he interrupted.

"What? Don't tell me you'll stay and finish the quest. This is what you wanted all along," he said bitterly, tossing me my bag.

"Oh," Marian said, looking at me. "Well, Gaelen, you can't exactly blame her for wanting to go home…" he said gently.

"Right, and I thought you wanted to come with me anyway!" I argued, standing as well now, setting the bag aside. Gaelen was quiet. Robin frowned.

"You…were going to go to the other world?" he asked Gaelen.

"I don't know. Yes," he said and sighed, crossing his arms. "Back when I had no one and nothing and no one cared about me. It's got horseless carriages and everyone can read! Why wouldn't I want to?" he said, looking at the ground again.

"Right, so why are you so upset? This means we can get back!" I argued, and Gaelen was silent again. Marian frowned a little more, looking between Robin and him.

"Unless…you've changed your mind," Marian realized, and Gaelen looked away a little more. Was he blushing? I couldn't tell from here but he seemed to blush a lot, even if it was kind of hard to tell sometimes. It was quiet for a moment.

"Gaelen?" Robin asked quietly. Gaelen slowly let out a sigh and spoke, still looking at the ground.

"I…I want to stay and…I don't know, I thought…now that I know you're here, I could…maybe join you…" he said, voice getting lower with each pause. He didn't give Robin much of a chance to answer. "I also want to finish this quest!" He turned to me. "The whole reason you're here is to save magic! Are you going to give that all up because you found a way home?" he demanded, and I put my hands up.

"Yes! Of course I am!" I shot back, incredulous. "Gaelen, I am a child. A twelve-year-old child! I never even meant to be here!" I ran a hand through my hair to get it out of my face. "I've barely seen any magic since I've been here, and it's all been terrible! Racist fairies and terrifying giants and deadly ghost women and a giant lake squid! Why would I want to save any of that???" I shouted. "Do you not remember an hour ago when we almost died?"

He looked at me with disdain and disappointment, and when he spoke, it was firm and unwavering. "Just because you haven't seen the good in something doesn't mean it isn't there, Althea."

It was quiet for a moment. I didn't know what to say to him, or what he wanted from me.

Robin broke the silence first. "Alright, well, it's been a long and difficult day for everyone; why don't we go to bed and figure this out in the morning?" he suggested, standing.

"Fine," Gaelen answered, not looking at anyone.

"Great. Ah. Gaelen, why don't you stay in my tent tonight, hmm?" he said warily, looking between us. "Marian, would you take the extra tent with Althea?"

Marian nodded with a smile. "Of course. It's—" He began, but Gaelen cut him off.

"Great," he said and starting walking away from the fire. I sighed as he did, groaning in frustration and annoyance and turning back to my stuff.

"Impossible, just impossible…" I mumbled, annoyed at how he was acting. He knew all along I wanted to get home. I thought he was trying to help me, but he just wanted me to fulfil this stupid prophecy… Robin sighed and followed Gaelen into the darkness.

I looked at Marian, who smiled sympathetically. "This way," he said quietly, picking up our stuff, bedrolls included, and heading away from the fire. I sighed and followed him, not knowing what else to do.

We reached a small tent that had some supplies in it but was mostly empty, and Marian held the flap open for me. I walked in and let out a breath, trying to calm my heightened heart rate.

Marian stepped in after and set down the bags, tossing me a bed roll.

"That all seemed like…a lot. Do you want to talk about it?" he asked as he started setting out Gaelen's for himself.

"I…I don't know. I'm mad. But also…I don't know!" I groaned, rolling out my bed for the night, on the other side of the tent. "I…I thought he was helping me get home! I get that the quest thing mattered but… The whole point was so that I could get home! I was never supposed to be here in the first place, it was an accident!" I ranted, plopping down onto my bed and putting my head in my hands.

"Well…an accident that was written in stone," Marian said gently, sitting on his own bed roll. "Is it possible, given the rock's powers…that you wanted to come here?" he asked. I shrugged.

"I…I mean, no, I don't think so, but I guess…I don't know, I could have been thinking about how we played adventurers in the woods, while we were chasing the cloaked guys? But I didn't even have the rock, Molly did!" I argued, looking at him. He shrugged.

"Well, maybe you were close enough it worked anyway," he said, and I sighed, rubbing my face.

"That still doesn't explain why we couldn't get back. We had the rock and everything!"

"Maybe you didn't actually want to go back yet?" he suggested and I shrugged.

"I mean…I'm pretty sure I did. I was super worried about my mom, and what she'd say when she found that we were gone… How worried she'd be…" I said, staring off to the side of the tent. "But…I guess maybe the adventure did feel a little short…I mean, we were in a whole 'nother world! I'm pretty sure that's never been documented as happening!

"And we'd seen magical beings, and been in a medieval town…I wanted to look at everything, and explore, and figure out why we were there, but we didn't have time and just needed to get back, and we didn't have our parents with us, and I wasn't sure how we were supposed to do all this on our own…" I threw my hand up. "The novels make it seem so easy! Like you get here and you know who you are and why you're here, but this…felt like an accident.

"Like we stumbled into something we were never supposed to see. There were no easy answers, and then suddenly I'm 'the chosen one' and supposed to save the world or something, but I have no idea what I'm doing or what I'm even saving and my best friend is sick and just…" I felt tears in my eyes, even if I didn't want them there. "How am I supposed to save anything when I don't even know what's going on?"

Marian listened quietly the whole time, and when I finished, he gave me a minute before he spoke.

"You know, Althea…life's kind of like that sometimes. You see a plan for your life, and something completely different happens and changes everything." He smiled a little, softly, to himself. "But sometimes those changes are for the better, even if it takes a while to settle into them."

He looked up at me. "If what you really want is to go home, then magic will still find a way. Someone else will step up, with an even cooler rock." He cracked a smile and I couldn't help but laugh softly, albeit bitterly, through tears. "And save magic or the world or whatever it ends up being. If this truly isn't what you want, you don't have to have it. Go home, live your life, and we'll figure out the rest, okay?" he said supportively, and I let out a breath slowly.

"What about Gaelen?" I asked, looking up at him. He smiled.

"Gaelen'll figure it out, but his happiness isn't your responsibility. He thought you were the chosen one, but him being wrong, or you choosing not to be…there isn't anything he can do about it. You told him you just wanted to go home, he knew that, it's his fault if he's mad about it now," Marian explained and I nodded slowly.

"Yeah…you're right. We didn't get to finish the quest; he can do it if he wants. I just want to go home…" I mumbled, lying back on my sleeping bag.

"Exactly. Now, get some sleep, and in the morning, we'll figure out the rest, alright?" he said, and the sound of someone clearing their throat could be heard just outside of our tent. I looked up to see the silhouette of a man in front of the door to our tent. "I'll be right back. Goodnight, Althea," Marian said to me and stood, stepping out of the tent.

"Goodnight," I replied.

I listened for their voices as the shape of Marian met the shape of Robin.

"How is she?" Robin asked in a hushed voice.

"Going to bed. She's dealing with quite a bit right now…I think she feels a little betrayed after Gaelen's explosion…" he said softly. *Oh most definitely*, I thought.

"Gaelen's the same, he thought she was in it to save magic, but I think it's more about the thought of her leaving after all that they've been through," Robin said, and I found myself frowning. *About me? Did he really care that much?* "But we can talk more in the morning," Robin said softly, and I watched the shadow of his hand come up to Marian's cheek, touching it softly. "You're sure you're okay with staying here tonight?" His voice was gentler now. I could tell Marian was smiling (and probably blushing) as he snorted softly, stepping closer to Robin.

"I can survive one night away from you, love," he teased, and Robin chuckled softly, in a warm sort of way.

"Very well. See you in the morning, Marian," he spoke gently, still touching his cheek, and they stepped together, kissing gently, their shadows melding together into one.

I let my head drop back onto the bed roll, deciding that this was a private moment that I probably shouldn't be watching. I let my eyes close as I heard quiet goodnights and the tent flap shuffle.

I heard Marian slipping back into his bedroll, and then it was quiet and only the sound of crickets and the wind coming down from the mountains and a distant fire crackling could be heard, and I let myself fall asleep slowly, deciding that whatever happened was going to have to happen tomorrow anyway.

Chapter Twenty
Gaelen

I woke up slowly the next morning to the sound of light snoring. Ugh, Althea's at it again...I rolled away, covering my head, but as I tried to drown out the snoring, I realized it wasn't Althea's. I frowned and opened my eyes and found myself inside a green tent. Wait, what?

I rolled to look at the person snoring next to me and found Robin, asleep on his back and snoring away. The memories of the day before came flooding back, including the ones from around the fire... I sighed softly, sitting up and rubbing my face as I tried to wake up and deal with my new reality. Althea was leaving.

We still had to get back to Emory's and get Molly, but... We had the shield, and that was so much further than anyone had gotten. We had the actual shield from a hundreds-of-years-old prophecy that no one had been successful in fulfilling, we had the Key to the Cosmos... What more evidence did she need?

But no, she just wants to go home... And I guess I get that... But that means leaving and ending the quest. If magic really was doomed, then her leaving meant terrible things for this world...

The choice between staying or going was one I didn't want to think about... If I stayed, I'd never see Althea again, but I'd also never see her world... I'd be in a world of magic, with Robin, and could be a thief like him... But I'd always know there was something greater out there. And I'd be trapped in a world that would lose its magic...

If I went, I could experience so much, but I'd be abandoning my world, and magic, and the quest... I'd never see Robin or Marian or Cecil again, and I'd already been through that once with Robin... While I wanted to learn everything, and see such a great world, I would be stuck there, and who knows if I'd even like it. There was no returning if I didn't… The choice was impossible and it was weighing me down.

I sighed softly into the quiet morning and decided to get up, leaving my bedroll unrolled. I picked Marian's coat up, glancing at my injured arm warily for a moment before pulling it on. Yesterday had been a mess.

I stepped out into the cold morning air, pulling the coat closed around me. It was early; none of the men seemed to be awake yet. I took a deep breath and made my way to the deserted fire, leaving Robin snoring in his tent.

When I reached the fire, I sighed softly. Althea's bag was still sitting on the log where it'd been last night. I didn't really want to think about all that just yet… I went about adding wood to the fire and throwing on dry, dead leaves, before pulling a flint and steel out of one of the fire bags and attempting to spark it. It took a while; it usually does.

When it was lit, I sat quietly next to it. I…felt bad about how I had acted last night. I shouldn't have been so mean to Althea…I should have been happy that she could go back to her family. I didn't want to stop being friends…

I heard shuffling footsteps and looked up from the slowly growing fire to see Althea, hugging Marian's cloak around her as she approached. I didn't know what to say. She nodded at me wordlessly and sat next to me on the log.

It was silent for a moment. The tension was high. She looked tired. I had a lot of things I wanted to say to her, but I didn't know where to start.

"How's your arm?" she asked me softly, and I glanced at it.

"Okay. A little sore," I answered. "How's your ankle?" I asked, noticing the cut on her cheek from my arrow had healed shut. She nodded.

"A little sore. Better."

It was quiet again, and felt awkward now. It had never been awkward to talk to her before… There was so much to say, and even though I couldn't pick, saying anything would be better than this silence. I let out a soft sigh, preparing to speak, but she beat me to it.

"I know this whole quest thing is important to you," she said, and I looked at her. I didn't know what she was going to say. She looked up at me after a moment, and in the early morning light, sitting this close, I had a hard time dealing with such direct eye contact. I looked forward, clearing my throat softly.

"Well—" I started, but she cut me off.

"I'm sorry," she said, and when I looked back up at her, she was looking at her hands in her lap. I frowned. What was she sorry for? She wasn't looking at me, face looking a bit guilty.

"Oh," I said as I realized. She's sorry because she isn't going to complete the quest. My heart started to pound as emotions rose in me, wanting to tell her all the reasons she needed to stay, how many people were relying on her, how I didn't want her to go… But I knew that wasn't what she needed, and it wouldn't change anything anyway. She'd made up her mind long ago. So I took a deep breath, tried to slow my heart rate, and spoke, "Okay."

She frowned and looked up at me. "Okay?" she asked suspiciously. I let out a breath and nodded a little, looking at the fire.

"Yeah," I said, and then softly added, "I get it."

I looked up at her, and she was just staring at me.

"So…" She started after a moment. "You're not gonna argue with me? Try to get me to stay?" I frowned at her.

"Do you want me to?" I asked in surprise, and she sighed, sitting back a little.

"I mean, no, I guess not, but…" She looked back at me. "Are you…sure you're gonna be okay with that?" she asked carefully. I looked down, shrugging a little.

"I…I'd still like you to complete the quest, but I understand that you'd like to go home…" I was kind of figuring this out as I went. Althea nodded a little in my periphery.

"And…and what now?" she asked, sitting forward, leaning on her knees. "Where…where do we go from here?" she asked, softer.

This definitely felt more like a conversation now, but it was filled with so many subtexts and undertones and unsaid things that it wasn't an easy one, but we seemed to be figuring it out together. I let out a slow sigh, sitting back a little.

"I…suppose I'll help you get back to town and get Molly and then…we'll part ways," I said, and glanced at her again. "You'll go home and I'll stay and finish the quest."

Althea looked up at me. "You're going to continue the quest? What about the key to the cosmos? Don't you need that to keep going?" she asked, and I shrugged, crossing my arms quietly.

"Maybe. But maybe I can just continue with the shield," I said. She was quiet, just looking at me for a moment. When she spoke, she spoke carefully.

"Gaelen, has it occurred to you that maybe the quest isn't supposed to be finished?" she asked. I knit my eyebrows. She sat up again. "Like, so far everything that's happened was supposed to happen, right? Maybe I'm supposed to go home…maybe just finding the shield was enough," she suggested with a little shrug.

I thought about it, but I couldn't be sure, not about any of this.

"I…I guess. Maybe," I conceded quietly, thinking about it. Everything else was so spot on; the rock, the pin, the hair and eyes…the prophecy even accounted for forgetting to give back a glowing pin…if it could account for all that, sure it would have accounted for this… I nodded a little.

"You should stay here with Robin and Marian," she added. I glanced quietly at the tents around me.

"Maybe," I said again. Althea didn't reply.

We stared at the fire for a while.

After about an hour, the men began to wake up and things warmed up a little, but it was still a chilly morning. Robin was up pretty early, and met us at the fire looking tired. I figured it was mostly from the early hour…but I remembered he'd been searching for me for a while too and decided it was probably a combination of both.

He stood in front of the fire, staring at it quietly, but acknowledged us with a nod. After a moment or two, he went about making coffee, and set the metal pot over the fire before sitting on a log across from us and quietly watching it boil. We were all tired today.

Althea quietly cleared her throat and stood. "I'm…gonna take a walk," she said quietly, and I nodded at her in response. She nodded back, hesitated awkwardly like she might say something, and instead nodded again and headed off toward the stream.

Robin and I were left, quietly staring at the fire. He glanced up at me across the flames, quiet for a moment before he spoke.

"How's your arm feeling today?" he asked, and I shrugged a little, because I wasn't really sure.

"Sore," I replied for the second time today. He nodded a little, looking back at the coffee.

"We'll have to rewrap it later."

It was quiet for a while. The coffee was finished eventually, and Robin poured himself some, and then poured another mug and came around the fire, sitting on the log next to me. He took a little sip of his coffee before offering me the other mug.

"Here, it seems like you need it as much as me today," he said, and I took it. I didn't really like coffee, but I had a feeling he was right. We were both quiet for a moment.

"It's kind of hard for me to wrap my mind around your… 'jump'," he said with a little smile, sipping his coffee little by little as it was still very hot. I held mine close to my chest as I waited for it to be drinkable.

"Mm? Why's that?" I asked softly, glancing at him. He was looking at me with sparkly eyes, like he was trying to understand me just by the way I looked right now.

"Well, to you, it's only been a few days since we first spoke. Since we… fought, and you left camp. It's been… well, it's been a few months for me," he said, and then glanced at the trees surrounding us, red and orange leaves quietly fluttering in the soft breeze coming off the mountains. "And for you, at least, you can look at the trees, and it'll feel like autumn, but for me…" He looked at me again. "It's hard to visualize. You basically didn't exist for three months." His tone was somewhere between amazed and amused, and I blinked quietly, trying to think about that.

"I guess you're right," I agreed, even though that was very strange to actually think about. It was quiet again. I sipped my coffee.

Men were milling around now, getting dressed and ready in their tents. In the daylight, I could see that about half the camp was here. I was flattered they all came out to look for us…

"Marian's wonderful, by the way," I said out of the blue. Robin looked up and smiled a little.

"Oh?" he asked brightly. "What makes you say that?"

"Well, we definitely would have been lost in the mountains and killed by wraiths if he hadn't shown up," I started, taking another sip from my coffee. "And he's very kind. I can tell he cares a lot about people," I decided aloud, and looked at him. "And I can tell you really care about him," I said genuinely, and a rare sight befell me.

Robin blushed a little and smiled shyly at his coffee. "Yes, well..." He started, taking a sip.

"You could have told me, you know," I said in a soft voice, and then held my coffee a little closer. "It might have taken me some time to understand...but..." I sighed quietly and looked up at him, bracing myself for...well, sharing feelings. "Robin, I don't have a father, but I've always kind of thought of you as—" I began, but his head raised quickly to look at me.

"Don't have a father? Of course you do, Gaelen. You didn't know?" he asked seriously, and I froze where I sat. My mind began to race. Did I have a father all along? Did Robin know him? Did no one ever tell me? Was it Cecil? Robin cracked a smile. "Why else would I have given you the best name in my arsenal if I wasn't going to be your father?" he joked and ruffled my hair. "That would just be a waste." I realized the joke and the sentiment, and cracked a little smile myself, chuckling softly, feeling warm from the coffee and the moment.

"Alright, I get it..." I laughed quietly, looking at the fire again. I smiled a little more. "Does that mean I get to go by Gaelen Hood?" I joked softly.

Robin chuckled and patted my shoulder, staring into the fire as well with a soft smile.

"If you want to, kid, if you want to..." he answered, and I smiled a little.

It was quiet for a moment longer and my smile slowly faded.

"But...seriously, Robin, I...I kind of understand what happened a little better now, but..." I looked up at him with a deathly serious expression, "...you have to promise me you aren't going to abandon me without a word ever again." Before I even finished speaking, he was shaking his head.

"Never again; I'm sorry it ever happened in the first place," he said seriously, and then gently put his arm around me in a fatherly sort of way, rubbing my arm. "I trust you and I'm not going to leave ever again without talking to you first or taking you along, okay?" He looked at me. "I promise."

I was quiet for a moment, making sure he genuinely meant it, but when I saw that he was sincere, I nodded a little.

"Okay. I trust you," I said.

"Thank you," he replied quietly, punctuated with a small smile. I smiled back a little before looking back at the fire. He left his arm around me for a while as we drank our coffees.

Eventually, he patted my back and stood.

"Alright. Let me show you my brand new cooking skills," he grinned and I groaned playfully.

"Wonderful, I've been craving burnt eggs and bacon for the last three years," I joked sarcastically and he laughed, waving me off.

"Prepare to be impressed, Son," he joked and cracked his knuckles.

Chapter Twenty-One
Althea

Gaelen is impossible! The whole time we spoke he barely said a word and he wouldn't agree or disagree with anything... It was maddening!

I just wanted him to be happy, but it was like no matter what I suggested, it wasn't enough! Would he really be happier having me trapped here for god-knows-how-long? For what, to complete some dumb prophecy? This wasn't even my world, why was it me that had to save the magic for it?

I walked to the stream, taking a breath as I reached it. I sat next to it quietly, watching it flow past. It was still pretty cold out, but now that the sun was coming out, it was getting warmer. I felt gross...I usually showered at least every other day, if not every day, and washed my hair once a week, but... Well, the last time I'd even gotten close was when we were attacked by that squid, and that was...well, more days ago then I even cared to count.

People here smelled...different. Well, worse, but it was interesting, because somehow it was less noticeable than back home? Back home if I didn't shower for the third day in a row, everyone around would know it, but it felt like, here, it didn't seem to matter as much? But after like, 8 days...

I touched the water with my hand and knew immediately there was no way I was getting all the way in... But I took off my shoes and socks and stood next to the creak, making sure no one else was around. *Okay, Althea. You can do this. For everyone's sake*. I braced myself, hiked up my skirts, and then stepped quickly into the water and let myself fall into a sitting position.

I gasped because it felt like ice, and then burned, but I needed to get clean. I was covered in cuts and bruises, and I washed them and any of my body I could reach in the water. My only thoughts the whole time were *hurry hurry hurry hurry* as I held my dress up from the water with one hand.

I got out as fast as I could, shivering, and sat on the bank, wrapping myself in my dress. I let myself recover and warm up for a second, but I knew I wasn't done.

I rolled up my sleeves and dipped my hands into the water, washing my arms and face as well as I could, but…something had to be done with my hair. I carefully unbraided it, running my fingers through it and letting it puff and fray… *Okay Althea, last thing, and then after this you can go home and use a real shower and never think of this again.*

I let out a breath…and then dunked my whole head into the freezing cold water.

It hurt, I don't know how else to explain it. I do not recommend sticking your head into a freezing cold creek.

Once my hair was soaked and I'd run my fingers through it, I whipped it back and cringed as the ice water ran down my back. I squeezed it out and then braided it as fast as I could, but by the end, I couldn't feel my fingers.

Shivering, I gathered myself up to go back to the fire, wrapping myself in the thankfully dry cloak.

This had all been…quite an experience. It wasn't like I had hated the whole thing, I had had a lot of fun, and Gaelen was a great friend, and someone gave me a sword, but…well, overall, I wouldn't ever choose to stay. No showers, not many bathrooms even, dangerous creatures and long walks…

I was still unclear on if people got married by my age here or not, but either way, weird and creepy. And the whole 'men being the strong ones and the ones with rights and respect'… not that I hadn't been treated with respect since I'd been here, but…well, maybe things here in this world were different than history in my world, but in any case, I didn't want to get stuck here. I wanted to be where I was supposed to be; home with my family. Where I was a kid and not expected to save the world or work or anything else.

I also missed the Internet.

I trudged back up to the fire to find Robin with his arm around Gaelen in a way that kind of touched my heart. They'd made up, I could tell.

I smiled to myself, stopping for a moment. Maybe Gaelen would be a little more okay now. Maybe he'd be happier. Maybe I didn't want to interrupt…pulling my cloak closer, I went for a quick walk, thinking that could warm me up, maybe. Just until breakfast was ready.

I rubbed my arms to try to warm up faster as I walked, thinking over everything so far. I glanced around at the trees and wondered if anything magical was lurking nearby.

If magic was so great, why had I only seen the bad stuff? Why hadn't I met any wizards or been able to cast any spells or shoot fire out of my hands or something?

But Althea, came the voice of Molly through my head, *have you even tried to shoot fire from your hands yet?*

No, Molly, I thought with a sigh, raising my hand in front of me, staring at the palm, *I haven't tried to—*

A flame flickered in the center of my palm, floating just off my skin.

I froze for a moment, staring widely at my hand as I tried to register what was happening. There's fire. In my hand. Not burning me. I made it. That's a thing I did.

What?

Okay, okay, let's think about this. I made…

…a flame…

…in my hand…

…with a thought.

I snapped my hand closed, rubbing my palm quickly against my cloak, as if it would get off whatever magic was there, and began to pace quietly, heart pounding.

Did I…

Did I just do magic?

Okay Althea, breathe and think about this. I'm sure it was just a fluke. I'm sure…my brain made that up. Yes. I'm just too cold and was thinking about the fire and… Yeah, yeah, I can't do magic, that'd be silly.

It doesn't change anything anyway, I'm still leaving, whether I'm a wizard or not (and I'm not) so let's just forget that ever happened and go see if breakfast is ready. Yup. Everything is fine and normal. Let's see how Gaelen's doing.

When I got back to the fire again, I found Robin cracking eggs onto their makeshift skillet thing, bacon already going. Gaelen was watching with a little smirk, sipping something from a mug. Coffee?

"I'm telling you, Robin, all the cooking lessons in the world couldn't change your amazing ability to burn everything you cook," he teased, and Robin scoffed.

"Get ready to eat your words, Hood. Literally," he joked back, and I noticed the use of a last name, which made me raise my eyebrows in an impressed way. Gaelen noticed and seemed to blush and roll his eyes a little, trying to play it off, but I knew he was pretty happy about it. He looked it, at least.

"Robin, you're stealing my job," came Marian's voice from between the tents as he approached, dressed for the day but still looking half awake. Robin laughed.

"No no, this is a one-time thing. Once a month at the most," he said and Marian chuckled, sitting on a log.

"Well then, I'll enjoy my break for the morning," he laughed, and then smiled at me with a nod. I was still just standing near the fire, so I moved to sit on a log. More men were up and moving around by now.

"Has he cooked for you before?" Gaelen asked with an incredulous laugh, leaning back on his log a little. "I'm getting the feeling he hasn't."

Marian made a kind of face when Robin wasn't looking. "He has. Believe me," he joked, and Robin tossed an empty egg container at him.

"Hey. Be supportive," he chuckled. "If I am still terrible, it's on you."

It wasn't long before we all were holding wooden plates of food, which looked more or less decent. Gaelen dared to take the first bite and shrugged a little as he ate it, looking impressed.

"Well," he said, swallowing it, "it's edible, so I'm impressed." Robin rolled his eyes and ate some of his own.

"It's better than edible," he said between bites, "but thank you."

Marian was smiling to himself as he chewed and Robin noticed me notice. He frowned at Marian.

"What?" he asked. "Why are you smirking at my breakfast?" He nudged him with a little grin.

"Ah, well… Just a note for next time…" Marian reached into his mouth and pulled out a bit of eggshell the size of a dime. "Maybe don't leave in the shell?" He giggled, and we all started to laugh light-heartedly.

Robin blushed and rolled his eyes. "Alright, alright, that was a fluke," he argued, and we laughed a little harder.

After breakfast, we packed up the camp to leave. It took a couple of hours overall, but by lunch time, we were ready to go. I pulled my bag on and attached the shield to the strap like Gaelen had done yesterday, letting it rest against my back. My ankle was feeling much better today, so I figured I'd handle it myself. It was my destiny quest after all…

We ate some fruits and jerky for lunch, which was good because Gaelen and I still had some left from…well, I guess it was three months ago at this point, back when they gave them to us. But it was all still good and everything, given it was only like, four-ish days old because we time-jumped… It didn't matter, we ate the fruit, bottom line.

We started walking back up the hill into the woods and Gaelen came to walk next to me, wearing bags on one side only, avoiding his bad arm. It would take a while to heal; Marion had looked at it earlier when he rewrapped it.

The line of men walking extended behind and in front of us for a while. I mostly watched my feet as we walked.

"It's weird, isn't it?" Gaelen asked and broke me out of my thoughts. I blinked and looked up at him.

"What is?" I asked, and he looked at me, smiling a little, thoughtfully.

"Just…going back with all of these people, with all the trees…the quest ending…I don't know. It's just different. I feel like it just started. I thought we'd be walking back like this in the summer and with just the two of us," he said softly, looking around. "It's just…"

"Weird," I finished for him with a little nod. A lot of things were weird right now. I was leaving, the quest was half done, things seemed to be better for Gaelen but we still weren't really talking about it, I could maybe do magic and was trying not to think about it in case my hand set itself on fire again, I could travel to different worlds but also maybe to different times…

Everything had happened so fast, but we had long enough until we could go home that I kind of got the chance to take in the world around us a little more. I hadn't been here for nearly as long as I thought I was gonna be…

"Is everything okay?" Gaelen broke through my thoughts with a frown. I blinked, looking up at him, and realized my trailing off might have seemed suspicious. I blushed as I tried to come up with an excuse.

"Um, yeah, yeah I'm good, sorry. Just thinking about…everything. I wonder if it's almost April back home now if it's November here…" Oh, wow, I hadn't actually thought about that. I thought about my mom, how warm and kind she was, already going through things with my dad and my brother, being horribly worried and thinking I was dead, and I was wracked with guilt. I hadn't realized how much I missed being hugged until just now, thinking about how she'd cry and hug me when I got back...

I felt a hand on my shoulder and looked up to see Gaelen with a very concerned expression.

"Hey. It'll be okay. You didn't leave her on purpose, and think of the prayers you'll be answering by coming back. It'll be okay." His voice was gentle.

I was kind of speechless for a moment, because I didn't really expect him to comfort me or anything, but then he did and I just... I nodded softly to him, with a little smile, and wiped the tears from my eyes. He smiled back and gently released my shoulder.

"You know..." I said softly after a moment. He looked up at me again. "You could...come with." I looked at him. He smiled a little sadly, but I stopped him before he could speak. "I mean, I think you'd really like it there...you could come to school with me, learn all about my world and the future, ride in cars and eat fast food..." He smiled, thinking about it. I noticed his arm again and nodded to it. "We've got modern healthcare, I'm sure they could take care of that in a snap."

"Althea." Gaelen stopped me, smiling softly at me, eyes equally soft. "I...can't." His eyes were shinier than usual.

I took in a breath and nodded a little, quietly. "Alright," I sighed, and looked up at Marian and Robin ahead. Marian and some of the men were laughing at something Robin had said. This was his family. "I understand."

Gaelen smiled at me a little more and then pulled me into a gentle side hug, before letting go and letting a silence fall between us as we walked.

It took around three days, but we reached the bandit camp. It was a quiet couple of days, walking together in the group of merry men, usually in silence or listening to the stories of the men. It was colder some days more than others, but walking together and keeping moving protected us from the cold mostly. Today was colder than it had been, and the clouds in the sky told me it was going to rain.

Gaelen and I didn't talk very much, but it didn't feel like we were avoiding each other as much. It was fun, talking and joking with the men, eating around a fire, sleeping in tents…but I was ready to get Molly and get home.

That night, all the men partied and drank and celebrated the safe return of everyone, and the safe return of Gaelen and I. It was a party honestly and I enjoyed it for a while, but once it got late and I felt myself getting tired and cold I checked out and went to bed. I wasn't sure how long Gaelen was there.

When I woke up to the silent camp that morning, it occurred to me it was my last one here. By this evening at the latest, we'd be back at the Tavern and Molly and I would be headed off. I took a deep breath and looked around the tent in the cool morning air, the fabric moving lightly in the wind.

I knew I wouldn't look back on this negatively. I would be really glad to be home, but I'd always remember that amazing time when I was in a magical world and stayed in Robin Hood's camp, fought off monsters, and adventured across a magical medieval Europe. The fairies I'd forget. Or try to forget, at least.

I yawned quietly and stretched, sitting up. I heard rustling behind me and turned to see Gaelen staring at me through his hair, lying on his side. I blushed a little.

"What?" I teased with a little smirk, fixing my own hair now that I was thinking about it.

"I'm gonna miss you," he said suddenly, and I looked up at him for real this time. I turned in my sleeping bag.

"I…I'm gonna miss you too, Gaelen." I admitted quietly. He pushed his hair from his face, moving to sit up. "I'm sorry that we're…well, parting ways," I said with a little shrug.

"Me too," he agreed quietly and looked up at me. "I've…really enjoyed this quest with you and…and…I think of you as a good friend," he said with a serious nod.

I smiled a little bit, in the quiet air of the morning. "Me too," I said, and he continued.

"I'm glad to have gotten to be friends with you, quest aside." He looked up at me. "I had a lot of fun."

"I did too," I replied softly, looking down a little. "And…I'll try to see if I can figure out coming back to visit…okay?" I tried, looking up at him. He nodded a little, but looked down, not replying. He didn't seem too hopeful but I didn't blame him. I didn't even know if it was possible. I wasn't sure how we got here in the first place.

"We'd better get ready then, for your last day here," he said, tying his hair back. I nodded.

"You're right," I breathed and looked around one more time before I would get up and ready and leave the tent for the last time. "Okay. Let's do this."

We left camp pretty early in the morning so we reached town with Robin and Marian in the early afternoon. They'd elected to come with us just to make sure we all got home safely.

When I saw the rooftops rising from behind the trees, my heart began to pound. Almost home, almost home, almost home.

We entered the pub and I looked around for Molly. I could tell she'd been here; in her months here she'd decorated, and cleaned, and there was a painting on the wall that looked like it'd been done with coffee stains and then nailed to the wall. I'd missed her on the quest, I really hope she was okay.

Thinking about it, she'd really missed the whole thing, which I felt really bad about. She was the one who had wanted this and was excited about it. And instead, she had spent months working for Emory…I'd have to buy her a lot of ice creams to make up for this.

Emory looked up from behind the bar when he saw us, and a look of relief washed over his face.

He approached quickly. "You're all safe. Thank God," he said, seeming genuinely glad we were, but looking around at the faces before him, he started to also look worried. "Where's Molly?"

I frowned. "She's not here?" I asked in surprise. Emory's face went pale, and he shook his head.

"No, she left when Robin did, over a week ago," he explained. Robin frowned. "She never caught up with you?"

"Once I left, I didn't see her again…" he said, looking at us. My eyes were wide now.

"Then…where is she?"

Chapter Twenty-Two
Molly

Okay, so, adventure on my own. Day one. Walking down a path…and that's it.

"Let the record show that there are trees," I mumbled to myself as I walked, looking around. "Wait, no, that's lawyers…" I frowned, trying to remember the Star Trek one.

"Oh! Right. Captain's log: day one. Trees. And…more of…them…" I sighed, looking out. "Captain's log: day one, part two. Everything is super boring. No magical creatures to be seen. Not sure how much further my friends are. First quest going well."

I walked, and walked, and eventually, I decided it was probably lunchtime given how hungry I was. I opened my bag to see what I brought with me. A roll and an apple. Hmm. Better save the apple.

I munched on the roll as I walked, looking around. Eventually, something had to happen, right? What were those directions he gave me? Was it…left? I remember something about left…was it because it was left or because I always guess left and wanted to remember not to this time? Hmmm…

Well, I'm sure once I reach the fork, I'll figure it out.

All this walking gave me a lot of time to think…and I started thinking about my family. I didn't want to…but it's been months. I really, really missed my mom and dad. And my brothers…I'd never been away from them this long. I had kinda gotten used to pretending Emory was my dad, because he tended to act like it, and it was easier than being alone for months…

I came here, and stayed here, because I wanted to go on an adventure. To meet a prince and fall in love. To sword-fight someone, or to learn how to shape-shift, or to use magic to help save the fairies or whatever. But instead, I'd just spent months helping Emory run his bar, which turns out was just to distract me from getting myself killed looking for my friends... But he was wrong! I am strong and I will get a magical destiny adventure if it kills me! —but it won't. Heh.

Hours later and the sun was setting and I was pretty hungry now, and hadn't ever caught up with that guy. I'm sure it's fine, he's probably just ahead of me.

Food-wise, how did people normally do this? I glanced around, looking for a berry bush or like...small animal or something to eat. Or maybe some carrots. What do carrots look like as plants?

There wasn't much other than trees and leaves covering the ground. Hmm...I opened my bag and saw my apple. I suppose there was no harm in eating it?

I ate as I walked, looking around. Okay. Sleeping. I...guess I didn't really think I would be on my own for that. I didn't bring anything...and there wasn't like any kind of building or structure out here to hide in... I pulled my cloak closer and glanced at the sky. The sun had already set and the light was fading fast... I didn't have a flashlight or torch or anything...

The path just kept going, so I knew I couldn't keep going blindly forever...I stepped off the path and into the trees, leaves crunching under my feet. I found a big tree and sat, pulling the cloak closer.

"I'm just like Wirt in *Over the Garden Wall*," I mumbled to myself. "Except with less death," I added, pulling the cloak hood up as I leaned back. "Well, hopefully."

I finished the apple way too quickly and tossed away the core, curling up. I fell asleep humming *Into the Unknown*.

Crunch!

I woke up in the middle of the night to the crunch of footsteps in the leaves, not far from me. I held my breath, eyes wide. What was that?

The night was cold and empty and the woods looked much scarier at this hour. Moonlight streamed through the leaves on the trees and created weird shadows and overall, I felt like a ghost would show up right in front of my face at any moment, but the footsteps were much more concerning at this moment. I slowly pulled my little knife from my cloak pocket and held it close to me, gulping softly.

My heart beat in my ears as I heard whatever was there, approaching from behind the tree. Images of monsters and ghouls and distorted ghosts

171

with glowing eyes filled my head. I gripped my knife tighter, and then watched in terror as the white head of a wolf rounded the corner.

Now, I don't know how common this knowledge is, but wolves are friggin gigantic. Like, I figured they were large dogs. I could probably ride the thing that rounded the corner.

It was brown and white and gray, and I held as still as I could as it passed me, sniffing the ground, it's dark eyes not focused on me. Okay. Okay. It's going to find me, so I have to strike first if I'm gonna—

"Wait a minute," I said aloud, and the wolf froze and spun to face me, growling. Its eyes glowed in the darkness in a way that made my heart pound in terror, but I stood anyway, ignoring it. "This is a magical fairy land," I said, taking a breath and then letting an easy grin pull up my lips. No magic or fun had been happening so far on this quest and I knew how it worked here. I knew how these adventures were supposed to go. Faith, and trust, and…well, I don't have any pixie dust, but you get the idea.

The wolf growled low, ears pressed back against its head. I cleared my throat and tried to ignore the careful part of my brain sounding off in the back of my head, telling me that I was going to be eaten. I stepped closer, and then dropped into a squat and offered my hand.

"Hey there, buddy! You're out here all alone, I am too." I smiled, and it growled again. "I don't have any food to offer, but I won't hurt you or anything." I put my knife away, voice gentle and soft and comforting like when I talked to my dog at home. "We can be friends?"

As I reached out to it and my eye contact didn't waver, the wolf seemed to get a little quieter. There was a moment of silence where I didn't know if the wolf would attack or back down. There was a thick tension hanging in the air.

I suddenly realized I could see the wolf in front of me a little better, something shining in the bottom of the wolf's eyes. I looked at my hand, and it had a very soft pink light coming from it. What was…going on with that?

The light flowed gently, seeping toward both of us slowly, like a mist, or dry ice on Halloween. The wolf and I watched as it fell out of my hand until we were both encircled. A soft, nearly see-through pink flower crown formed on the wolf's head, and I realized that this may be fairy magic at play. The wolf was quiet now and so was I, and then the light was gone.

Light? I heard an echo in my head, and I frowned. That didn't sound like my normal inner dialogue...

"Was that you?" I asked the wolf in front of me. It looked at me.

I can understand you, came that voice in my head. My eyes went a little wide.

"Is my brain connected with a wolf's?" I asked excitedly. The wolf blinked, staring me down.

Yes, it answered and I grinned.

"Finally, something real and magical adventure-y," I sighed happily, sitting back against my tree again. I looked up at the wolf. "You aren't going to eat me, are you?" I asked it warily.

No, it replied.

"Were you going to before?" I asked with a frown, raising an eyebrow.

Yes, it replied and I gulped a little. Its voice sounded like...well, it sounded indescribable. It didn't sound like a human's voice. It was like it was speaking a different language, and yet I could understand it.

"Hmm. Good thing I had that fairy magic then, I guess." I pulled my cloak around me because now that it was the middle of the night it was pretty cold out here. "Why are you all alone?"

Lost my pack, it replied, and I nodded sympathetically, patting the ground next to me.

"Sucks, man. Well, I can be your pack now. My name is Molly," I introduced myself. The wolf stared at me.

I am Silent-as-the-Breeze, he replied. I frowned.

"Can I call you Silent for short? Or Si? Or Silo—" I gasped "Silas?"

The wolf slowly sat in front of me.

Can I call you Soft-of-Hand? Or Quiet-of-Voice? it asked me almost sarcastically back and I frowned.

"I mean...I guess," I replied, and it nodded, lying down. "But that's kind of long."

I will just call you Soft then, for short. I felt like it was smirking but it's a wolf, so I couldn't really tell.

"I have a couple of problems with this, but okay." I yawned sleepily, tired now that all the adrenaline was going away. "Can I pet you?"

What does that mean? it asked, so I sleepily put my hand on its head and ruffled its fur gently. Its eyes opened and looked up at me. *Oh. Yes, you may.*

"I should call you soft because you're the soft one…have you felt yourself…" I mumbled, eyes closing. "Or marshmallow, because you look like a toasted marshmallow…with all that…brown and white…" Silent shifted closer to the tree, curling up next to me. I leaned on him a little. "Thanks for not eating me, Marshmallow…" I mumbled, feeling my head get heavy.

We'll see, it answered, and I smirked sleepily before falling asleep on my new wolf friend.

The next morning I woke up on a wolf, which was new. It wasn't what I expected to wake up to, coming out of a nice dream about superheroes and school, but eh. Magical destiny adventure is like that sometimes.

I winced as I began to move because my whole body was sore from sleeping against a tree and on the ground and at an awkward angle.

As I began to move and wake up, Silent seemed to as well, eyes blinking open. It shook its head, making its ears flop against the side of its head and causing hair to fly everywhere.

I groaned and turned away before pushing my way up to stand, stretching and cracking my neck. Ugh, sleeping on trees is not fun. Or wolves. Quests have to get better than this.

I yawned and my stomach growled. I hadn't eaten much yesterday…I looked around me, and then at Silent, who was standing now as well.

"Any ideas on breakfast or…" I asked it, but it didn't answer. "New wolf buddy? Silent? Marshmallow? Nothing?" He stared at me. I sighed. "Alright."

I turned back to the road and began trudging back up to it, crunching loudly through the leaves.

"Okay, so I don't know what you're up to, but I'm on a quest to find my friends and save mag—" I glanced behind me to see if he was following to see; he had completely disappeared. I glanced around but didn't see him anywhere. "Wow, he wasn't kidding when he said silent as a breeze."

Now alone again, I turned back to the road and started walking up it. I'm sure I'll come across something or someone soon. Right?

Nope. Hours later, the sun was much higher in the sky, and I was sooooo hungryyyy. All there was were leaves and the song stuck in my head wasn't helping the situation.

"Young man," I started to the tune of YMCA, "there's no need to feel down I said young man, there are leaves all around I said young man, eat a leaf off the ground cause you…love…to…eat them…I don't know…" I trailed off with a sigh when I couldn't remember the words anymore.

I stopped walking for a moment with a heavy sigh. I wasn't even at the fork yet. I couldn't have taken a wrong turn 'cause there hadn't even been a turn yet. I need to eat something, right? I was running out of energy to keep walking.

I slowly looked at one of the red leaves on the ground. Was it even edible? Would it poison me? Maybe I should look for small animals again…

I picked up the leaf and held it in front of my face. Surely, it can't taste that bad. Salad isn't that bad, and it's made of leaves. Right? Right?

I ate the leaf.

I chewed it slowly and shuddered as the flavor settled in. It crunched as I chewed, but it tasted so bad and I was mad at myself for ever thinking that it was a good idea. There's gotta be something else around here though, right? What do the animals here eat? It can't be leaves.

I heard a soft ribbit and looked down to see a small little toad-frog guy sitting on a leaf and looking up at me. Oh. Oh.

"Hello there, little frog. Don't mind me…" I said, reaching down and gently picking it up. It didn't jump away. I held it, looking into its eyes. Okay. Just…pop it into your mouth. People eat frog legs or something right? I swear my grandpa has said that before.

I gulped as I looked down at it.

"Okay Molly, it's…it's just a little chicken nugget. You can eat a chicken nugget, right?" The frog (toad?) croaked in my hand and I nodded. "See, the nugget agrees, just…put it in your mouth. It's that easy." I nodded once more, firmly, and raised it toward my mouth.

I didn't eat the toad.

Sighing, I held him gently and stroked his head. "Alright nugget. You're safe. I can't eat you." I set him back in the mud gently and he jumped away. I wiped my hands on my pants. "You were just too cute…"

I continued down the path, resigning myself to just finding this stupid fork and hopefully food very quickly after. "Nuggets aren't supposed to be cute…" I mumbled to myself, rubbing my face. "Except the dinosaur ones, but that's besides the point."

It was only about another hour until I found the fork that that one guy had told me about. Okay. Now I just have to go down it. I smiled and took a step—wait. Was it right? Or…or left?

Left or right? Why can't I remember?

"Left is always right, I guess," I mumbled with a sigh and headed that way a couple of steps before suddenly a man stepped out of the bushes and blocked my path, making me jump a little.

He was kind of tall and skinny, wearing a white button-up shirt with a blue sweater over it, which after months of being in medieval times I knew was kind of out of place, but I guess I couldn't be sure. He also had a big dark gray wool-looking peacoat on, and looked very nervous.

"Hey…hey there," he said awkwardly, not really making eye contact. I frowned at him. He looked like he was maybe 20. But I couldn't be sure. Is he sweating?

"Hey?" I asked, confused.

"Heyyy…" He trailed awkwardly, and honestly, I was really confused.

"Hi…" I said again, looking around nervously. "What, uh, can I help you?" I asked. He gulped and nodded.

"Right, yes, uh, I'm a…fellow traveler…and uh, well…you look a little lost, am I wrong?" He had short, curly light brown hair that kind of fell out of place when he talked and he tucked it back away immediately. It was well cut, like freshly trimmed, going short on the back and sides and longer on the top, and I started wondering if he was a traveler traveler.

His eyes were light blue and were flickering around nervously, not meeting mine. I…didn't feel scared? I knew I was small and he was a good foot taller than me but I still got the feeling I could knock him over if I wanted to. He was really pretty too. And kind of awkward? In a nerdy sort of way. I liked it.

I shrugged a little. "I mean… No, I guess you aren't, I'm not…well, I wasn't sure whether to go left or right."

"Well, that depends on if you want to get into town or not," he said, kind of bouncing up on his toes.

"I… Yes, that sounds right. Or was I supposed to go to the ruins?" I suddenly couldn't remember. I really should have written it down…

He smiled nervously. "Well, don't worry, we'll figure it out! What are you looking for?" he asked, and my stomach made a very loud noise. It was getting mad…the leaf had only offended it.

"Food, to begin with," I sighed. He frowned, looking at me for real for the first time since he'd jumped out in front of me.

"You... don't have any food? Town's only like a day and a half away from here each way…" he said, and I nodded, then this eyebrow rose in surprise. "Did you not actually bring any food with you?"

I shook my head, feeling sheepish and embarrassed but not really caring about what this random well-dressed stranger said at the same time. His shoes and the bottom of his pants were covered in mud, so I'm not sure how much he can judge me, but…

"I ate a leaf," I admitted for no reason, pushing my glasses up a little. Why did I say that? He made a face.

"Man, what was I thinking?" He seemingly mumbled to himself, before rummaging through his pockets. He reached into one of his big coat pockets and pulled out a protein bar. "This might help." The packaging told me he was definitely from my world. I lit up, and then felt like crying. Chocolate flavor. I took it and tore it open, taking a big bite.

"Thank you," I mumbled through it, crying a little. It tasted so goooooood. He chuckled and nodded.

"Of course, happy to help," he said brightly. He was much more relaxed now.

"I'm Molly," I said as I chewed.

"Oh," he said with a little nod and awkward smile, previous ease and confidence hopping right back into awkward shyness. "Nice to meet you, Molly." His voice was tense as he said my name.

"Nice to meet you too…" I trailed off, waiting for him to tell me his name.

"Oh!" he said like he had just realized he hadn't told me, after a couple seconds. "Right. It's, ah…it's Cecil," he said nervously.

"Oh. Cool. Nice to meet you, Cecil."

Chapter Twenty-Three
Molly

"So, ruins or city?" he pondered as I chewed on the protein bar he'd given me, saving my life, probably. Saving me from eating more leaves, at least. Ugh. Never doing that again.

"Right," I said as I ate, "it's a destiny quest."

"Oh," His eyes lit up with intrigue. "Right, like for the prophecy? Saving magic and all?" he asked in a bright tone. I nodded. "It's a pretty cool prophecy, isn't it?" he asked in a tone that sounded like he was trying to conceal his excitement, but he wasn't trying very hard, seeming…proud almost? I don't know. I shrugged.

"I don't know, I didn't really see it," I admitted. He frowned.

"Oh. No? Huh," he was quiet for a moment, frowning. "So, why are you coming this way, then? The first step is in the mountains," he explained, looking at me curiously. I shrugged again.

"I don't know, my friends went into the mountains months ago and so I figured they probably just went on to do the rest of the quest when they got done, so I was heading to the next step to look for them," I explained back, between bites of protein bar.

"Oh," he said again (he seemed to say that a lot). "Okay, well, if it's destiny quest, it could be either, I suppose. The town is still a day and a half walk that way…" He pointed down the right side of the path, which I hadn't gone down. "But the ruins are only a couple of hours' walk this way, if you're not sure which?"

I thought about it, looking down both. I felt like it was the town, but the ruins sounded cooler, and I kind of wanted to explore them…

"Let's do the ruins," I decided with a nod.

"Oh, y-you…me? I'm…going somewhere else," he explained awkwardly, looking around.

"Oh," I said back (I guess he's rubbing off on me). "Okay. Thank you for the bar." I'm sure I'll figure it out. I started walking down the path past him.

"Um…well…okay, bye," he said, seeming unsure, but didn't stop me from passing. His unsureness didn't stop me though; I had to find my friends.

"Okay, bye," I said without turning, "Nice to meet you, Cecil."

"You too…" he trailed from behind.

It was literally maybe two minutes later when he came jogging up to me, stopping when he had caught up.

"Maybe I'll go with! I haven't seen the ruins yet and…no harm in walking you there, right?" He seemed like he was talking mostly to himself.

"Right. I guess," I agreed, glancing up at him.

"Right," he replied with a nod, seeming reassured, though I guess I didn't really know what about. I was getting the impression he was more of a young adult than an adult adult.

We walked in silence for a couple minutes. It was nicer out today, a little warmer.

"So Cecil," I started after a while, "where're ya from?" It was a casual way to start a conversation, but I was also very curious.

"Ah, well, the Time Hub," he said, looking around at the woods, seemingly distracted. He seemed nervous again.

"Oh cool! Gaelen was telling me about that. The Time Hub and the Prophecy. You aren't the…what did he call it…Time Prince or something, are you?" I asked with a little teasing grin. He blushed red and laughed in a strangled kind of way.

"Me? No, I'm not…I mean, no, look at me. I wish," he laughed and I decided he was kind of a weird guy. Or maybe he was on his first quest too. Or just a nervous type of person.

"Okay," I said with a shrug. "It doesn't matter anyway."

Cecil frowned a little and looked at me.

"What?" he asked. "Why not?"

"Oh, well, I'm not the 'chosen one', that's Althea. So whoever the prince guy is would fall for her anyway," I answered, and then, "Well, I guess he is our way home, but…" I shrugged. He was quiet for a moment.

"Huh. Okay, well, if you're trying to get home, maybe I can help? You aren't from here, right?" he asked, and I nodded a little.

"What was your first guess?" I joked lightly.

"The leaf," he joked back with a chuckle. I smiled.

"No, we're from another world. Our clothes look more like yours." I gestured at his outfit.

"World? You mean time," he corrected easily. He seemed a lot more relaxed, but suddenly I wasn't.

"Wait, what?" I asked in surprise.

"Yeah. Wait, you thought this was a different world?" he asked in surprised, seeming somewhat amused as well. "No, this is just—what year are you from?" he asked suddenly.

"2022," I answered. He whistled.

"Yeah, wow, this is just the distant past for you then," he explained, looking at me. I let that sink in a little.

"Huh. Then…why don't we have fairies or anything like that in the future?" That didn't make sense, if he was even telling the truth. "Why does everyone think magic isn't real?"

"Oh, because of the Magic Wars," he said, looking at me. "In less than a hundred years, the kings and lords and queens of the lands, all over the world, will begin a war on magic," he said with a shrug, and I looked at him in surprise.

"Why? Why wouldn't they want magic?" I asked incredulously.

"Well, because they'll see it as a weakness in themselves," he said, watching the ground as he walked, hands in his coat pockets. "Having something out there more powerful than them, just by being born. It's a threat," he explained. "Any peasant could be more powerful than them just by existing. So they'll try to kill off every magical anything they can find, they'll pay hunters to hunt them down and kill them, they'll send armies through the enchanted forests and send assassins after anyone even suspected of being magical."

I blinked, listening. "How…how could they do that? Wouldn't someone magical survive that? Wouldn't more magical people be born anyway?" I asked. He shrugged.

"Some live. But they're hunted down as witches, or hiding in unnamed societies shrouded in secrecy," he explained softly, but his tone was somber.

"And more are born, yes. Well, for a while anyway. But as time goes on, the less magic there is in the world, the less magical people are born. Until eventually, they'll be no one…so far into the future that the idea of magic is insane, and no one even believes it was ever commonly believed in."

I shivered as I thought about my friends back home, all not believing in magic anymore. It was already happening…

"And…and this prophecy can stop that?" I asked seriously, looking up at him. He nodded quietly.

"Well, not the prophecy exactly, but the person doing it. It's supposed to, at least," he said, and then froze for a moment, "I probably shouldn't be telling you this. I…" then shook his head. "It's fine. It's supposed to be completed by someone who can go back in time and change things; most of us can go back, but like a drop in a bucket, we can't make much of a difference. Anything we would be able to go back in time and do would already have been done by the time we were born in the future. Does that make sense?" He looked at me.

"I…I think so…like if you went back in time and stole a necklace before you were born, when you were born, it's already stolen…or…something…" I frowned, and then shook my head. "I…I get the concept. Everything's kinda already predestined, even time travel."

"Well, yes, I…" He paused for a moment, thinking. "It's like if time was just one continuous line, and you went back in time to change it, you'd only be adding to the line without knowing. Like, you might be going back to change things, but your actions inevitably only lead to the future you knew anyway," he explained slowly, and I nodded.

"Okay, yeah, that makes sense." I nodded, "So…chosen one can go back and actually change things for the future?" I asked.

"In theory, yes," he replied. "Also—oh shoot!" he said suddenly, glancing back behind us. "I forgot something," he looked at me for a moment, like he was deciding whether or not to go back. He sighed. "I guess it's too late now, anyway." He relaxed a little. I looked at him.

"Is it really too late if you're a time traveler?" I asked, kind of a joke. He smirked a little at me.

"No, but I personally don't have time." He looked around us. "We're…not far." He looked at me again. "So if you didn't bring any actual food, what did you bring?"

"Oh," I said, and looked in my bag. "Well, I did bring food, but I ate it, and now I have a journal and quill, but I didn't actually remember the ink, so I guess that doesn't matter. I also have a knife and this cloak. And somewhere, a wolf, I think," I added with a nod, glancing around the forest. He frowned.

"Wolf, okay…but that isn't much…" He trailed thoughtfully, looking at me and then the path ahead. He was quiet for a moment. I shrugged.

"Well, it isn't like these adventures come with manuals. If they did, I would have read it already," I decided, and he nodded a little, quietly. I looked at him. No reaction.

"So, why Time Hub? Why not, like, Time City?" I asked and he glanced at me finally, and a smile broke through his concerned face.

"That's what I've been saying!" He giggled, looking at me again. I shrugged, smiling as well.

"There's gotta be something with a better ring to it. Like…Timeville. Clockburg…" He was laughing now, as I threw these out. "Era-topia."

"Era-topia? Clockburg?" he asked through his laugh, looking forward as he calmed down a little. "Maybe if you ever go there, you can ask them to rename—" He gasped before he could finish his sentence, noticing something in front of us. He quickly covered my eyes with his hand. "Don't look now, but there's a boggart!" he explained in a hushed voice. My heart began to pound.

"Like Harry Potter? What do I do?" I whispered back urgently, but he was still walking, so I kept up with him.

"Keep your eyes closed, cover them with your hands; if you look, you'll be paralyzed with fear!" he said in a loud whisper, a hand on my back, guiding me forward.

"Aren't you in danger too?" I asked as he led me forward, keeping my own eyes covered now.

"My eyes are closed too; I've walked this path enough to know the way. We're almost past, don't worry," he said, and I felt the air get colder. I pulled my cloak closer against it and after what felt like forever, his hand fell off my back. "Okay, we're safe. You can open your eyes," he said and I did, but was careful not to look behind us.

"Thank you," I said seriously, hugging myself a little. "I probably wouldn't have made it past that alone…" The thought came to my head and

I felt…a lot of fear, from everything that had happened so far, rush through me. I could have been eaten by that wolf, or starved to death, or frozen last night, or—a hand landed on my shoulder.

"Hey, don't worry about it. I'm sure you would have made it past on bravery alone," Cecil said in a comforting tone, smiling gently. I wasn't so sure, but his tone didn't seem to leave a lot of room for doubt, so I just smiled softly.

"Well, thanks, but either way… Thank you," I said genuinely. He smiled.

"No worries. Anything for another traveler," he said with a playful wink. I smiled, and when I looked back at the path, the ruins were coming into sight.

They were tall and gray and looked like the remnants of a huge castle, sitting in pieces, some pieces still fully intact, some destroyed.

"Wow…" I breathed as I looked at them. Cecil smiled sadly.

"There they are. Well…" He smiled at me, less sadly. "It was really nice to meet you J—Just randomly on this path here," he laughed nervously. "I'm going to head back and take care of that boggart, good luck with the ruins, you know the way back if they aren't here. I've got to get moving on my own quest. Lovely to meet you, Molly," he said with a wave as he started to leave.

"Right, nice to meet you too, Cecil," I said with a little snort because he's still just an awkward funny guy, "Thanks again for the protein bar!" I called with a wave. He was really handsome. But I hadn't noticed any weapons on him…hmm…

I turned back to the broken pieces of mansion or castle once he was gone, and took a deep breath before approaching them, wondering whether or not to enter.

"Althea? Gaelen?" I called into the dark ruins. The sun was still out, but it would be gone in a couple hours and I didn't really want to be alone here when they did.

I circled the whole thing and found nothing but an entrance, so after taking a deep breath, I stepped inside hesitantly and began to make my way into the darkness.

It was dark inside, but a nice break from the cold wind. It hadn't warmed up again since we passed the boggart, and I wondered if I should hide here for the night in case it was going to rain or something. The sky was pretty gray…

My foot hit something and I heard it clank away in the darkness. I looked down at my feet and saw something shimmering in the light peeking through a crack in the wall. I bent down and picked it up, finding it was a gold coin.

"Awesome!" I said brightly and stuck it in my pocket. That's when I heard a low growl somewhere deep in the ruins, shaking everything, and began to smell smoke. There was movement somewhere in the darkness before me and my eyes went wide as the mass slowly started to take shape.

"I knew there'd be a dragon…" I mumbled to myself as it rose up in front of me.

Chapter Twenty-Four

Althea

Robin, Marian, Emory, Gaelen, and I were now walking back toward the hovel where we had started this journey. We knew Molly didn't head north toward the camp, because she would have inevitably crossed paths with either Robin or the Merry Men that stayed behind.

Emory helped us realize that Molly had taken almost no food with her and given it'd been over a week since she'd set off… We were more than a little worried. He'd grabbed an axe off the wall before we had left.

Was Molly even still alive? Had she died while we were camping with the Merry Men? What would I do if she had? My best friend…

It was easy to not worry or think about her when I was on a destiny quest and she was safe with Emory, but now that I knew she was in danger…I was incredibly worried.

I didn't know if Molly had the capabilities to survive out in the woods on her own. And I didn't know what I'd do if she hadn't survived on her own…I couldn't go back home without her. I couldn't go to school every day…knowing…

What would her parents say? What would I say to them?

"Althea." I heard Gaelen's voice to my left, and glanced at him. "We'll find her," he said in a reassuring tone, and I nodded very quietly. Maybe. But, he's right. For now, I've got to focus. I've got to do everything I can to find her until I'm sure there isn't anything else I could do.

We reached the hovel to find the men harvesting the fields of corn and wheat. As we approached, some of the men caught sight of Robin Hood first. A sour look came over their faces. Well, some of their faces. Others were expressionless and some looked happy to see him.

Then they noticed Gaelen and broke into grins.

"Gaelen! You're okay!" One of them, tall with blond fluffy hair, called to us. A group of men formed, surrounding him excitedly and patting his back or ruffling his hair. I didn't get off without a couple hair rufflings, though.

"And you got the shield! You completed your first quest. Good job!" One of them said brightly, hand still on his head. He smiled a little and looked kind of proud, but then looked up at Robin, whose face was expressionless, but whose eyes were cast down, and got a little more serious.

Gaelen cleared his throat. "Yes, but now we're looking for our friend. Did anyone pass by here on a quest?" He asked, looking between them.

The brown haired man paused, thinking. "Actually..." He started, and then nodded, "Yeah, a little boy with brown hair passed by nearly a fortnight ago, looking ready for adventure."

"Yeah, he asked me about you two!" Another guy said, blond and a little younger.

Gaelen and I looked at each other. "He asked about both of us?" I asked, knowing that no one really knew about me. He nodded.

"Yeah, both of you. I told him to go take the path there..." He pointed. "And go right at the fork and he went on his way."

Emory spoke up. "Did he have light brown hair tied back in a ponytail? And eyeglasses?" he asked, looking closely at him. The guy thought for a moment before nodding.

"Yeah, little round brown ones? Yeah." Emory and I looked at each other.

"Molly."

We knew where she went then and we knew where to go.

"Is Cecil still here, by the way?" Gaelen asked, looking around at the men. The blond man shook his head.

"No, he left just after you. Haven't seen him since." Gaelen frowned at his response.

"Robin." The older brown haired man greeted in a serious, unfriendly tone, interrupting any other interaction. Robin looked back just as coldly.

"Henry. Long time no see," he replied, crossing his arms. Henry's eyes turned to Marian, looking over him with cold judgement.

"This is why you left us?" he asked, one eyebrow raised. I could see a sneer forming on Robin's face, and Marian just kind of looked sad and upset, and I was about to throw down, but it was Gaelen who spoke up first.

"Yes, and he's why I'm leaving too," Gaelen said in an unwavering tone, looking up at Henry and stepping over to stand in front of Robin and Marian. Henry frowned and looked at him.

"Gaelen, what do you mean?" he asked, concerned. His eyes flicked between Gaelen and Robin.

"I'm not staying with a group of people that kicked someone out for loving someone they didn't approve of." Gaelen stared him down, an anger and hurt rising into his eyes that was kind of indescribable. "Had you even met him? He's great. He cooks amazing food, and he's kind and smart, and an insanely strong warrior. If he hadn't showed up to help me and Althea fight off fifty wraiths, we'd be dead. He definitely killed more than half of them himself." Henry looked grudgingly impressed, arms crossed, looking away now.

"So, what, you're gonna leave and go join their band of thieves? After everything we did for you?" he asked quietly. Gaelen's jaw set angrily.

"Yes, thank you for taking care of me for three years after you kicked my father figure out of the group," he glared, and the men around us started to look uncomfortable. The blond one spoke up first.

"I mean, he kind of has a point, Henry," he said in a quiet voice.

"Shut up, Simon," Henry snapped back and headed back toward the hovel without another word. I could tell he wanted to fight, but he did seem to care about Gaelen enough to know not to.

Most of the men followed him, some still congratulating Gaelen on his quest, some saying nothing, but three men stayed behind, including Simon. Robin and Marian looked at them.

"Got room for a couple more?" Simon asked, rubbing the back of his neck. Robin smiled a little, but Marian spoke first, smiling brighter.

"Always," he replied and they smiled. I smiled a little too, happy that the whole interaction hadn't ended in a fight or tears.

Marian looked between Gaelen, Robin, and I with a smile. "I think I'll head back with them to the camp and gather some men. If the last step in the quest involved locking caves and an army of wraiths, I can only imagine what this one will have. We'll be a day or so behind you, but if you get into trouble, we'll be back up to get you out," he explained, and Robin nodded a little.

"That sounds like a good idea," he agreed, and glanced at us for approval. I nodded a little, glancing at Gaelen who was doing the same. Marian nodded back, smiling softly, before turning to Robin.

"Great. See you soon?" he asked Robin, who agreed with a soft smile, kissing his cheek quickly. Marian squeezed his hand before turning to Gaelen. "Thank you for that…" he said softly to him and gave Gaelen a quick hug.

"Anytime, Marian," he said with a little smile, hugging back.

Marian waved as he left with the men and Robin, Emory, Gaelen, and I headed for the trail.

It was a few hours later that it was starting to get dark and there hadn't been a single sign of Molly. That means she kept going…I took it as a good sign. If we'd found her already…I didn't let myself think about it.

It rained a little as the evening passed, but nothing too bad. I reminded myself to look up when umbrellas were invented when I got home. If I ever got home…

I'd spent most of the journey thinking about my mom, and getting back to her, but after that display, and Emory with Molly, I was thinking about my dad…

After he moved out, we didn't see each other nearly as much. He didn't live too far away, but he was busy a lot with work… Either way, my brother and I stayed with my mom because she stayed in our house, and my parents agreed they didn't want to uproot us, but… Well, that meant only seeing my dad when he brought us out to lunches or fun things every once in a while, on weekends. And… Well, I hadn't talked to him for a while.

Glancing at Emory and Robin, I knew I wanted to call. Once I got home. Once everything was okay again. I hoped that me going missing wasn't too hard on him, but I couldn't know…

When he and my mom first separated, I was mad at him. It felt like he was leaving, abandoning us. I learned later that my parents had grown apart, and it was best for both of them, but…it still hurt. And it was still so easy to blame him for it. I did, for a long time. I didn't want to see him. But now, all I wanted to do was get home and hug him and tell him I was okay. But I will. Soon. After we find Molly.

I straightened as I walked, walking a little faster. We're gonna find you, Molly.

We hadn't planned on a whole journey, so we didn't have a lot to sleep with, but as we set up camp for the night, Emory pulled out a few extra blankets from his bag. They weren't big, but they were warm. We found a little dry clearing and slept close together for warmth, under the stars.

I stared up at them as everyone began to fall asleep, Gaelen on one side of me and Emory on the other. I didn't think I'd be here tonight. I thought I'd be back home, in my bed. But here I was…and I felt relief, almost. I got another night. The quest wasn't quite over. I had a little more time.

I felt Gaelen shift next to me and turned my head to see him looking at me. He smiled at me softly. I smiled back a little. Everything felt calm, for a moment. Gaelen quietly curled up next to me, his knees touching my side and his forehead touching my shoulder. I looked back up at the stars and fell asleep, warm and content.

In the morning, we ate a quick breakfast of jerky and rolls, because we didn't have time to make a fire or cook over it. We got moving very early because we didn't know how long it would take us to find her or where she'd even be by now. Nobody talked much.

As we walked, I tried to figure out what Molly would have eaten, walking this same road. All I saw were leaves and dying trees…I was worried.

"How will we know which way she's gone?" I asked as we walked, getting closer to noon now.

"Didn't the guy say he told her to go right, toward the town?" Robin asked with a frown.

"But she always goes left," Emory and I said at the same time. I looked up at him in surprise, and he shrugged. "After three months, you notice things," he added. I nodded a little, slowly.

"Right…so, if she forgot the directions, she'd pick left…but if she remembered, she'd pick right…" I frowned. We couldn't know what she did. We couldn't just assume she forgot…if we were wrong, we might not ever find her. "Should we split up and look for clues then?" I asked, looking at them. Robin nodded a little.

"Perhaps Gaelen and I could go left, toward the ruins, and Althea and Emory could go right, toward town? We could meet back at the fork?" Robin suggested, and Emory nodded.

"That seems like a good idea." He looked at me for approval and I nodded, glancing at Gaelen.

"I think that makes sense…" I said, and he nodded slowly, even if it didn't seem like he wanted to.

We were in the process of eating beef jerky and apples as we walked when we suddenly reached the fork… And a huge, brown and white wolf, sitting just as the road forked. Its coloring looked a bit like a toasted marshmallow, the brown color just on top and the rest of the wolf being white. I knew that was the first thing Molly would have thought of.

We all froze in place, but the wolf simply sat there, as if it was waiting. Robin and Gaelen were slowly raising his bow…but I put my hand up.

"Wait…" If I squinted, I could almost make out a pink flower crown on its head. It didn't look threatening. The wolf, not the flowers. "Marshmallow?" I asked hesitantly.

The wolf's ears perked up, but it kind of almost rolled its eyes. It stood and turned toward the left path, looking down it. I slowly approached and stood next to the wolf. It didn't move or growl. It looked pretty relaxed…I carefully put my hand on its head, to make sure it really was friendly, and it just kind of looked at me.

"How…how did you know its name was Marshmallow?" Robin asked in surprise, lowering its bow.

"That's what Molly would have named him," I replied. "I think it wants to show us the way." That sounded so stupid, even to me, but the wolf nodded, and we all looked at each other.

"Let's follow Marshmallow," Emory said with a shrug. Robin and Gaelen looked at each other, but I think they were the only ones who weren't aware that a quest to find Molly was going to be weird.

Marshmallow the wolf seemed to roll its eyes again before walking forward down the path in an almost annoyed way. I'm guessing its real name was not Marshmallow. It also seemed to have a lot of sass for a wolf, but I haven't met a wolf before.

We followed it as it walked, down the empty dirt path. We hadn't run into anyone, and it made me wonder why. Did no one trade or travel between towns? Or was it just a bad time for them? I figured it probably didn't matter.

It wasn't very long before we reached the ruins of some sort of mansion or castle.

"Oh my god…" I mumbled as I looked at it. It was huge and destroyed, pieces of wood and whole chunks of beautifully designed walls scattered across the area. The structure of the house remained mostly intact, but I could see through to the wood floors on the third floor from where I stood. Frayed curtains, torn and burnt in places, waved quietly in the wind. It looked like they might have been red once. I wondered what could do this; could cause this much destruction. "What was this, before it was ruins?" I asked Emory.

"No one really knows," he said, looking at it. "Someone just found it one day, seemingly out of nowhere. We aren't sure where it came from or what it used to be. Some sort of manor house," he explained. Robin nodded quietly. "It's said to be haunted or cursed, though."

"There's all sorts of legends surrounding it. But the only recent ones I've heard have been about a—" The ground rumbled and we all stumbled back, watching as smoke rolled through the gaps in the roof. My eyes went wide. "—a dragon."

Chapter Twenty-Five
Molly

I was sitting on a pile of gold coins, hugging my legs to my chest. There were melted photos on the walls and a big trophy case, which made me wonder if this had been some kind of school or club. It was dark except for the daylight finding its way through holes in the roof above.

"So, let me get this straight…" I started again, looking up at the large gold/brown and mint green scaled creature.

Must we? the dragon sighed in annoyance, voice echoing around the room. I guessed earlier that the fairy magic must still be working.

"You took me and I'm part of your stash because…I'm…important? Or something?" I asked with a frown. The dragon groaned.

No. Yes. No, we've been over this—you're valuable, traveler. You'll bring me the rock, it said.

"And…how am I supposed to get the Cool Rock if you're forcing me to stay here and not feeding me?" I asked.

Because they'll come for—I've already answered these questions! it boomed, closing its huge, violet eyes in annoyance. I put my hands up.

"Okay, okay, I get it, but I slept in a dragon's den on hard metal coins and I haven't eaten since yesterday, so forgive me for asking questions." I sighed. It was quiet for a moment. "…and you're gonna kill them when they get here?"

YES, I'M GOING TO KILL THEM WHEN THEY GET HERE!

"Okay, okay, just checking, jeez…" For the moment, it seemed I could talk to most animals and creatures. The dragon wasn't used to having to entertain its(her?) prisoners. "…and can I talk you out of this at all?" I asked quietly. I growled.

If you talk anymore, I'll eat you just to get you to stop TALKING. This was different than with the wolf. That was in my head. This was a lot more out loud. And also the dragon was going to eat me, so overall, not as helpful.

"Why do you want the rock?" I asked after a good long pause. It sighed angrily.

I thought you were done talking, it boomed.

"Well, I mean, I'm gonna die either way, right?" I shrugged. It groaned.

Fine. It's the most valuable of the treasures, known across all the lands, and I want it, it said. I frowned.

"That's it?" I asked in surprise. "You're gonna kill all of us…because it's a pretty rock and you want it?"

Yeah. I'm a dragon, it said, raising an eyebrow, probably. *Also, it's said to have amazing powers for dragons. Shapeshifting, walls of fire, eternal life…*

I sighed. "Look, I've seen this rock and it does nothing. It couldn't even get us home."

Are you a dragon? it asked me.

"…no," I answered begrudgingly.

That's what I thought, it answered. I groaned and put my head down on my knees.

"I just…my friends don't even know I'm here. What makes you think they'll find me?" I asked it, looking up again.

Dragons can see bits of the future, it replied, voice in my head deep and wise-sounding. *I have seen them coming. They will be here soon.*

"Do you see yourself killing us?" I asked it curiously, raising an eyebrow. It looked at me for a moment, before turning away, causing multiple landslides in the pile of coins.

…No, it replied hesitantly. *But I also do not foresee you living.*

"That's not really proof that we'll die though…" I pointed out, raising an eyebrow. It was quiet for a moment. "Althea's the chosen one, she's prophesized to do stuff. She isn't just gonna die by some random dragon," I argued, and it growled loudly, almost an angry shout. It was loud enough that I covered my ears, wincing away. Smoke filled the room as the dragon's mouth caught fire, and I coughed and tried to use my cloak to protect my from the smoke.

THAT'S IT, I'M KILLING YOU NOW! it roared and its head came toward me. I dug around my pockets for my knife but an arrow struck it in the head and bounced off before anything could happen.

The dragon froze and then slowly looked over at the group that had entered the dragon's den.

"Althea!" I said brightly. She's okay! Her and Gaelen! And…Emory is with them. "Emory?" I asked in surprise. What's going on? How did he find them first? Did that other guy come back?

"Let my friend go," Althea demanded, standing next to Gaelen who had another arrow leveled at the dragon, the one guy just behind them with an arrow ready as well. Althea had a sword and Emory had an axe… My eyes sparkled because this was the coolest thing ever.

"Oh my god," I whispered excitedly.

Finally, the dragon's voice said into my head, and it turned to look at them. I could see the smoke starting to pour from its nostrils… My eyes went wide.

"Guys, watch out!" I shouted and they all dove as the fire scorched where they'd just been standing. Emory stumbled up behind a piece of rubble. I felt tears forming in my eyes.

Since yesterday, I'd been stuck here. I didn't bring food…I didn't know what I was doing, and when Emory tried to tell me that, I yelled at him. And he still came to save me.

"Emory, you were right! I shouldn't have gone off on my own. I didn't even bring food! I'm sorry I yelled at you!" I shouted across the large room as the dragon recovered from breathing fire.

"It's…it's okay, Molly. I shouldn't have held you back from helping your friends," he called back from behind the rubble, carefully looking at me around the side of it. "If I've learned anything over the past months, it's that you're strong and capable." He gave me a small, supportive smile from across the rubble and coins.

I sniffled and nodded a little, smiling, but we had bigger problems right now. The dragon clawed at Althea, leaving huge marks down the piece of marble wall she was hiding behind.

"Why is it trying to kill us???" Althea called, ducking down. The dragon was moving to snap up Gaelen, who had stepped out and was firing arrows at it as fast as he could.

"It wants the Cool Rock!" I yelled back, scrambling to get off the pile of coins but it was a lot harder than it looked. I slipped and fell and pushed my way back up, just trying not to sink into it.

"What? Why?" Althea hit its tail with her sword but it just kind of bounced off the thick scales.

"Something about telling the future and shapeshifting powers and eternal life, I don't know, she won't listen to reason!" I called, sliding haphazardly down the pile.

"She?" Althea yelled back, before fire came her way and she had to hide again. I barely avoided it this time and ran to hide with Emory and the other guy near the entrance, but was knocked away with the force of the dragon's tail, back into the coin pile.

You stay here, pesk! it growled at me as I landed, taking a particularly sharp gem to the back. Ouch.

"We have to retreat for now!" the archer from the tavern shouted.

"We can't leave Molly!" Emory shouted back.

"We can't defeat a dragon!" the man exclaimed, rolling away as the dragon bit at him.

"Robin, we don't have a choice!" Althea shouted as she jumped out from behind her wall, stabbing at the dragon's face. It snapped at her, catching the end of her dress, but she sliced it off with her sword and stumbled back into the dilapidated hall.

"Why did you wear a dress to a dragon fight?" I asked incredulously.

"MOLLY!" Althea shouted from somewhere on the other side of the wall.

"Right, dragon, sorry."

I stumbled back up from the pile of gold as the dragon snapped at Emory, and took out my little dagger knife. I looked at its tail carefully, looking for a soft spot. It was all thick scale…except for this gap between two scales! I stabbed it between the two scales with all my might, and the dragon roared and yanked its tail away, leaving me free to run. I took the opening and ran for the exit.

"Go!" Emory shouted as he ran at the dragon, brandishing his axe. "We'll hold her off!"

Althea, Gaelen, and I did what he said, and the archer fired endless arrows at it, covering us. We made it out the door and then into the grass.

Light rain was falling and after the heat of the fire and that room, it felt amazing.

We kept running until we were far enough away to not get hurt. I fell into the grass, trying to catch my breath. My head was spinning.

"Oh my god…I'm so glad you showed up," I said, turning to look at the mansion in the distance. I glanced up at Althea. "After waiting for you for months in the tavern, I wasn't sure if you would. The dragon had faith in you though," I panted. Althea smirked just a little.

"Good to see you too," she answered, looking back at the mansion. Her smile fell and her face became serious. "They aren't coming out."

Gaelen frowned too, watching the smoke rise out the top of the ruins.

"Well, I don't have a weapon anymore, and we didn't seem to be doing much… Maybe we should just give her the Cool Rock and then come up with a plan?" I suggested, and Althea shook her head.

"It's our only way home… If we give it to her, we're trapped here," she explained, her eyes not leaving the mansion ruins and I frowned.

"Oh. Well…I mean, if we knew how to use it, we could—" I started, but she cut me off.

"We do; we figured it out." My eyes got a little wide.

"Oh," I said in surprise, "that's good. Well then, we can open up the way home and escape. Right?" I asked. They looked at me, and then Althea looked at Gaelen.

"I…I guess that could work, but we'd have to give her the rock to stop her attack, and then you wouldn't be able to get back," he said, looking at Althea. Althea frowned a little, thoughtfully.

"I…I can't think of a better plan though. This is…insane," she said, looking back at him. I could tell they'd gotten close. But they'd had months together so I guess I wasn't too surprised. He's pretty cute too. Not shocked.

"You can't give her the rock," I said suddenly. "She said she'd kill you anyway."

We were quiet for a moment, and looked back at the mansion. No one had come out yet… We couldn't hear much from over here, but that didn't comfort me either.

"Maybe…we should try to fight it," I said, standing. "And surrender the rock only if we have to." Althea nodded a little, gripping her sword.

"That's the best idea we have…" she said, and Gaelen prepared an arrow, looking up at the ruins. The earth shook, and through one of the walls, the dragon came crashing.

"Can I please have a weapon though? Mine's still in the dragon." I gulped as it noticed us and began to approach at terrifying speeds. Althea looked at Gaelen and then took the shield off her back and offered it to me.

"Sorry, that's all I have." I took it with a nod and looked up at the quickly approaching dragon. It stopped in front of us, smoke rolling from its nostrils.

Give me the rock, its voice was dangerously low. I knew it wouldn't ask again.

"No," I replied. Althea looked at me like I was crazy. I shrugged. "Fairy magic, don't worry about it."

Then I will simply take it from your dead, burnt hands! the dragon roared and swiped its giant claw at Althea. With nothing to hide behind, I knew it would be deadly.

In a moment of stupid adrenaline, I dove forward with my shield and the huge claws, bigger than my head, raked across the metal shield instead. I was knocked to the side by the force of the claw, but had succeeded in protecting Althea at least. Gaelen began firing arrows, aiming at the eyes.

Insolent humans! Give me the rock! it boomed, voice filled with anger and rage that I was pretty sure I was no small part of.

One of Gaelen's arrows finally hit and the dragon cried out, falling back for a moment. That was when Althea moved in, raising her sword.

I jumped up, running in to cover her. We might not be very strong, or trained, but we had to at least try.

I blocked the dragon's tail as it came swinging around, deflecting it away from us with the shield, only stumbling a little. Althea took the chance to drive her sword into the dragon's chest, between scales.

The dragon roared, a sound louder than any I'd ever heard before and that I could feel throughout my entire body, and swung at us with its huge foot. I raised my shield, but was thrown into Althea and then Gaelen, who was still firing arrows.

We hit the ground, tumbling over each other just as the dragon began to shoot fire at us. I barely had time to block it and some came through, singeing my ponytail, which had been swinging above my head at the time, completely off.

Gaelen cried out and pulled his leg in as the flames hit it and Althea's sword turned red with the heat from the fire and the dragon's blood, sticking out the other side. Althea stamped the fire out of her dress, but it was still swirling around us, getting incredibly hot.

I held onto the shield as it got hotter and hotter, until I could feel it burning my arm. But I knew I couldn't let go, because that would burn a lot more than this did, and so I grit my teeth and held on. Come on, come on, she's gotta run out soon...

Suddenly, the fire stopped and I cried out loudly, dropping the shield as fast as I could. It was glowing red with heat.

My arm was burned badly from the side of my hand up to nearly my elbow, through my sleeve. Gaelen's leg was severely burned, and Althea was covered in various cuts and bruises.

I looked at Althea and Gaelen. Their eyes said it all: we weren't winning this battle. We needed to run.

Althea opened her bag, digging for the rock. I pushed myself up from the ground and grabbed Gaelen's hand, pulling him up while the dragon recovered from breathing fire, but I knew it wouldn't be out for long.

"It's not here!" Althea cried, looking up at us, face paled with horror. "The rock isn't in my bag."

"What?!" I asked in shock, holding my arm. "Where is it then?"

Gaelen's eyes were wide, but he didn't have time to say anything as we were hit with a blast of air, the dragon's wings opening wide and thrusting it into the air.

GIVE ME THE ROCK! it screeched.

"We don't have it!" I shouted back, trying to pick up the shield again, but it immediately burned my hand and I had to leave it. The dragon knocked me to the side.

THEN YOU WILL DIE. its voice echoed through the valley, and I was pretty sure it wasn't just me who could hear it anymore.

"No!" I heard Althea scream as the dragon bit at Gaelen. I looked up in time to see Althea burn it with the red-hot sword. It roared and pulled back, only to knock Gaelen away and into me. It wasn't messing around anymore. The dragon then turned its attention to us, preparing to blast us again.

"No!" I heard Althea scream again, and then closed my eyes as fire lit up the sky.

…but it never hit us. My eyes opened again.

Althea was standing, fire seemed to be blasting at her from the dragon, but she wasn't burning… In fact, the dragon was the one bellowing with pain and falling back.

The…the fire was coming from Althea. My jaw dropped.

"Did you know she could do that?" I asked Gaelen in surprise, over the roar of the flames. He shook his head, watching in amazement, the fire reflecting off his dark eyes.

Althea roared over the sound of the fire, and the dragon fell back. But by the end of the attack, the trees surrounding us were on fire. The ruins were also on fire, but I think that was a separate fire that the dragon did earlier.

Everything was burning and Gaelen and I scrambled up as fast as we could. The dragon was burning, and for a moment, I was hopeful that this whole thing was over. But the dragon wasn't falling. I was stumbling back, and then recovering. My jaw dropped in horror.

"If that didn't stop it…" I looked at Gaelen, who looked just as hopeless as I felt. Soon it would be out and coming at us again. It was wearing down, but we were wearing down faster. I looked at Althea just as the archer and Emory stumbled up from the burning ruins.

"Robin!" Gaelen called and they looked up. They were jogging over now.

"Robin?" I asked as I caught it and looked at Gaelen. My jaw dropped. "Don't you tell me that's Robin Hood." He nodded, but moved to run over to them. A huge, burning tree fell between us before he could, nearly hitting him. He stumbled back into me, and Robin stumbled back into Emory, both a near miss.

Althea ran over to us. "What are we gonna do???" she shouted over the sound of burning forest. The light rain was helping nothing.

"Get out of here!" Robin shouted, raising his bow. "We'll hold off the dragon; go!"

"It's not gonna stop!" Althea yelled back, nearly in tears. "It's just gonna keep coming after us, and we don't have the rock!"

"We won't leave you to die!" I called back and Gaelen nodded.

"We'll fight it together!" he added, raising his bow. Robins face was grim, but proud in a way. He nodded. There wasn't a better choice to take here.

I turned to the dragon, a burning, glowing creature, who was now stumbling toward us, the fire going out. We'd need an army to even have a chance…I looked at Althea.

"Are you absolutely sure the rock isn't in there?" I asked as a last resort. She shook her head, tears in her eyes.

"It isn't, I promise." She opened the bag to us, and Gaelen frowned.

"The glowing pin isn't in there either." He looked at her. "And you left your bag out overnight…"

"Frank," they both said at the same time, Althea anxiously and Gaelen annoyed.

"How could I leave my bag out at a camp of thieves???" She hit herself in the head, but the dragon was here now, and we didn't have much to fight back with.

"Althea, use your flames, it's here!" I shouted, stumbling back as I had no weapons. She put up her right hand, sword still raised in her left, but nothing happened.

"It isn't working!" she cried, trying again, but we were out of time.

The dragon stopped in front of us, glaring down with its piercing eyes, still on fire. We were surrounded by burning woods, and Emory and Robin were bracing to fight it.

It was too late to do anything else; the dragon was here and it was going to kill us.

Chapter Twenty-Six

The dragon, burning, stabbed in the tail and in the chest, bleeding and with one eye blinded, towered over the three children. The adults trying to save them knew there wasn't much they could do; setting the dragon on fire was already so much more than the five of them ever thought they could do, and that hadn't done anything to stop the dragon from advancing on them. There wasn't anything else they could do. They braced themselves for the inevitable final attack, knowing they wouldn't be the one delivering it.

Suddenly, an arrow hit the beast in the side of its head. Gaelen and Robin looked at each other; it hadn't been either of them, arrows nocked and at the ready. Then who?

Out of the burning forest to the right of them came a hundred men, firing arrow after arrow and charging the creature. And at the front, leading them all? Marian, with a broad grin on his face.

"Marian!" Robin breathed in relief. He turned and winked at Robin as he charged.

"Told you I'd be your backup! Don't look so surprised," he grinned, and threw a knife that landed itself in the dragon's mouth as it roared.

I'LL KILL YOU ALL!

The men laughed heartily and didn't flinch, raining arrows down on the dragon and slicing at it once they reached it. The towering monster fell back into burning trees, roaring in pain but still slicing at the men with its claws. The fight was taking a turn.

As the three young warriors took a step toward the fight, ready to join it, a burning tree fell in front of them, knocked over by the falling dragon. They were surrounded by flames that were only growing, their only way out being through the burning forest behind them.

"What now?" Molly shouted over the flames, looking to Emory.

"Frank's got the rock!" Althea shouted to Robin.

"I'm sorry!" A shout came over the fight and Frank appeared next to Emory and Robin. "I went for my pin and it was just there, so easily, so pretty…" He held the rock out to Robin, who yanked it from his hand, making an annoyed and disappointed face.

"We'll talk about this later," he said and tossed the rock over the burning trees to Althea. She caught it, barely. "Get out of here!"

Gaelen didn't want to leave and didn't plan to, he was supposed to stay, but they were trapped in a burning forest, and suddenly there was snow on the path behind them, leading through the burning trees. It hadn't been there a moment ago. The rock in Althea's hands was glowing.

"Go!" Robin insisted as Gaelen opened his mouth to argue uselessly. Robin glanced at the dragon and Marian, who gave a battle cry as he led the winning fight. "We've got this, just go!" He said with a soft little smirk, "It's okay!"

Frank tossed the pin in, which Gaelen caught. "Here, I'm sorry, take this!" he shouted and ran back to the fight.

Gaelen hesitated, tears in his eyes, but he knew Robin was right. As the grass beneath them began to catch fire and burn, he ran for the snow. Althea went with him, but ran past when he stopped for a moment, turning to Robin. "I'll be back," he shouted over the flames, "I promise!" His voice broke.

They were gone and Molly moved to run down the path after them, but stopped, looking at Emory. There was so much she wanted to say, but there wasn't time now. She found the only words she could manage, the most important ones. "Thank you!" she called over the noise, eyes meeting his. "For everything."

He had tears in his eyes as he nodded, and though she couldn't hear the words, she knew they were 'you too'.

Molly wiped her eyes and turned and ran down the snowy path, a burning tree falling behind her the moment she was through.

Chapter Twenty-Seven

Three children, burning and exhausted, coughing from the smoke, stumbled onto the silent, snow-covered road, silent alpine woods surrounding them.

"Are we home?" Molly asked with a cough as she stumbled up to Gaelen and Althea, who were catching their breaths now, out of the flames. Althea tossed her sword, still red hot, into the snow. It sizzled and melted where the sword touched it.

"I think so," Althea replied, panting. She straightened, looking around. "This...looks like the road to your house, doesn't it?" she asked, turning. Gaelen wiped his eyes as he caught his breath and prepared himself for the new world.

"Yeah, this is my road..." It was early evening, wherever they were. The snow fell silently around them, gentle and soft, the sun covered by a soft layer of clouds. "Why are we on my road?"

"I don't know...I wasn't sure what it'd be like to turn up like this at my house and I just..." Althea shrugged, tripping over a piece of her dress that had torn. She sighed and just sort of tore the whole bottom off, tossing it aside.

"I don't know what my parents'll say either..." Molly argued, looking down the road that led to her house. "I don't know how long we've been gone..."

"Let's just stop there first, maybe your parents can drive me home..." Althea said, and the three began to walk that way, but then Gaelen cried out and had to stop. Althea and Molly looked at him with concern.

"My leg..." he explained, looking down. It was burned pretty good, down his calf to his ankle, his shoe half burnt.

"Oh, that doesn't look good..." Molly said, and Althea looked down the road.

"Okay, let's…let's just get you to Molly's and then we'll figure out the burns." Althea knew Molly's had to be pretty bad too, but she could at least walk.

Molly went on Gaelen's right, supporting him with her good arm. Althea picked up her sword from the snow, no longer red or glowing, and tucked it back into its sheath on her belt, and went on Gaelen's left, despite the arm injury still healing there.

"First quest," Gaelen said softly, in a sort of tired-but-celebratory way. Althea let out a soft snort.

"Look at us. Wow. Maybe I should have used the magic rock to get us to a hospital…" she mumbled and they started making their way.

"Eh, I'm sure we're fine," Molly replied positively as they made their way through the snowy wood together. "We just fought a dragon and lived."

When they reached Molly's house, there were no cars in the driveway. Molly frowned as they walked up it.

"Huh, no one's home. I wonder why…" She led them to the downstairs door, taking the hidden key from the old Pepsi machine her dad bought in the 80s. Gaelen looked at it with interest but didn't say anything.

"Okay, take off your shoes though or my mom will get mad," Molly said as she slid the door open and wiped her feet on the rug, slipping off the boots Emory had gotten her a couple of months ago. "It feels really weird to say that now."

Althea helped Gaelen get his shoes off, and Molly helped him onto the carpet and to the small leather couch. He was looking around in amazement.

"Things are so different here…" he marveled. Althea looked up from her place sitting on the rug, pulling at her shoes.

"Yeah, they are. Remind me to show you the bathrooms," she teased, and he looked up with sparkling eyes.

"Bathroom?" he asked. She nodded with a little grin.

"We could all probably use a shower, actually…" Althea admitted, looking around at the group. Molly smiled.

"Oh man, I missed those. Me. I don't even like showers, but not showering…well, ever…will really change that for you. Baths too." She yawned a little, and then turned and walked into the bathroom, the door next to hers, and pulled out a first aid kit. "I don't know if you'll want to shower with a burn or not…" Molly looked at Althea. She shrugged.

"Cold shower? Or…just warm maybe." She wasn't worried; she just wanted to clean up and go home.

Molly nodded. "Okay. Gaelen, I've got two brothers, so I'll help you with this," she said, and Althea frowned.

"Molly, I've got a brother too," she pointed out.

"Yeah, but were you bathed with him when you were younger?" She put her hands on her hips. Althea stuck out her tongue.

"No. Whatever. I'll shower upstairs." Althea sighed and stood, pausing. "Can I borrow some clean clothes?" she asked. Molly nodded.

"If my parents didn't throw them all out," she commented, peeking into her room. Everything was exactly the same. "Huh."

Molly pulled out a sweater and pants for her. Althea took them and headed up the stairs, where the other bathroom was.

"Okay, I'll be back. Good luck, both of you." Althea said, ready to be clean and then go hug her mom and make sure everyone was okay.

"Okay," Molly said with a nod, helping Gaelen into the bathroom. "So this is a bathroom and that's a shower; basically, water comes out at any temperature you want."

"Really?" Gaelen asked in amazement. Then he pointed at the toilet. "What's that?" Molly smiled brightly.

"So, get this; it's an indoor outhouse. It flushes away everything with water so you don't even have to go outside or clean anything!" She grinned, understanding after three months just how exciting that was.

"That is amazing," he said genuinely, head spinning from all the new things, but in a good way. "I might never leave."

A couple of showers later, everyone was clean, bandaged, and changed, sitting in the upstairs living room. Molly was digging through the fridge for food, still starving from her terrible quest.

"So, Silent led you to me? Because you knew I'd call him Marshmallow?" she asked as she pulled out leftover spaghetti, putting it in the microwave. Gaelen, dressed in one of Molly's older brothers dark blue Henley's and a pair of gray joggers from her closet, watched in amazement, holding his cup of tea she'd just finished making in wonder.

"This world is so cool…" he mumbled as he took it all in, feeling cleaner and softer than he'd ever felt. Althea chuckled softly as she looked at him, thinking about how adorable his excitement and wonder was for everything she used to find mundane.

"Yeah," she answered Molly, "I know you well enough to know what you'd name a wolf that looked like a toasted marshmallow," she giggled. "Speaking of food and toasting though, what did the dragon feed you the whole time you were there?"

Molly snorted. "Nothing. She said she'd kill me anyway, so it didn't matter what condition I was in when you got there."

Althea frowned. "Wait... How did you fight after not eating for a week?" she asked, shocked.

"I'd just pass out," Gaelen added quietly with a nod, sipping his tea. He raised his eyebrows and looked at it. It was really good.

"What? No, I was only there for like a day," Molly answered, looking up as she pulled a plate out and dumped the pasta onto it. Althea frowned.

"A day? How?" She knit her eyebrows. Molly frowned.

"What do you mean, how? I left Emory's to find you, slept on a wolf, got there, was kidnapped by a dragon, sat on a pile of coins overnight, and then the next day you showed up." She shrugged. Althea shook her head slowly.

"No...but we didn't even leave to find you until, like a week after you left," Althea explained. Molly stopped, frowning.

"That...doesn't make any sense, I was at Emory's three days ago," she said, and Althea shook her head. Molly nodded. "No, it's only been three days, I promise."

Gaelen chimed in, "That must mean one of us jumped." Molly looked at him.

"Like, through time?"

Gaelen nodded. Molly thought.

"Well, it could have been you guys..." she thought aloud, but Althea was starting to shake her head again.

"No, because Frank had the rock..." She looked at Gaelen and then they both looked at Molly.

"I...I guess it could have been...but I didn't have—oh!" She looked up at Althea and Gaelen. "I met another 'traveler' like us at the fork!" She did the finger quotes around traveler, and they understood. "Maybe...he jumped us?"

"But wouldn't you notice?" Althea frowned. "And why would he?"

"Maybe he knew I'd starve to death before you found me?" Molly asked, thinking back to him. "But I don't know why he'd know that…"

"Did he seem…creepy? Or mean?" Althea asked.

"Or evil?" Gaelen added. Molly laughed a little.

"Cecil? No, he was a total dork," she giggled, waving her hand and turning toward the microwave.

"Cecil?" Althea and Gaelen blurted at the same time in amazement. Molly stopped, looking back at them with confusion.

"Yeah…you knew Cecil too?" she asked slowly, and they nodded.

"Cecil's a traveler…" Gaelen sat back in his chair a little. It was quiet for a moment.

Molly didn't know how to respond, so she moved back to the jumping problem. "He did make me close my eyes at one point to protect me from a boggart, it could have been then?"

"This is all so strange…" Althea mumbled to herself, and things were quiet again. Althea glanced up at Molly, planning to ask more questions. She frowned as she saw her. "What's up?"

Molly was staring at the food spinning in the microwave, quiet.

"This…I'm pretty sure this is the same spaghetti my mom made for us the night before I came to your house and we ended up in Althalamist." She glanced at Althea. "We can't be more than a couple of days past when we left."

Althea pondered that, glancing out the window. "Maybe…I…I don't know. My mom keeps a calendar, but either way…we need to go there. It shouldn't take us more than an hour to walk there," she said, looking up at Molly, before cracking a smile. "That sounds so short to me now, but back before we left, I never would have even considered trying to walk it."

Molly smiled too, before looking at Gaelen, who had gone back to sipping his tea and then looked down at it in amazement. "I don't think he's making the hour walk with his leg like that…" she said softly. "Maybe he should stay until we get back."

Althea nodded a little, looking at him. "Gaelen, are you okay staying here while we check on my family? We'll be right back," she insisted. "Oh! And…" She picked up the house phone Molly's parents kept. "I'll write down a number, and if you click the buttons in the right order, another one at my house will ring and we can talk through them. Uh…does that make sense?" she asked hopefully. Molly ate her warmed spaghetti as Althea explained.

Gaelen nodded uncertainly, taking the new and strangely light device. "Numbers. Yeah, I can handle that."

"Okay, and if it makes noise, and the screen part…that's here…says Achebe, click the green button and you can talk to us. Does that make sense?" she asked hopefully, and he nodded. She paused, looking at him for a moment, before going back to the pad she was writing on. "Okay, I'm gonna write it down anyway…"

A couple of post-its later and Molly and Althea had gone downstairs again.

"Okay, I'm wearing my actual snow gear out this time," Molly said and opened the closet. She frowned. "Huh. My coat's gone." She frowned more. "Oh, I think it's still in my parents' car. I left it there when they dropped me off…or maybe my parents donated it."

Althea frowned. "Huh. Okay, well…what are we gonna wear then?" she asked, looking at Molly. Molly shrugged and looked back at her.

They trudged up the driveway in their medieval boots and cloaks as Gaelen watched through the windows, sipping tea.

As they made their way back up the snowy road, things were quiet.

"We're home," Molly mumbled mostly to herself, looking around at the snowy trees.

"Yeah," Althea replied. "I can't wait to be home…"

"How are we going to explain Gaelen to my parents? Where will he stay?" Molly wondered out loud.

"I don't know," Althea admitted with a frown. "Maybe…maybe we tell them…he was abandoned? Or…hmm…" she trailed off.

"We could tell them his parents dumped him in an orphanage but we snuck him out, or something?" Molly said. Althea frowned.

"Do you think one of our parents would take him?" She was worried about her friend now, wondering what would happen if he was given away.

"I think, if I asked really nicely and explained…" Molly said, trailing as she wondered. "Well, we'll figure it out, I guess. We could always just try bringing him back."

They were quiet for a while, trudging through the thick snow, thinking to themselves *Where do we stash a twelve-year-old?*

We could make a bed for him under my bed...but my parents would notice him leaving the house for school and stuff... Molly thought to herself as they walked.

If I was going to convince my mom to adopt him and all that, he'd have to have papers and I'd have to explain where he came from and how I know him... Althea pondered as she nearly slipped on ice but caught herself. Molly looked at her.

"Now, imagine that in flip flops."

"That was months ago for you now, Molly, let it go," Althea scoffed.

Molly put her hands up in surrender. "I'm just saying." Althea rolled her eyes with a smirk despite the situation and didn't respond.

It was quiet again, until Althea's face brightened.

"Molly! Didn't your grandma just move in down the street from you?" Althea turned to look at Molly. "Gaelen could go there!"

Molly frowned, thinking, before nodding slowly in response. "Yeah, you know, you're right! She wouldn't ask too many questions... We could tell her his parents kicked him out or something!" she agreed, glancing back down the road.

"Great! Once we figure out my parents, we can figure all that out..." Althea sighed, looking up to the approaching hill. She was anxious to get home, both because she missed her home and family and because she was dreading what she would find. Had it been a couple days since they left? Or months? Or years? Would her mom be old and dying? She knew, based on Molly's house, that it'd probably only been a year at the longest, but... The possibility still scared her.

"Well," Molly started after a second, "until we get him back, at least."

"What?" Althea asked, looking up at her. Molly looked at her.

"Gaelen. He wanted to go back, right?" she asked. Althea nodded slowly.

"Oh. Yeah. You're right," she looked down at the Cool Rock, which she'd tucked into her bag once they were back.

Around thirty minutes later, they were walking up Althea's drive. It was early evening by now, and Althea wondered if her family would be eating dinner. There were no cars in the driveway...

"I don't think anyone's home…" Althea said as they approached the window, peeking in. "There aren't any—" She stopped talking with a gasp as someone entered the living room. Althea suddenly realized they were here much earlier than she thought.

"That's you," Molly said in amazement, looking between her friend setting movies out on the coffee table inside and her friend standing on the porch with a sword. She was grinning. "That's you, right before I—oh crap!" Her smile dropped and she grabbed Althea's hand and pulled her down to sit on the porch, headlights approaching in the distance.

Chapter Twenty-Eight

Headlights came and passed, and Althea and Molly both let out the breath they'd been holding.

"Seriously though," Molly said, looking at Althea, sitting on the porch next to her, "I'm about to pull up with my parents, walk up your slippery sidewalk, find the rock in the snow, and then knock on your door," she explained, looking to each place in amazement. Althea's eyes widened.

"You found the rock...here?" she asked, looking at Molly. Molly nodded.

"Yeah, right there, near the door," she said, pointing.

"How did it get there?" Althea asked, and Molly shrugged.

"I don't know, it was already there when I got here," she said. Althea frowned.

"Is it there now?" she asked. Molly shrugged.

"I mean, it has to be, right? I'm about to find it," she said, and Althea nodded toward where Molly pointed in the snow.

"But, look. Is it there?" she asked. Molly sighed, pushing herself up.

"I'll check, but where else would it have come from if not..." She went quiet as she realized the rock wasn't there. "Wait, what?" she asked, and approached. There was no rock. Not a sign it had ever been there.

Althea looked around quickly. "Whoever put that rock there for us to find has to still be coming then," she decided, turning slowly. "Whoever it was hasn't been by. If we wait, I'm sure we'll meet them."

It was silent for a moment as they waited in the falling snow, sucking up any ambience there may have been. Molly frowned slowly.

"Althea?" she asked quietly.

"Mm?" Althea replied, watching the trees. There was no path in the woods next to her house.

"I think…I think we left the rock here," Molly said slowly, looking at the place where the rock had been, but never was in the time they were in now. It was a little hard to think about.

"What?" Althea asked in surprise. Molly looked up at her.

"Think about it. My parents and I are about to pull up your driveway, any minute now, and there's no sign of anyone else. And who has the rock right now?" she asked.

"Us," Althea answered with a frown. She slowly looked down at the bag. "How…but…then where did the rock come from? And if we leave it here, we have no way to get back." She looked up at Molly. Molly nodded grimly.

"No, we don't. But if we don't leave it, it'll be like we never went. I'll walk in, and we'll just have a sleepover, and nothing happened, and we'll never know any of what happened or could happen," she said, looking up at the house in distress. "We'll never know magic exists."

Althea was quiet for a moment, taking the rock out of her bag and holding it for a moment in her hand before finally speaking up, "Molly…wouldn't that be…better?" she asked, and Molly looked at her in shocked surprise. "Wait, just…I know, I know, but… You spent three months just waiting for us to get back. I spent the whole time just missing my family, stressed and scared that I'd never get back here. If we'd never gone, we wouldn't be standing here, covered in cuts and bruises and burns and exhausted from walking for days," she said, gesturing at herself.

"Althea, you fought a dragon. You're telling me, in all your time there, you never had fun? Don't you feel stronger? Like you could do anything?" she asked and gestured at Althea's sword, attached to her hip. "You have a sword, for crying out loud, and we did get home. You want to just forget all that? Forget that magic exists? Forget Gaelen?" She looked up at Althea, searching her eyes. They only had moments to make a decision. "We don't even know what will happen if I don't find it. We might just stop existing."

Althea slowly let out a breath, looking at the rock in her hand. Closing her eyes, she gave it to Molly.

"Here," she said, crossing her arms, looking away. "It's technically yours, right? Since I gave it to you? You decide."

Molly nodded seriously, looking at it for a moment, before dropping it into the snow where she had found it all those months ago, so she could find it in a couple minutes.

"Well, our quests were fun while they lasted," she said with a smile, feeling the magic in the air and in the snow, and sunk into the snow waiting to be found. Headlights approached. "Come on," she said softly, pulling Althea around the corner of the house and out of sight.

Althea and Molly stood, backs against the side of the house, as they heard a car crunch through the driveways snow, and heard a car door open and slam shut. They listened as the footsteps crunched up the sidewalk, paused, and then continued on to knock on the door.

"Molly," came Althea's voice from the doorway. Althea smiled reminiscently, then glanced at her friend as her voice came from around the corner.

"Yeah?" Molly mouthed ridiculously, and Althea had to cover her mouth to stop from giggling, and pulled enough of a straight face to mouth over her own voice.

"This better be the Thai Chicken pizza that I asked for." Molly was crying with the effort to not laugh, covering her mouth with both hands.

The sound of the front door closing and a soft "Well, hello to you too" came next and both girls started laughing.

"Oh, oh man..." Molly laughed, sliding back down against the wall and sitting in the snow with a giggle. "That was so long ago..."

"Yeah..." Althea giggled, sitting next to Molly. "So now we just have to wait for them...us...to leave," she said and glanced at Molly. "Catch me up on the last three months. What did you do at Emory's tavern to keep yourself from dying of boredom?" Molly's eyes lit up.

"I got pretty creative..."

An hour and fifty-three minutes later, Althea and Molly were both basically caught up on each other's adventures and were sitting quietly next to the heater, waiting. Althea was beginning to frown, as they still weren't coming out.

"Molly..." she said slowly, and Molly looked up from drawing a smiley face in the snow. Althea looked at her. "They aren't coming out."

Molly shrugged. "I'm sure they will." She stood and peeked in the window but the blinds were closed and she couldn't really see anything. She listened a moment as Althea got up and stood next to her. "See, I can hear the credits music. You're about to wake me up and run outside." She smiled easily. Althea's eyes went wide.

"Molly," she said, deadpan, "we're wearing cloaks."

Molly's eyes went wide. "Oh, crap."

"What?" came Molly's voice from inside, and Althea and Molly threw their hoods up, making their way quickly toward the woods.

"There's no path! What do we do?" Molly whispered urgently to Althea as they neared the spot the trail had been.

"I...I don't know! Maybe we made it appear!" Althea panicked, shooting a glance back to see herself moving toward them, ducking behind a tree. Althea pulled Molly into the woods with her quickly, and they watched Molly, a few months younger, slipping around in the snow, follow behind other Althea. From this distance, they couldn't hear what they were saying, but could see Molly's sweater hanging out from around the tree. The pocket was glowing.

Molly frowned. Why was it glowing? A path formed in the woods next to them.

"It was...it was us? Or me?" she said in surprise, looking at Althea. Althea grabbed Molly's not-burnt arm and pulled her up the hill.

"We don't have time to check," she insisted, and they ran up the path as far as they could, but ducked to hide in the trees at the top of a hill when they heard crunches in the snow behind them and distant voices.

They caught their breaths as they waited.

"What now?" Molly asked at a whisper, looking at Althea hiding on the other side of the path.

"Now...now I'm gonna insist we go up the trail, and we're gonna run until...I don't know," Althea said as she panted. Molly glanced back.

"No...no, you went up the trail, stopped, saw the figures, and then ran after them up the trail," she said, looking carefully at Althea. Althea looked at her, and down the path, before stepping out onto it. Molly did too.

"There!" They heard from down the path, and Althea and Molly sprinted down the path, away from Althea and Molly.

In front of them, the snow started fading. Molly's eyes went wide as she suddenly realized they could end up stuck in the other world again.

She grabbed Althea's hand as they turned a corner on the trail and dragged her off the path, diving into the snow behind a bush.

Footsteps ran past them in the snow as they lay there, panting. Althea realized before she had to ask why they had to stop. When they couldn't hear themselves up the path anymore, they climbed out of the bushes. The snow was still disappearing up the path. Molly and Althea glanced at each other quietly, before turning down the path and walking back toward Althea's house. They'd be staying in their own world today.

When they got home, they pulled off their boots and set them on the rug, which had just recovered from the last load of snow deposited on it. Althea plopped down on the couch and set her sword on the coffee table, pushing aside the Disney movies and pizza plates still there. Molly picked up a slice of cold pizza as she sat. The room was silent for a moment, in a happy sort of way.

"So," Molly said after a moment, "we did it."

Althea smiled. "We did it."

It was quiet again.

"What now? Just...sleep over and wait for my parents to pick me up tomorrow and...go back to normal?" Molly asked, shifting in her seat to face Althea a little more. Althea shrugged a little.

"Yeah, I guess," she paused, smiling. "That's so weird. That's...wow," she grinned a little, shrugging. "We're home. Everything's fine. We just...we almost got eaten by a dragon, but we're fine," she was grinning now, and laughed. "It's over."

Molly laughed too, grinning, before it slowly fell. "Over," she repeated, looking at the sword on the table. It was quiet again as she thought about it. "Oh! But we gotta call my grandma first. To pick up Gaelen."

"Oh!" Althea exclaimed as she sat up again, "You're right, but let's call Gaelen first." Althea grabbed the phone and dialed, but paused before hitting the call button. "I hope your parents aren't home yet."

Molly waved her off as she finished off the pizza's crust. "Nah, they were going to a movie and then dancing. My brothers are at friends' houses too, so it's just Gaelen for the evening." Althea nodded.

"Cool." She hit call and the phone rang. Gaelen managed to pick it up, and the message came across after a couple of tries. Gaelen didn't even try to understand how any of this was working, he was just happy they were safe.

Afterward, Molly dialed her grandmother.

"Hello?" came her voice.

"Grandma! It's Molly, I have a favor to ask," she said, straightening in her couch.

"Oh! Straight to the point, huh… What's going on?" her grandmother asked, concerned.

"Well, one of my friends…his dad kicked him out and he came to my house, but I'm at Althea's, and he knew where the key was, so—" Molly began to explain, trying her best to sound convincing and doing a surprisingly good job, but her grandma cut her off.

"Does this friend's name happen to be Gaelen?" she asked in a knowing way. Molly frowned, knitting her eyebrows.

"I…uh…how…did you know that?" she asked in surprise, looking up at Althea.

"Oh, dear, it is. Wonderful. I'll go pick him up right now, his room is already set up," she continued easily as Molly blinked in confusion. Althea gestured to ask what was happening, and Molly in turn put the phone on speaker.

"Grandma, how…how did…Did you know Gaelen was coming???" Molly asked in disbelief, and Althea's eyebrows rose.

"Oh, dear, of course. I've known for years. Now, tell me, how was your adventure?" she asked brightly, and Molly and Althea looked at each other.

"How was our adventure?" Molly asked Althea with an incredulous shrug, cracking a disbelieving grin at the insanity of the situation. Althea giggled.

"Where do we even begin?"

CPSIA information can be obtained
at www.ICGtesting.com
Printed in the USA
BVHW040042030921
615904BV00009B/1041